Contents

Preface iii
Acknowledgement iv
Prologue – Jack 1
Chapter One – Jack 5
Chapter Two – Leo 22
Chapter Three – Jack 26
Chapter Four - Leo 31
Chapter Five - Jack 46
Chapter Six - Leo 64
Chapter Seven - Jack 79
Chapter Eight - Leo 87
Chapter Nine - Jack 98
Chapter Ten - Leo 113
Chapter Eleven – Jack 124
Chapter Twelve – Leo 139
Chapter Thirteen – Jack 151
Chapter Fourteen – Leo 163
Chapter Fifteen – Jack 173
Chapter Sixteen – Leo 188
Chapter Seventeen – Jack 198
Chapter Eighteen – Leo 209
Chapter Nineteen – Jack 218
Chapter Twenty – Leo 234
Epilogue – Jack 255

Sneak Peek: A Match Made In Evan	263
About the Author	268
Also by Anna Sparrows	270

ANNA SPARROWS

You Don't Know Jack

Dads & Adages Book 2

Copyright © 2024 by Anna Sparrows

All rights reserved. No part of this publication may be reproduced, stored or transmitted in any form or by any means, electronic, mechanical, photocopying, recording, scanning, or otherwise without written permission from the publisher. It is illegal to copy this book, post it to a website, or distribute it by any other means without permission.

This novel is entirely a work of fiction. The names, characters and incidents portrayed in it are the work of the author's imagination. Any resemblance to actual persons, living or dead, events or localities is entirely coincidental.

Anna Sparrows asserts the moral right to be identified as the author of this work.

Anna Sparrows has no responsibility for the persistence or accuracy of URLs for external or third-party Internet Websites referred to in this publication and does not guarantee that any content on such Websites is, or will remain, accurate or appropriate.

Designations used by companies to distinguish their products are often claimed as trademarks. All brand names and product names used in this book and on its cover are trade names, service marks, trademarks and registered trademarks of their respective owners. The publishers and the book are not associated with any product or vendor mentioned in this book. None of the companies referenced within the book have endorsed the book.

Anna Sparrows acknowledges that all of her writing is 100% her own. No part of it is generated by Artificial Intelligence (AI) software of any kind. Yes, that means that it's sometimes flawed, but she's okay with that.

Cover Design by: Joe Satoria

Cover Model: Robbie Siclari

Cover Photography by: Christopher John/CJC Photography

First edition

*This book was professionally typeset on Reedsy.
Find out more at reedsy.com*

For my kids, who I will always think of as being just as adorable (and troublesome) as the pair in this book.

Preface

Dear reader, please be aware that this is a book set in Australia with predominantly Australian characters. As such, it is written in Australian English, with Australian spelling, not the American you are most likely used to reading from me. Yes, this is a bit of a mindfuck when half the book is from an American character's POV. (I never said I was clever.) I'm sorry in advance for the extra 'u's, and the 's's instead of 'z's. Don't even get me started on the word 'storey' in terms of building structure. I hope you still enjoy it anyway!

Also, despite the bulk of the romance being ridiculously sweet, this book does touch on some **potentially triggering topics**. These include some chauvinistic behaviours, 'outing' someone without their consent, the stress/trauma of raising children, self-doubt/anxiety, parental meddling, brief mentions of custody negotiations, mentions of cheating/infidelity (not on page or between the MCs), and discussion of homophobia and parental rejection.

Acknowledgement

Firstly, thank you to my amazing alpha readers, Ky, Claire, & Megan. Without your thoughts while this was in development, I would still be growling at my laptop about the boys being stubborn. Your reader reactions give me life!

Similarly, to my beautiful beta readers, Amanda & Cindy, the tweaks you suggested really polished this story to a place where I can honestly say I'm the happiest I've been with a final draft.

Speaking of polishing, thank you to Helle for your amazing proofreading/editing services. I apologise for dropping the ball on so many commas. I'll do better, I swear. Haha.

Joe Satoria, thank you for another amazing cover, and for putting up with me being a nitpicky so-and-so. You don't charge enough for your work!

Thank you to Robbie Siclari for being my second ever exclusive cover image, and for being the perfect fit for Jack's description.

And a huge thank you to Christopher John (CJC Photography) for taking the cover photo! I love what you do, and I'm so excited to keep working with you. This will be the first of many projects!

Finally, as always, thank you —the person currently reading this— for picking my book up. With time being in short supply for people these days, it means so much to me that you've chosen to give my book a go.

Prologue – Jack

"I had a lot of fun last night," Steph says as I try to usher her out through the front door of my studio apartment. She's angling for more, her smile equal parts sweet and sultry, but I made my position perfectly clear when we started chatting on the hookup app. Even my profile is very clear about what I'm looking for.

Sex.

That's it.

One-night stands, no commitment, just a bit of fun and done, *thanks*.

Steph's profile had said she was after the same thing. So we spent a couple of days messaging back and forth and eventually arranged to meet in person at a pub a few blocks away from my apartment. We had a few drinks, just enough to feel buzzed and comfortable, and it was clear that the chemistry we'd shared via our online chat was also present in person, so I invited her back to my place.

Obviously, she spent the night.

You Don't Know Jack

Steph's an attractive woman. With brown hair a shade or two lighter than my own, big brown eyes, and full pouty lips, she's definitely my type. But I'm not the dating or settling down type. Hell, I'm not the type to bring the same woman home more than once. Maybe twice if the sex was off the charts.

And, while Steph and I certainly had fun last night, I can't say it was anything mind blowing.

Yeah, okay, I'm a bit of a dick. But I want it on record that I never led this woman on, okay? My profile clearly states I am not interested in anything more than sexual release. I don't even want anything casual and ongoing.

My life is great just the way it is. At twenty-seven, I love my job, I have close friends and family, I get to play and watch a lot of sports, and I live in paradise. Literally. My apartment, tiny and run down as it might be, is in the middle of Surfers Paradise on Australia's Gold Coast.

When my brother and I moved halfway around the world with our dad as teenagers, I was just excited to have the chance to see more of the world. I never imagined that I'd feel at home in a country so far from the one I grew up in, but this is a beautiful place to live.

Yes, the wildlife here can be a little daunting, but there were rattlers and scorpions back home, so I can't say there's that much of a difference. In the time that I've lived here, I haven't come across many venomous snakes or spiders, and most of the encounters that I've had have happened while I was at work. Snakes, like most creatures, don't like fires destroying their habitats.

Anyway, more to the point: the weather in Queensland is subtropical, the winters short and not exactly what I would

Prologue – Jack

call freezing. The summers are hot and humid, but I live so close to the beach that the weather is a blessing rather than a curse.

Oh, and my accent gets me a lot of attention from the ladies here, too.

So.

Paradise.

It would be a lot more like utopia if I didn't have to let this poor woman down gently, though.

"I had a lot of fun, too," I tell her because I'm not a complete asshole.

Nevertheless, her smile falters at the 'but' I'm sure she can sense coming. Still, I'll give her props for shrugging it off and shooting her shot anyway when she cocks her head, walks her fingers up my bare chest and asks, "Wanna go for round two sometime this week?"

My hand closes over hers between my pecs. My smile is rueful as I shake my head. "I don't do ongoing flings," I remind her gently, giving her hand a soft squeeze. "I'm not into commitment. And," I add before she can tell me that she's totally just interested in being *casual*, "I don't want to risk things going from fun to serious right under my nose."

That's happening to my twin brother right now. Wes started dating his girlfriend on a casual basis, and now he's talking about moving in with her.

Ugh. No thank you.

Wes and I might have been born identical, but we've taken vastly different paths since our early teens. He's a nerd and I'm a jock. He's bookish, and I, after years spent in the gym and playing sports, am broad and, dare I say it, *beefy*. We're the same height, and our faces are similar (I like to think mine has filled out a little alongside my body), but we are otherwise polar opposites. Even in sex and romance, he's all about monogamy and settling down and I...well, I am very much *not*.

Steph sighs and pulls her hand out from underneath mine. "Fine," she bites out, and I try not to wince at the sharpness in her tone. "I'll lose your number, then."

There's no point in reminding her that we had both agreed to a one-nighter from the beginning. I get that feelings can change and that people can get attached unexpectedly. I do. But I haven't. I can't help that.

So, instead of trying to placate her, or protesting, I just nod. "That's probably for the best."

She growls at the back of her throat, stomps to the door and wrenches it open with obvious irritation. I'm not a complete idiot: I know that a lot of the attitude probably stems from her hurt pride and embarrassment and is not an indication of how invested she was in the idea of being with me. I don't know if that makes my mild feelings of guilt worse or not.

"Don't worry," she spits at me as she crosses the threshold into the dim hallway, her heels dangling from the index and middle fingers of her left hand by their straps, "you won't hear from me again, Jack."

Those parting words are designed to hurt me, but they're secretly a relief.

Until four and a half years pass, and those words turn out to be a lie.

Chapter One – Jack

Most thirty-ish-year-old men might not be excited to go to a one-year-old's birthday party, but I am. Vicky is a bright spot in my dad's life, and she has therefore become one in my life, too. It's true that I feel more like an uncle than a stepbrother, but that little girl has me wrapped around her finger and I'm pretty sure everyone knows it.

My dad, Will, met his soon-to-be husband, Connor, when they were neighbours, but fell in love with him after a tragic accident left Con in sole custody of his newborn niece. When I realised just how serious Dad was about him, I supported their relationship wholeheartedly. After all, for my entire life, Dad had never so much as hinted at dating anyone, let alone considering a serious relationship.

He'd worried that Connor's age —only three years older than me and Wes— might be an issue, but I told him that age was just a number and he needed to put his happiness first for once.

You Don't Know Jack

See, I'm not anti-romance. Just because I have no interest in commitment, it doesn't mean I don't support my friends and family in their own romantic endeavours.

Even Wes, though I think he jumped in *way* too early with Vanna. Dude didn't even try to sow his wild oats or anything. The idiot.

But I digress. Dad and Connor got their shit together and are now living happily ever after. I'm happy for them. Plus, it's a lot of fun having a cute little sister in the picture. I tease Dad mercilessly about starting over from scratch at his age, but seeing him truly enjoy fatherhood when his first (unexpected) round was less than ideal, no matter how much I know he loves me and Wes, is heartwarming. Con's good for Dad, too, which makes it even easier to like the guy.

So, yeah, I'm excited for my stepsister's first birthday party. I've bought her the coolest pink *Batman* costume and a matching plush toy, and I'm campaigning for Dad and Con to buy her a puppy. They're not on board.

A knock at my apartment door while I'm rushing around making sure I'm ready to head out to the beachside party gives me pause. My place is starting to feel cramped, considering it's no more than a dated hotel room, and I'm starting to think that I should consider moving to a one-bedroom unit instead of this studio space.

Is that maturity kicking in? Surely not.

I swing the door open and blink at the harried woman on the other side. She looks vaguely familiar, with light brown hair swept up on top of her head in a messy bun, and pretty brown eyes which are lined with dark circles. Her makeup-free face is drawn and tired…and I can see why.

On one hip, a little boy with a mop of dark hair sits propped

Chapter One — Jack

up, sucking his thumb and glaring while, on her opposite hand, an identical boy tugs and whines for her to head in the other direction.

"Can I help you?" I ask cautiously, a tingle of nervous anticipation drilling into the back of my brain.

The woman rolls her eyes. "You could invite us in, Jack," she answers. She even sounds tired, but there's a sort of vitriol in the way she speaks my name that sparks a memory.

"Steph?" Her name comes out as a question, even though I have a pretty damn good recollection of most of my hookups.

"Oh, good, at least we don't have to have *that* awkward discussion," she muses bitterly, and I frown.

Even though I don't usually repeat my one-night stands, it's not like there have been so many women that I would forget the details. Who does she think she is just assuming I'm some kind of manwhore? She only knew me over a few texts and a single night like four years ago.

Suddenly, it's like a switch goes off in my brain.

Four years ago.

Those kids can't be older than three. And they're twins. Twins with dark hair and blue eyes and… *fuck.*

Fuck, fuck, fuckity fuck.

I take a stumbling step back and she bustles inside with the two boys, heaving a relieved sigh when she drops down onto my sad, worn couch.

The kid not on her hip takes off at a run towards the glass sliding door which leads to my tiny little balcony overlooking the city side of the coast.

"Hudson," Steph barks at him sharply. "No. Come sit next to Mummy, okay?"

My last hope that these kids aren't hers withers and dies.

You Don't Know Jack

"Mommy?" I choke out, praying that maybe I misheard her.

With a roll of her eyes, and her hand still held out, beckoning the kid she called 'Hudson' to return to her, Steph says, "Yep. That's me. And you are—"

"Daddy?" The kid curled up to her side asks.

She smooths her hand through his hair —hair which looks way too much like mine for my comfort— and smiles softly down at him. "Well," she tells the kid, and I have half a moment where my hope flares again, only to be smashed into smithereens when she continues, "he didn't know that until now, but, yes, Prez. This is your daddy."

I would like to say that I do not stagger backwards dramatically until my back hits the closed apartment door, but that would be a lie.

"What?" I demand, as though I haven't been suspecting to hear those words from the moment I realised who she was. "You're not serious."

Prez —and, seriously, what kind of name is that?— starts to sniffle, his cute little face crumpling into one of deep upset.

"Butthead! You made Preston cry," the other kid stomps up to my side and kicks at my shin, and any thoughts that the way he pronounces his 'r's as 'w's is cute fly out the window as I flinch in pain.

"We don't kick, Huddy," Steph says with a sigh. "And we don't call people names, either." She waves her hand vaguely in my direction. "Say sorry to your dad."

No. Nope. I am not someone's dad. I'm not. I can't be.

Hudson sighs heavily and glares up at me. "Sorry," he mutters with blatant petulance, the 'r's once again curled into 'w's. Damned adorable demon child.

"Uh…" I manage, then shake my head. "You're, um, it's fine."

Chapter One – Jack

I am so far out of my element right now, it's not even funny.

I look over at Steph, bewildered. "How could you not have told me about them?" It's probably *not* the first question I should have asked, but it's the only one that comes blurting past my lips.

"Oh, gee, I don't know, Jack. Maybe it's the fact that you blocked my profile on the app and, when I tried to create new profiles, you ignored my messages. And I'd already deleted your number when you practically kicked me out of here, so…"

I cringe as she trails off.

So much for not being an asshole.

(I might have been a *little bit* of an asshole.)

But, honestly, how was I to know that she'd gotten pregnant? We used condoms. I'm a stickler for safe sex. In fact, these kids might not even be—

"I can get you a DNA test if you need proof," she says, almost as if she read my mind. "But they're definitely yours."

Shit.

Fuck.

What do I do here?

"Okay," I exhale, looking down at the hellion whose scowl does actually remind me a lot of my own. Or, rather, of Wes's, considering that's where I usually see it. *Crap.* "Okay," I repeat again, sounding a little more sure of myself. I look back over at Steph. "You obviously remembered my address, though. So…?"

With a huff, she shrugs. "Turning up on your doorstep wasn't something I wanted to do. And I didn't want to write you a letter that might get lost in the mail, or forgotten about, or…I don't know. I guess after my third attempt to message you on chat, I just gave up."

"Until now."

She nods. "Until now."

"Is that Batman?" Hudson asks, and it takes me a moment to realise that he's no longer beside me but is climbing onto my bed to tug at the framed poster on my wall instead.

"Hudson," Steph groans, "get off the bed. Now. Come here."

"So," I prod, my eyes tracking the kid as he continues to ignore his mother, "why now, then?"

"I..." her voice cracks and my attention is once again solely on her. She clears her throat. "I've just been laid off work. We're getting evicted. My parents...well, they said I can come crash on their couch, but the boys..." Her shoulders fall and tears track down her cheeks. "They don't have the space or the energy to deal with them. The boys can't come."

Wait...*what?*

"What kind of grandparents would say something like that? Especially when you have no other options? Also, pretty sure I owe you a backlog of parental support payments, right?" It's an avalanche of questions that go straight from my brain to my mouth, bypassing my filter entirely.

Steph sniffs and shrugs. "To be honest, I can't really handle them anyway," she starts, and there's a crash and a yelp from the bed to punctuate the sentiment. I turn to find that Hudson has knocked over my bedside lamp and then fallen off the bed himself.

He's crying loudly by the time I get to him. I crouch down and check for injuries, but he just seems to be in shock. Then his little arms are wound around my neck and he's clinging to me like a sobbing spider monkey. "S-sorry, Daddy," he says, wiping his snotty face into the fabric of my t-shirt, and

Chapter One — Jack

the sound of the title coming from his little mouth stuns me enough that I barely notice his actions, "it was a accident."

"I know, kiddo," I tell him, pushing back to my feet with him still wrapped around me. I rub his back. "It's okay. It was an ugly lamp anyway."

He giggles. It's a watery little sound but it makes me feel strangely warm to hear it. I look back down at Steph, who is refusing to meet my gaze.

"I'm sorry, but it sounded like you were leading up to—"

"They're going to have to stay with you for a while," she cuts me off. "I've done three and a half years. It's your turn."

The other one —Preston?— clings tightly to his mother, howling out a bereaved, "I don't wanna stay with him, I wanna stay with you!"

"I'll still come visit," she promises, and I don't know whether that's for my benefit or his.

Either way, neither me nor the kid seem to think it's enough. We both shake our heads and protest at the same time. Hudson just tucks his face into my neck and sniffles.

Steph holds up her hands. "No. No. *I can't.* Boys, you have to stay with your daddy for a while. This is non-negotiable."

My heart aches for these boys, being thrust at a stranger they've never met and told that the only parent they've ever known won't be hanging around. Panicked, I glance around my cramped apartment and ask, "Where are they supposed to sleep?"

Steph bounces on the couch. "Does this pull out?"

I bite back the bitter definitely-an-asshole retort in my head that sounds suspiciously like 'I wish I had', and I nod. "Yeah."

"Then there you go. They can share."

Preston whimpers and clings to her and she pats his head.

"They're still toilet training right now, so I recommend nighttime pull-ups and a mattress protector. I've got their clothes and toys in the car. I'm keeping the car seats, so you'll have to work that out yourself." While I remain stunned under the onslaught of information, she points to the backpack at her feet. "There are some daytime pull-ups, snacks, and a couple of changes of clothes in there, too, to get you started."

This is insane.

"Steph..." I start, trying to reason with her. I feel frantic, but the little arms around my neck tighten and, oddly, that calms me down some. "Steph," I try again, "come on. I'm a firefighter. My shifts are erratic. I live in this tiny space and I have nothing more than my car to my name. How am I supposed to make this work?"

"I made it work for three effing years, Jack!" she hurls at me.

"You should have tried harder to tell me," I hiss back. "I would have..." What? Freaked out. Denied paternity. Run for the hills. All the things I want to do right this second. I swallow. "I would have at least helped financially."

"I don't need your money, Jack. I need a break."

That can't be healthy for these kids to hear. Something in my expression must convey that because she has the grace to look guilty.

"I love my...*our* boys," she corrects herself, and tears slide down her cheeks again. "I do. But it's been a rough three years. They deserve better. *I* deserve better." Her shoulders slump. "I'm not walking out of their lives here, Jack. I'm just...I can't take them with me while I get back on my feet, and I don't have any other options than to surrender them to foster care or whatever, and I don't want to do that."

Jesus Christ.

Chapter One – Jack

Looking down at Preston, his little face similar to my own in so many ways, I know I'm going to agree before my brain has fully computed the decision.

"I'm going to have to get a lawyer involved," I tell her, and she cringes but nods.

"I can't afford one," she says.

I feel guilty because I can ask Wes to use his contacts, or I can reach out to Henry, a friend I've made through Connor. Henry actually practises family law and has also helped Connor and Dad out these past few months. He's probably going to be my best bet, and I doubt it's going to cost me anywhere near as much as it would if he wasn't my friend.

Still, the situation Steph has gotten herself into isn't my fault. It was her choice not to tell me that I was a father. I would have stepped up and fulfilled my obligations, even if I was panicked and stressed about it.

I sigh. "We'll work it out."

* * *

Pandemonium breaks out pretty much the second Steph leaves. She hugs the boys, tearfully telling them that she's going to visit them when she can, but that it's Daddy's turn to spend time with them. She's been selfish, she says, using the logic of toddlers. She's been keeping them all to herself and now Daddy deserves to have fun with them.

The logic doesn't help them.

Their tiny hearts break as soon as the door closes, and I'm left with two screaming three-year-olds and an ache in my chest which won't quit. It's half panic and half empathy for these poor boys.

You Don't Know Jack

I'm also *not* going to make it to Vicky's birthday party.

That's going to upset Dad.

Dad, who has been a grandfather for three and a half years and hasn't known it.

He's great with kids, don't get me wrong, but he's not going to love that 'g' word ageing him.

And *of course* it's me that has managed to do that. Not Wes, the golden child. Nope. *Me*. The troublemaker.

I drop to the floor so I can be at the same level as the twins, reality slowly sinking in.

I have kids. Sons. I'm a father.

I am *way* too immature to be someone's dad, and the universe has seen fit to burden *two* someones with me as their glorified sperm donor.

These poor kids.

"Hey," I try to soothe them, feeling so out of my depth I could cry. "Guys, it's going to be okay."

If I repeat that enough, I might even convince myself.

"I want Mummy!" one of them screams.

I've already lost track of which one is which. Was Hudson wearing the red shirt or the blue one? *Think, Jack. Think!*

"I know, bud," I placate. "I miss my mom sometimes, too."

The other one stops his crying and frowns at me. "Where's your mummy?"

"And why do you say 'mummy' funny?" demands the first.

"You say all the words funny," accuses the other one.

They're standing side by side now, faces scrunched up in matching red, blotchy, snotty, suspicious expressions.

"You sound like S*esame Street*," nods the one in the red shirt.

I can't help but crack a grin. "I do," I nod. "That's because I grew up in America, so my accent —that's the way I pronounce

Chapter One – Jack

words, uh, *say* words— is different than yours. Because you are growing up in Australia."

The one in the blue seems to digest this while the one in the red snorts.

"That's silly," says Red.

At least they're not crying.

"Is your mummy at 'Merica?" asks Blue.

Bobbing my head, I can't help but make comparisons between this pair and me and Wes. Blue is Wes all over. Analytical and clever. Red seems a little more like me, quick to lash out or joke. "My mom does live in America, yes."

"Is that far away?" That's Red. He's still cocking his head, as if he's unsure whether I'm telling the truth or not.

I swear to God, the way these kids turn the letter 'r' into 'w's is going to kill me with cuteness.

"It is," I acknowledge. "If I want to visit her, I have to get on a plane."

"Mummy said she's gonna visit," Blue says, and then his eyes water all over again. "I want Mummy!"

And that sets the pair of them off once more.

* * *

When my phone rings, the boys are *still* crying. I haven't been able to bribe them with food, or a walk to the nearest park with a playground, or even a trip to buy toys. They want their mom and nothing else will do.

I answer the call distractedly, and Wes's voice is gruff and full of irritation. "Where are you?"

"Um, something's come up," I tell him, unsure of how to drop this bomb on him. I should really be telling him and

Dad in person. "It's…I—" Blue —who, I have worked out, is Preston— gives another cry of frustration and throws himself at the floor.

To add insult to injury, Wes must have me on speaker because his fiancée, Vanna, starts, "Was that…"

"…a baby?" Dad's voice finishes.

I cringe. So much for doing this in person. "Not, uh, not *a baby*, no…" I'm still trying to find the words when Hudson, who has been throwing a much more violent tantrum than his brother, stomps into the kitchenette and yanks on the dish towel overhanging the counter. The dish towel upon which my morning bowl and coffee mug have been drying. "Shit, no, don't touch—"

It's too late. The bowl, mug and spoons come crashing down to the ground, the ceramic items smashing on the tiles. Hudson leaps back, having scared himself. He starts to cry. I pinch the bridge of my nose. "Damn it."

"*Jack*," Dad hasn't sounded like this since I was a kid. I have to admit, I feel like an errant teenager right now. "What's going on?"

Hudson and Preston are still crying and I have no idea what to do. I sigh heavily and scrub my hand over my face. "I think I'm going to need some help."

* * *

Dad pulls me into a tight hug the second I open the door. There's practically a parade behind him, and there's no way we're all going to fit comfortably in my combined bedroom/living area/kitchen/dining space, but none of the people who have arrived will care about that. Especially not

Chapter One — Jack

when they see the two little boys clinging to each of my pants legs.

When Dad lets me go, my hands drop to brush over the dark heads of hair which barely reach my mid-thighs. The boys tuck in next to each other, huddling behind me, understandably overwhelmed.

"Jesus, Jack," Dad breathes, but there's no disappointment or disparagement. He just sounds a little taken aback. He can join the club. I'm a card-carrying member right now. "You really didn't know?"

I shake my head and attempt to waddle backwards to let my family in. It's not as easy to do as you'd think with a small human gripping tightly to the back of each leg. "Not a clue," I tell him. Then I rub the back of my neck, feeling a little sheepish as I confess, "I was a bit of a di...er...*not great guy* to her that morning after. She made a couple of attempts to connect, and I brushed her off. So, this is all on me."

Dad exhales and shakes his head. "What's done is done, you can't change the past." He tries to peer around me, smiling warmly at the two boys. "Hi, guys," he says in that overly bright tone we all use around small children, "I'm your grandpa."

His nose scrunches as he says it and then glares up at me. "I am too young for that title."

"We could call you Pops? Or, *ooh*, Pop-pop?" I suggest helpfully.

"How are either of those better?" he asks me, but I'm saved from having to answer when Connor finally gives in and sets Vicky on the ground. She barrels towards me, squealing her version of my name, and I grin down at her.

"Happy birthday, princess," I declare, carefully bending to swoop her up. A glance down shows that the two three-year-olds are suddenly *very* interested in this newcomer.

"Daddy," Preston tugs at my shirt, ignorant of the intakes of breath from the adults around us. My heart still leaps into my throat to be referred to by the title, but I'm not going to discourage it. These kids have been through enough today, regardless of my own personal freakouts. "Who's that?"

"This is Vicky," I tell him, moving over to the couch so I can drop down and hold my stepsister on my lap. "She's my sister."

Hudson bursts into a series of staccato giggles. The sound is music to my ears after a morning filled with screaming. "She's little," he says in a tone that conveys how stupid he thinks I am. "She's not your sister."

It is hard to explain to them that they are older than their own aunt, so I don't do it. I just grin impishly at them. "Our family is special. So," I bounce the smaller toddler on my knee, and she squeals and giggles, "this is my sister. Can you play nicely with her? It's her birthday today. She just turned one."

"We is big boys," Preston declares haughtily. He holds up his pinky finger and the two beside it. It's an awkward move, but he doesn't seem bothered. "We is *three*."

"You *are* three," I nod and subtly correct him. "Very good."

"For a guy afraid of commitment, he's good with kids," I hear Wes mutter somewhere near Dad. When I glance up and narrow my gaze at him, he shrugs. "Well, you are on both accounts, aren't you?"

Vanna swats at him. Her dark hair has blonde streaks through it now, and it's up in a high ponytail. She places a hand on the ample curve of her hip. "Be nice. He's been hit with a lot today."

Her empathy makes me feel a tiny pang of guilt for how much I openly resent her. It's not that she's not a nice person,

Chapter One – Jack

but she came along and suddenly my time with my twin brother seemed to evaporate. I know we were in our twenties, and we lived a couple of hours' drive apart, but Vanna's entrance into Wes's life seemed to close a door on my time with him. And, for a twin, that was hard to reconcile. It still is, to be honest. I still don't understand why Wes can't go anywhere without her nowadays.

But I have other things to focus on right now.

Wes mumbles an apology and I dismiss it with a wave of my hand. If anyone's allowed to tease me, it's him.

Behind Connor, Henry and his wife, Sarah, enter my apartment. Thankfully, they're the last of the crew to be a part of this bizarre moment in my life. I'm not embarrassed, per se, but it does sting to admit that I was enough of a douche that it put a woman off informing me about my children for over four years.

Not my proudest moment, for sure.

I look over at Henry and offer him a hopeful smile. "So, I'm going to need your expertise."

"You Bradford boys are going to buy me a new car with all the work you're bringing my way," he teases me back, knocking shoulders with Dad.

I snort. "Thanks, man."

I set Vicky down on the carpet and Dad immediately squats down to her level, encouraging the boys to join in as he pulls a tub of Duplo blocks out of one of the bags that he and Connor brought with them. My heart does a funny little flip when I watch them all interacting together, and I wonder what things might have been like if I'd known about the twins from the start.

But, as Dad always says, we can't change the past. I can only go forward from here.

"So, is this a weekend thing, or…?" Wes asks, and I flop backwards against the back of the couch, already shaking my head.

I recap the morning's events, trying not to sound too frustrated when I express my heartache for the boys and the situation that they've been left in.

"What am I supposed to do about childcare?" I lament, the feeling of panic kicking back up again. "Never mind finding a bigger apartment. This place isn't even big enough for me anymore, let alone me and two growing boys. I have to *work*. Otherwise I won't be able to feed them, or keep a roof over their heads, or…or…"

Wes drops into the seat beside me and wraps me in a one-armed hug. Even though we're not really the same size anymore, there's a comfort I get from him which nobody else can match. I guess that's a twin thing? Either way, it helps calm me back down.

"The tenants in Will's apartment are leaving next week," Connor suggests when I'm no longer on the verge of hyperventilating. He shares a look with Dad. "Pretty sure we'd be happy to have you living upstairs. And that way we can help with the boys a bit easier, too."

Dad nods. "Once you've sold this place, we can talk about maybe buying me out, or, rather, talk to your brother about buying out the half he stands to inherit. I was keeping it in trust for the both of you anyway. You can buy out his half and then inherit the other half when I die."

"Well, that's not morbid," I sass him sarcastically. Then I turn to Wes. "Would you be down with that?"

Wes nods. "It makes sense to me, and I don't need to own

Chapter One — Jack

half an apartment on the coast." He grins. "Especially when Van and I can come crash in your guest room whenever we want anyway."

"Guest room?" I cock an eyebrow. "I have two sons. They can each have their own room." Wes and I grew up sharing a room which worked just fine until puberty hit. Then things got awkward. If I can manage to spare my boys that trauma, I will.

"Actually," Connor interjects with emphasis before Wes can argue with me. "With the costs of childcare, the fact that you have *two* little ones *and* you're on a single income… and considering that your shifts aren't standard nine-to-five Monday-to-Friday shifts, would you think about having a live-in nanny? Like…an au pair?"

We all swivel our heads to look at him and he shrugs. "We looked into it at one point. It's moot now with Will retired, but it would have worked better for his roster."

I honestly hadn't considered the fact that daycare doesn't really cater to parents in my position.

Shit.

The idea of inviting a stranger to live with me when I have spent the better part of the past ten years living happily on my own is not appealing. But I have the twins to consider now, and I can't expect Dad to look after them forever, even if he is retired.

Breathing out and rubbing my palm over my face, I nod. "Guess I'm going to need your help looking into that, too."

Chapter Two – Leo

Telling people that I like children usually earns me one of three predictable responses.

The first: bewilderment and disbelief. Like, why would a guy in his early twenties want to spend the prime of his life looking after other people's loud, sticky, stinky offspring? Most men my age are running from the very thought of dealing with the responsibilities that come with caring for small humans, not seeking them out.

The second: similar to the first, only laughter at my 'great joke'. Because, again, how the actual fuck could I enjoy 'babysitting' so much?

And, finally, the third: disgust, or the accusation that I must have some sort of perverse intentions. This is the reaction I hate the most for obvious reasons, and that's without going into my rant about the stigma of gay men being linked to pedophilia. Like, *hello*, statistics prove that's all based on fearmongering, but idiots will be idiots.

So, okay, I know it's not typical for a twenty-one-year-old

Chapter Two – Leo

guy to love being a nanny (or manny, as the cool kids say), but it's super rewarding. I mean, I'm being paid to cuddle and play and be silly all day. No stuffy office job for me! Additionally, because I've just signed up as a live-in au pair, I'll also be provided with room and board as part of my next contract…which is great, because I've been living out of a motel for the past couple of weeks ever since I walked in on my ex banging *his* ex. The ex before me, I mean. Who, it turns out, wasn't *actually* his ex, they were just 'on a break'.

Ugh. I never really got into *FRIENDS*, but I'll refer to my ex here forth as Ross because…why not? I've already forgotten his real name, considering he forgot that we were living together in a committed relationship. So. There's that.

Anyway, I manage to contain my excitement until I'm off the phone from the call with the agency. Then I dance around my dingy motel room, with its stereotypically moth-eaten carpet and the moulding shower curtain, and practically count the minutes until I can move into my new employer's home.

Angie, the lovely lady I just spoke to, gave me a brief rundown of the home into which I will be moving with the promise that she'll email me the contract and complete dossier 'soon'. From what I gathered, it's a single dad and his twin three-year-old boys, and there's been a bit of upheaval in their lives recently. I'll be moving into their Burleigh Heads apartment in three days' time, and I'll be paid a little more than industry standard because the dad is a firefighter. His hours, and therefore my hours, can be unpredictable, meaning additional pay in compensation.

To be honest, since *Ross* (I'm sticking with it) took most of my social group in our breakup, it's not like I have much of a life outside of my job anyway. And, hey, it sounds like this apartment is close to the beach, a playground, and the shops, so the kids and I will make our own fun.

Honestly, I can't wait. I've been going a little stir-crazy on my own these past weeks. I'd been in between contracts when my life went to shit. Living out of a motel, subsisting on a diet of instant ramen and home-brand cereal, I've also been chewing through my savings.

I've kept active by jogging and making use of the public exercise equipment along the beachfront esplanade, but that can only take up so much of one's day. I binge-watched all three seasons of *Ted Lasso*, though. I considered watching the fictional characters to be my daily social interaction. How sad is that?

(And let's not mention the way I ugly-cried over the series finale.)

So, yes, I am a little desperate for actual human interaction, even if it does come in the form of two people who aren't even potty-trained yet. I've met some adults who have proven not to be after a few drinks, too.

My phone pings with the notification of an incoming email. I dive into the information Angie has sent me with a gusto, memorising key details.

The boys are named Hudson and Preston, their dad is Jack. The twins are struggling with potty-training and are also suffering from night terrors. They haven't lived with Jack long, and there's a note that suggests he wasn't expecting to gain sole custody, but it's vague and I'm instantly curious.

Trying not to speculate, I read on about the boys I'll be looking after. The information is sparse, but it sounds like they're fairly average three-year-olds. They like to run around, play with blocks, draw, and paint. You know, the usual.

Chapter Two — Leo

Preston loves dogs and Hudson likes turtles. They both like *Sesame Street*.

I'm particularly happy about that last fact because I consider myself a Henson aficionado. I wonder if they've been introduced to the magic of The Muppets yet. If not, I'll start them with *A Muppet Treasure Island.* Who doesn't love the combination of classic literature and Muppet humour?

Great. Now I have the song 'Sailing For Adventure' stuck in my head. I'll be humming that for days.

I start thinking of icebreaker ideas and decide that, even though I'm an employee, I can't move into their home empty-handed. Especially when the employer himself hasn't interviewed me personally. Usually, we would meet before the contract with the agency is finalised, but in this case time was of the essence. Because of that, I want to make the best impression possible. I don't want to wind up being a stopgap. I want this to become a long-term contract. So, I need to take gifts of some kind. Books for the kids, maybe? We can read them together at bedtime.

With a plan in mind, I snatch up my keys and leave my motel room. I have supplies to buy!

Chapter Three – Jack

"Daddy!" The little voice is shrill and loud in the otherwise eerie silence of the apartment. I'm still not used to living in such a large space again, and I'm disoriented when I open my eyes blearily against the darkness. "Daddy!"

I'm not used to that word applying to me, either, so it takes a moment to understand that I'm being summoned.

I groan and scrub my palm over my face before leaning over to tap on my phone screen, where it's sitting on my bedside table, to wake it up. I squint at the bright display and groan again at the numbers. 2:13 a.m.

"*Daaaaaaaddy!*" The voice has multiplied, turning stereo as it echoes down the hallway and into my room.

Forcing myself up, I heft my legs over the side of the mattress and push to my feet.

Not all that long ago, being up at two in the morning on a non-workday would have meant I was doing something enjoyable. Now, it means I probably need to change the sheets

Chapter Three — Jack

on a kid's bed. Again.

I try to bite back the frustration over that thought as I stumble my way out of my room and into the bedroom next to mine. Sure enough, when I make my way past the threshold and flip the light switch, I'm greeted with the sight of both of my three-year-olds huddled in the middle of Hudson's bed, the fabric of their pyjama pants visibly wet, and a round dark patch on the blue sheets beneath them.

I even put them in pull-ups, but they seem to wet through most nights.

It's exhausting to deal with.

However, one look at their little tearstained faces and I remind myself that I can't lose my temper with them. They've already let it slip that Steph used to get cranky when they had nights like these, and I want them to feel safe with me.

Even if I don't have a fucking clue what I'm doing.

"Sorry, Daddy," Preston sniffles and then throws himself at me as I approach the bed. "I had bad dreams."

"Me too," Hudson echoes miserably and adds himself to the hug.

It takes a lot of coaxing to get them into the bathroom to get changed out of their soaked clothes, and I feel my irritation pick back up when the tantrums over having a quick shower start up.

I'm not built for this, and I hate that I can understand why Steph threw in the towel.

"*Please*," I resort to begging, wishing I could just climb back into my bed and tug the covers over my head. "Boys, you need to get cleaned up."

Preston seems to realise how close I am to my breaking point because he stops stomping his feet and his shoulders slump with defeat. "Can I sleep in your bed, Daddy? After the shower?"

The question silences Hudson's crocodile tears and he nods. "And me?"

At this point, if they asked me to feed them nothing but chocolate and ice cream for the next three months, I'd agree if it meant they'd get in the Goddamn shower and then let me get back to bed. Even though I know I run the risk of having to change my sheets —which do not have a waterproof mattress protector beneath them yet— I nod readily.

"Yeah," I agree tiredly. "But you've gotta get cleaned up first."

The fear that this is going to be my life for the foreseeable future roils my gut as I quickly rinse and scrub their little bodies down with the Spider-Man body wash Connor bought for them. They're cute, and I love them because they're mine, but I feel trapped in this new reality and it's *hard*. I miss sleep. I miss my independence. I miss my life before urine-stained bedding and midnight tantrums. Before my search history was full of questions like 'can I bribe a three-year-old to potty train?' and 'how can I get kids to stay asleep?' which, admittedly, may have been followed by questions asking why nighttime daycare isn't a thing.

There's also the fact that I spent the first couple of days talking to the boys as if they were adults and not quite wrapping my head around the fact that they were not on the same page as me. It turns out, expecting small humans to behave like grown-ups is a recipe for disaster.

"It's going to be an adjustment," Dad had said after the first night, when I had called him on the verge of tears to tell him I wasn't going to be able to manage this, "but they're not going to be three-year-olds forever. It gets easier, I promise."

Chapter Three – Jack

God, I can only hope he's right.

It's three a.m. by the time I get the boys in my bed, with one of them snuggled up on either side of me, their identical heads pillowed on each of my shoulders. Their eyelids have drooped, and their breathing is evening out, and I'm overwhelmed with guilt for being so frustrated with them.

I suck at being a dad.

I know it's really only been a handful of days, and maybe if I'd raised them from birth it might be different, but they're harder work than I had anticipated and I'm already run ragged trying to look after them.

My throat tightens as Huddy's little hand stretches across my chest, searching for his twin's. When he finds Preston's and then links their fingers together as he releases a little sigh, I have to blink back tears.

They deserve better parents than Steph and me.

Unfortunately, we're what they've got.

Prez nuzzles his forehead into the crook of my neck, little puffs of air tickling my skin, and he murmurs something that sounds suspiciously like 'Love you, Daddy', and I'm officially a goner.

The tears I've been trying to hold back slide down the sides of my face and trickle into my ears, but I don't care. I try not to make a sound while I let go of my emotions, feeling overwhelmed by the responsibility of sudden, unexpected parenthood and also the weight of my love for these kids.

If I'm all they've got, then I'm damn sure going to try and step up my game. I don't have any other choice now, and I am the adult. Change starts with me.

And, hey, the nanny will be starting soon. That's bound to help me become the best dad possible, right?

Right.

At least, that's the plan. It's not as though hiring a male nanny is going to complicate things more, right?

Chapter Four – Leo

On the day I've been told to move in, I pull my car into an on-street spot just down the hill from the apartment building which will be my home for the —hopefully— foreseeable future. The location is honestly fantastic. Yeah, parking in this area can suck, especially on a weekend, but it's such a short walk to the beach, local restaurants, and shops that it is worth the minor inconvenience of struggling to find a spot.

The building itself is midway up the steep hill and is fairly unassuming. Built maybe in the 90s, it's got that coastal vibe about it: a rendered brick façade, four stories of apartments, each with a street-facing balcony, and an underground car park for residents, as well as a little paved area in front of the building for visitors to park.

I shoulder my backpack, grab my rolling suitcase from the boot of my beaten up Corolla, and then snatch up the two matching gift bags by their handles. I travel light, but that might change if I can put down roots here for a year or two.

I drag myself and my meagre belongings up the hill to the apartment building and then buzz Apartment 4 on the boxy intercom when I reach the door to the main foyer.

"Hello?" a deep voice asks.

"Hi, is this Mr Bradford?" I start, and then forge on when I don't automatically get a response. "My name's Leo. Leo Martin. I'm here for the nanny position."

"Oh, you're early. Awesome. I'll buzz you up."

There's a click as the intercom disconnects, then the door to the lobby buzzes. I hurry to turn the handle before I miss my opportunity to get in. There's nothing more awkward than having to call back up and explain that you're an uncoordinated loser.

I wait for the lift and catch it up to the third floor, then step out into the hallway and knock on the apartment door. It swings open before I can fully retract my hand, and I do my best not to swallow my own tongue.

Christ on a cracker, this guy is gorgeous.

He's tall, well and truly eclipsing my 5'7" frame to the point where I actually have to tilt my head back to meet his stunning blue eyes. The dark beard is thick but trimmed neatly along his squared jaw, and the matching dark hair on his head is slightly curled on top, though the sides are cropped short. He's broad and muscular, with the kind of build that says 'working out isn't just a hobby, it's a lifestyle', and his smile is setting off a freaking flock of seagulls in my belly, bypassing butterflies completely.

"Leo?" He asks when words fail me and, fuck it all, even his voice makes me weak at the knees. It's deep and warm and…was that an accent?

"Hi, yeah, that's me." I immediately cringe at my awkward

Chapter Four - Leo

reply.

You want him to trust you with his kids, Martin. Get it together.

Giving myself a shake, I extend my hand and hope my smile doesn't give away my sudden burst of 'you're too fucking hot for my sanity' nerves. "Sorry, hi. Mr Bradford, yeah?"

Better, but not by much.

He laughs and shakes his head, "Jack, please." He takes my hand in his calloused palm and gives it a firm, but thankfully not aggressive, shake. Then he steps back and gestures for me to head inside. "Come on in. The boys are with my dad and his partner for now. It's not that I don't trust the agency, but…" He rubs the back of his neck and offers me a chagrined grin while I try not to salivate because, yep, that's definitely an accent. "This all happened pretty fast, and I was hoping to interview candidates before I settled on one, y'know? And I guess I just want to at least talk to you first before I introduce you to the kids."

I hold up my hands with my palms facing outwards. "No need to explain," I assure him, feeling more comfortable after his info dump. It's cute that he also babbles. Humanising. "I'd rather talk to you before meeting them anyway. We both need to be comfortable and confident in this arrangement." Admittedly, if he decides that he's not, I'll be up shit creek without a paddle, but I don't think it's going to come to that.

I hope.

"Great," he replies, then sweeps his hand through the air, motioning towards the couch in the middle of the living area. "Please, sit. Coffee work for you? Or tea?"

"Coffee's great. White with two, if that's okay?"

"Comin' right up."

I sit down on the end of the black leather couch and survey

the space as he putters around the adjoining kitchen. This half of the apartment is all open-plan and modern, with a glass-topped four-seater dining table taking up the space beside the kitchen, right in front of the sliding glass door that leads to the apartment balcony. The colour scheme is all neutral tones, and the flooring is that false wood click-clack laminate plank stuff. (Yeah, I'm not great with renovation terminology, but ask me about makeup and I'm your guy.)

The wall in front of me has a large TV mounted on it, and there's a large pile of toys in the corner — evidence that children do really live here. If I had turned left when I entered the apartment, I would have found myself in the hallway which I assume leads to the bedrooms and bathroom. It's quite a spacious layout, and part of me wonders how a single firefighter can afford a place like this on his own, especially when he's going to be paying me, too.

"Sorry there's no coffee table," Jack says, handing me a mug and pulling me out of my thoughts as he comes to sit on the opposite end of the couch, turning his body in to face me. "It was glass topped and Hudson…" He trails off and shakes his head ruefully. "Let's just say it was safer to get rid of it. So, yeah, you'll have to hold on to your mug for now."

I sip at the hot drink and try not to moan. Jack's got the good stuff and I've been living on sachets of Instant Roast for the past few weeks. It's not until after I've savoured a few mouthfuls that I realise I had closed my eyes…and that I have an audience.

"Good?" Jack asks with amusement, not even trying to hide his smirk behind his own mug.

I feel my cheeks burn. "Yeah. Sorry. I've been making do with instant crap for a few weeks and this is heaven in a cup."

Chapter Four – Leo

My handsome new employer screws up his face in commiseration. "The station doesn't stock great stuff, either. So if I want good coffee, I've gotta make it here and take it with me."

I peer over into his mug, and I'm unsurprised to find that he drinks his brew black. "Well, if you're drinking it straight like that, you need the nicer stuff."

"Anyway," Jack changes the topic without fanfare, "tell me about yourself. Forgive me for generalising, but young guys aren't usually…"

"Au pairs?" I offer. "Mannies? Interested in a career in childcare in general?"

"Exactly."

Even though I hate having to justify my chosen career, I appreciate how direct Jack is. He didn't sound judgemental, just curious. I can't say I blame him.

"I've always enjoyed looking after kids," I answer honestly, shrugging. "I'm an only child, so I used to love going to my friends' houses and playing with their younger siblings. Babysitting was my first job, and I loved it. Playing with toys, colouring in, playing dress-ups and other imaginative play…it doesn't feel like real work, you know? Watching littlies get excited about stuff we take for granted, watching them learn new things and grow up in front of my eyes…it's just so rewarding."

Jack blinks at me. "No shit?"

I frown. "No. I'm serious. Working with children feels like I'm cheating the system. I basically spend my days being a big kid." I pause. At twenty-one, I know I'm probably barely an adult in his eyes. I need him to trust that I'm not going to spend my days goofing off. That I'm a responsible choice. "That's not to say I don't also do educational or serious stuff with them, either. But I make it fun. Or at least I try to. Like…like Mary Poppins."

The second the words leave my mouth I want to snatch them back.

Like Mary Poppins? Who says shit like that?

Jack snorts. "You're going to get on really well with my dad, at least. He's all over making learning fun."

I smile at the fondness in his tone. "Is he a teacher?"

"Nah. Retired firefighter. But he has a one-year-old daughter with his partner, and he's a stay-at-home dad, so…" he shrugs.

Meanwhile, I blink. "You have a one-year-old sister?"

"Technically she's my stepsister, but Dad will adopt her as soon as he can. And he's been helping to raise her since she was born, so I think of her as my sister, yeah."

Once again, his tone is practically dripping with affection for his family. It fills my stomach with a fluttery feeling which I try to drown with coffee. "It's awesome that you're close with your family."

His gaze turns shrewd. I'm guessing something in my tone gave my own situation away. "You're not close with yours?"

I shake my head, sighing. This was a bridge I was going to have to cross eventually. "My parents kicked me out as soon as I turned eighteen, but things were strained for years before that." I shrug, trying to play off the old sting of rejection as though it's nothing. I force myself to meet his gaze.

Even though it's illegal to discriminate based on sexuality, I always double check that my employers aren't homophobic. If he's uncomfortable with me being gay, I'd rather give him an out now. I refuse to hide who I am for anyone…not that it's possible for me to really hide it. Gesturing vaguely over

Chapter Four - Leo

my body, I give my practised, self-deprecating spiel. "So, it's pretty obvious I'm gay. I've been like this forever. Hence being kicked out as soon as it was legal."

Jack's handsome face pulls into a scowl. I can't read whether it's on my behalf or directed at me.

"So, if my being gay is a problem—"

He holds up his hand, shaking his head. "Yeah, I'm gonna stop you right there." When he pushes to his feet, my heart sinks. I can usually pick the homophobic arseholes before we even sit down. I honestly didn't think he was one of them, but he's gesturing for me to follow him to the door, so I guess I was wrong.

Shortest lived contract ever.

I open my mouth to scathingly thank him for nothing as he opens the door, but he steps through it before I can and says, "Come on. It's easier to just introduce you."

"Huh?" I ask, tailing him as he bypasses the lift and heads down the stairs to the floor below.

I follow with my thoughts whirring.

Oh, God, are his neighbours going to gang up on me with him? Preach at me about my *lifestyle*? Sadly, it would not be the first time. I've been working in childcare since I was sixteen (longer, if you include the babysitting gigs) and I've heard it all and then some.

Jack knocks on the door to the apartment directly beneath his, shooting me a reassuring smile, while I wonder if I should have let someone —*anyone*— know where I was going to be this morning.

The door swings open to reveal an older man with steely blue-grey eyes and a silver fox beard. He has the same jawline as Jack, and the same warm smile. He's got to only be in his late forties, and I can see that he and Jack are related in some way. The similarities are too close for it to be a coincidence.

"Dad," Jack greets the guy with affection, confirming my suspicions, "this is Leo. Leo, this is my dad, Will. Can we come in?"

"It's feeding time at the zoo," Will warns with a chuckle, his accent matching his son's, but he steps aside. "Your boys are teaching my girl a ton of bad habits." He looks at me curiously as I follow Jack inside the apartment, but I'm too busy taking in the new space.

This apartment has the same layout as the one upstairs, but the colour scheme is starker, with greys, whites, and black accents. The living room here is also carpeted where upstairs is not. At the dining table, positioned in the same spot as Jack's, two little boys are making a mess of their meals while a toddler in a highchair claps and squeals. I can't help smiling at the sight.

Feeding time at the zoo indeed.

"Nice to meet you, Leo," Will says with a genuine smile. "You're the nanny?"

"I, uh, yeah." I'm so far out of my depth now, it's not even funny. "Sorry. I wasn't expecting…I mean, we were talking about…" I glance at Jack in askance.

What the hell even is this? I tell him my parents kicked me out because I'm gay and he takes me downstairs to…what, exactly? Gloat that he practically still lives with his? Because that's weird.

"Is Con around?" Jack asks his dad, ignoring my obvious confusion.

Will grins and nods, then cranes his head back towards the hallway behind him. "Sweetheart? Jack's here to collect his

Chapter Four – Leo

hellions."

"I wish you wouldn't call your grandkids that within their earshot," a higher pitched Australian voice complains with amusement before the owner appears, smiling widely.

'Con' is not at all what I expected.

He's a guy, for one thing. And he's young. He couldn't be any older than Jack.

Roughly my height but somewhat slimmer, he has light brown hair, pale skin and bright hazel eyes. He's dressed in skinny jeans and a grey polo shirt, and as he nears, I catch a smattering of freckles over his ski-dip nose and cheeks. He's handsome, I have to admit it, even if he's not my type.

Not that I should be checking him out, considering he seems beyond smitten with Will, kissing the older man's bearded cheek when he finally reaches us. Then he smiles at me, extending his hand. "Hi, I'm Connor. You must be Leo."

"Uh," is all I can manage as I shake his hand.

He misinterprets my gaping. Chuckling, he says, "Not a stalker: I did most of the groundwork with the agency, what with how much Jack had to organise with no notice."

"We haven't gotten that far," Jack tells him when I continue to flounder.

Professionalism, thy name is *not* Leonard Xavier Martin.

Connor looks between us, arching an eyebrow.

"I asked if Mister Brad—*Jack* had an issue with my sexuality," I blurt, correcting myself mid-sentence at Jack's glare. Then I cringe as the other two men look at Jack with wide eyes. "Not that he gave me any reason to think he might. I just…I always bring it up with prospective employers. I'd rather not agree to work or, in this case, *live* in a house where I'm not really welcome, you know?"

Great. I'm rambling. I don't have to worry that being gay will be a problem: I have to be concerned that I'll sound too much like a crazy person.

Surprisingly, Connor laughs. "Let me guess! Then he dragged you down here instead of saying 'it's all good, my dad is gay'?"

Relief sweeps through me at the knowing expression on Connor's face. "Exactly! I had no idea what the hel—*er*—heck," I glance back over at the table, but none of the kids seem to be paying attention to us, "was going on."

"Let's just say Jack's lucky he's pretty," Connor teases.

Jack offers an affronted, "Hey!" but there's no real emotion behind it. He's grinning at Connor. "Careful, or I'll start calling you 'stepfather'." He clears his throat and affects a really dodgy accent that sounds more British than Australian. "Oh, stepfather, please don't mock me so."

The expression on Connor's face says everything I need to know about how he feels about being addressed that way, and I can't blame him.

"Okay, okay," Will intervenes, but it's clear he's trying to keep a straight face, "don't go making things weird, Jack." He sighs as though the request is a lost cause and directs his attention back to me. "So, no. It's safe to assume being gay won't be an issue under Jack's roof."

"Yeah, I gathered as much. Well, once I got with the program."

Connor's expression sobers and he reaches out a hand, placing it on my bicep. It's a comforting gesture to go with the question, "Do many people take issue?"

I shake my head. "There was one family early on who made snide comments, especially when the dad noticed that I

Chapter Four - Leo

occasionally dabble with light makeup because it makes me feel good, but I learned my lesson after that. Now I'm very clear about it before I settle into a job. If you're not okay with it, I'm not comfortable working with you, and that means I'm not a good fit to look after your kids."

Connor nods. "Still, it's stupid that you even have to say as much in this day and age. And unfair." He frowns. "Those people are discriminating, really."

Sighing, I acknowledge, "I know, but I'd rather just find somewhere else to work than make a huge legal thing out of it. That's not going to change their opinions, either."

"Ugh, fair point," he says, but he still looks put out on my behalf.

"Anyway," Jack cuts in. His tone is filled with forced brightness, like he's uncomfortable with the path the conversation took. "Wanna meet the kids?"

I practically bounce on my heels. "Yes! Oh," I stop before Jack can lead me across the apartment to the dining area, "I bought them gifts. They're upstairs with my bag. It's just books, but—what?" I interrupt my own ramble with the question when I realise Jack is staring at me, mouth agape.

"You bought them presents?" he asks me.

I nod.

He blinks. "You didn't even know if I'd be okay with who you are, but you bought my boys presents?"

"Well, it wouldn't have been their fault if you turned out to be a raging tool."

Behind me, Will laughs while Connor says "Awww."

My attention is completely on Jack, though. He seems genuinely touched, if slightly bewildered. "Wow. That's awesome, man. Thanks."

"Hopefully they'll like them. Do they enjoy it when you read to them?"

"They seem to," he answers. Then he runs a hand through his thick, dark hair and looks over to where the boys are starting to shove at each other. Will passes by us to tend to them as Jack extrapolates. "The thing is, I didn't know about them until a couple of weeks ago. Their mom just turned up one day, dropped them on me and then took off. We've all been just trying to get our bearings."

Now it's my turn to gape. "Oh my God," my mouth runs before I can stop it, "that's…" I don't have the words.

Jack just nods anyway. "Yeah. It's been rough on them."

"And on you," Connor interjects softly. "You're allowed to admit that." There's an edge to the way he says it. It's knowing and empathetic all at once, but also firm, as though he's trying to convince Jack that it won't make him a failure or weak to acknowledge that the change to his circumstances has been difficult for him.

I let my gaze drift over to the table where Will is attempting to wipe little hands and faces clean. The toddler in the highchair is covered in mush. She's going to need a bath.

Then it clicks that she's the baby sister Jack spoke of earlier, and that Connor is speaking from experience. Though I'm curious about his story, I'm much more concerned with Jack's.

"Kids are hard work," I back Connor up. "I love them, and they're totally worth it, but when you're thrust into looking after them with no warning or experience, it's not always fun." I focus on the two little boys, identical save for the colours of their shirts and the smudges of food on their faces.

They look just like Jack. Dark hair, blue eyes, angular jawlines. They're adorable.

Chapter Four – Leo

Lips pulling up of their own volition, I continue, "They seem remarkably well adjusted for kids who have gone through that kind of upheaval. But then kids are resilient little things, aren't they?"

Jack exhales heavily. "We're getting there," he reiterates his earlier sentiments. "Huddy —he's in green today— is volatile. His tantrums are epic, and he likes to smash stuff. Prez," the one in yellow, I reason, "is withdrawn. Outside of Hudson, he'll only really talk to me, Dad, or Vicky. Uh, Vicky's the toddler. My sister." He juts his chin towards the highchair. "They've both completely given up on potty-training. *Nothing* is working there. They have night terrors, and they refuse to sleep in separate beds. Hell, half the time they refuse to sleep anywhere but in my bed with me." He swallows and sighs. "But now that Steph and I have got custody sorted out, we've agreed to weekly FaceTime calls, and I think that'll help. At least, I hope it will." Wiping a big palm over his face, he groans. "You sure you want to sign up for this?"

My heart aches for him in this moment. It's like the blinders of 'look at the hot man' have fallen away, and suddenly I notice the dark circles under his eyes and the lines of exhaustion making him appear drawn and weary.

"I'm more than sure," I answer, fighting the instinct to lay a comforting palm on his arm the same way Connor did for me only a couple of minutes ago. "And all those behaviours are normal for kids their age, let alone kids who have gone through the unexpected changes that they have. But if they're clinging to you, that's a good sign that they trust you. Even if you are new to them, you're their safe space."

I'm no child psychologist, mind you. But I know things could have been far worse under these circumstances.

You Don't Know Jack

I have so many questions I want to ask him. Probing, wildly inappropriate questions that I have no right to ask. Questions about how he is taking the sudden change in his life, from (I assume) carefree bachelor to dad of two three-year-olds. Questions about why the twins' mother never told him about them, and why she suddenly changed her mind and left them with him, all but walking out of their lives completely. Questions about whether he ever wanted kids, or if he resents them.

I keep my mouth shut.

"Thanks," Jack says with a sad little smile. He looks back over to the table just as the boys finally look over and seem to notice him.

They clamber off their seats, calling out "Daddy!" in matching high-pitched little voices and make a beeline for him.

His smile brightens, and it's good to note that the expression is genuine.

Even if he does resent them, it's clear that he cares about them.

"Hey, monsters," Jack tousles their hair as they each choose a leg to cling to, "have you been having fun with Grandpa?"

Preston shrugs and presses his face into Jack's hip, while Hudson says, "We drawed pictures, then Vicky cried an' Grampa gave us snacks." Like a lot of children his age, he can't quite get the 'r' sound down. It's insanely cute.

"That sounds like a lot of fun," Jack tells him with exaggerated enthusiasm.

Hudson looks sceptical.

"Anyway," Jack is still using the 'get excited' voice, "I want you to meet someone special."

Chapter Four - Leo

If anything, the boys seem to try and press in closer to his big body, studiously avoiding my existence. That doesn't deter my new employer.

"This is Leo," he introduces me. "He's going to be staying with us for a while."

That gets their attention. Hudson pulls his face away from Jack's hip to peer up at me curiously. I crouch down to meet him at his level.

"Hi," I say brightly. "I hope you'll be my friend."

Hudson ignores my statement, his big, blue eyes drilling into mine. When he speaks, the words are like a sucker-punch to my gut.

"Did your mummy go far away, too?"

Chapter Five – Jack

My new manny's eyes flash with pain before he schools his expression and pastes on a super-fake smile in response to Hudson's question.

"Nope," Leo says easily, "but I need to make new friends and your daddy says you like all the same things I do."

I have to hand it to him; he seems to be a natural with kids. Or he's just that good at his job. The lady I spoke to at the agency did say that, despite his young age, he was one of their best-rated nannies.

Huddy narrows his eyes. "Do you like turtles?"

Leo nods. "Yup. The Teenage Mutant Ninja Turtles are my favourite."

"I mean *real* turtles," Hudson huffs impatiently.

Leo's lips twitch with suppressed amusement. "Oh, of course, I love real turtles. I love dogs, too."

From where he's been hiding at Dad's side, Prez moves a fraction closer to Leo. "Dogs?" he repeats hopefully.

Leo beams and nods excitedly. "Yup. I love dogs *and* turtles."

Chapter Five – Jack

He reaches into his pocket and pulls out his phone. "Want to watch a video of a dog seeing a turtle for the first time?"

Oh, he's really good. Tension I didn't know I was holding in my shoulders melts away as he seems to easily draw the boys out of their shells. It gives me a moment to observe him properly.

Leo's a cute kid. He's got rounded cheeks, and long eyelashes framing wide brown eyes. Floppy dark blond hair which curls at the ends. A sweet smile and an equally sweet demeanour… and I'm pretty sure he's wearing lip gloss and maybe a bit of rouge. It suits him.

I think about what he said earlier, about his parents disowning him after he came out, and my heart hurts on his behalf.

I don't understand people sometimes. How could anyone treat someone as sweet as this kid so badly? And a parent no less! I've only known my boys for a couple of weeks, but I already know there is nothing they could do to make me love them any less.

No, I didn't want to be a parent. I never planned on it. But that's not because I hate kids. I'm just a realist. I'm a big kid myself, and my lifestyle has never been conducive to being responsible for the well-being of small, defenceless humans.

From the moment I realised what Steph and I had done, I accepted that my life —my plans, my outlook, my priorities— had to change. I've known some men to resent their kids for that. I can't help thinking that's dumb. The kids' existence was out of their own control. You know who could have controlled it? Me. If I'd bought a different pack of condoms or abstained completely, they wouldn't exist. The fact that I didn't is on me and not on the kids who are in this world because their mother and I created them, no matter how unexpectedly.

I still love them. I love their curiosity. Their adorable, if slightly hilarious, high-pitched chipmunk voices. I love their unbridled energy. Their complete lack of biases. I love their pudgy little fingers, still stuck between toddlerhood and being 'big boys'. I love their cheeky smiles. I love the way it feels when they throw their little arms around me, squeezing me tight. I love how quickly they accepted me as their dad when it was obvious I was just as lost as they were.

"And you is staying with us now?" Hudson asks, narrowing his eyes at Leo. He looks at me when Leo nods. "You staying, too? Not leaving us with him?"

My heart hurts all over again. I have to ignore Connor's strangled sob because I might just cry, too. I squat to my sons' level, making sure to look both the boys in the eye, one after the other. "I'll need to leave you with Leo when I go to work," I tell them honestly, "but I will always come home to you. Every day. I promise."

Hudson looks sceptical while Preston just looks resigned.

I hate that these are their go-to emotions now. That their life experiences have led them to have so little trust in the adults around them. They're only three, for Christ's sake!

"I promise," I repeat emphatically. "And if I don't, I'm not allowed to have ice cream for a whole month."

Predictably, the boys gasp. "That's forever!" Prez says, and I work hard not to laugh.

"Yep," I agree solemnly. "That's how serious I am." Reaching out, I take one of each of their hands in mine and tug gently. "So, will you be nice to Leo and make him feel welcome in our home?"

They do their cute little twin thing and nod in unison. I

Chapter Five - Jack

wonder if Wes and I were ever that adorable.

* * *

Leo's first night in our apartment is uneventful, but the first morning sees my heart leaping into my throat within an hour of Leo waking up. Really, it starts even before that.

It takes all my powers of persuasion to convince the boys —who once again slept in my room— not to barge into their new nanny's room and wake him up before the sun has properly risen. They start complaining about wanting to 'help' make breakfast as I try to herd them past the doorway to the third bedroom, but then sounds of life drift towards us from the kitchen.

Their little legs race towards the sounds of cupboards quietly shutting and cutlery tinkling and I follow them at an equally quick pace, not wanting them to do any damage.

Leo, wearing long, loose pyjama pants and a worn P!nk concert t-shirt meets my eyes and he cringes. "I'm so sorry," he says, confusing me. "I didn't mean to wake you."

"You didn't," I respond honestly, then make a grab for Huddy who is opening the cutlery drawer.

"You sure?" Leo gently pries Hudson's hand away from the knives and, instead, passes him two empty plastic plates. "Can you put those on the table for me?"

Hudson nods and turns around to complete his task. Leo passes two empty plastic cups to Preston. "And can you take them to the table for me? Brekkie's almost ready."

"Yeah, we were already up," I answer his first question, a little baffled by how easily he dealt with what could have been impending disaster. Then I give myself a little shake and question, "You made breakfast?"

"I hope that's okay? I didn't want to overstep, but it's been ages since I've been able to cook a proper brekkie…and as soon as I saw the eggs and the ham I couldn't stop thinking about a toastie. I was just gonna make them and reheat them when you got up." He turns back to the stove where he flips two sandwiches in a pan, revealing their golden brown tops. The smell hits my nose next and makes my mouth water. "I just went basic for the boys, thought half a toastie each would be enough," he nods at the sandwich cooling on a plate beside him, "and then I just kind of assumed you eat everything in your fridge so I put some onion and tomato on ours. I hope that's okay, too?"

"You know you don't have to cook for me, right? Like…that's not part of your job."

"Well I was cooking for myself anyway, and they're your ingredients." He shrugs. "Plus it *is* part of my job to cook for the boys—"

"When I'm at work," I interrupt, shaking my head and fighting a smile at his obvious exasperation.

He plants one hand on his hip and brandishes the spatula at me. "Do you want the sandwich or not, Jack?"

The boys giggle, and seeing the opportunity to acknowledge Leo's role and authority, I immediately act contrite. With exaggeration, I apologise and tell him I'll behave and eat my breakfast, and he plays along, patting me on the head and sending me to my seat at the table.

We all eat, and things go well as I offer to do the dishes and he takes the boys to clean up and get ready for the day. But, as I'm wandering down the hallway to check on their progress, I overhear their conversation.

Chapter Five - Jack

"What's that?" asks one of my chipmunk clones from the bathroom, his voice filled with curiosity.

"It's makeup," Leo answers easily. "Foundation, to be exact."

There's a brief pause and this is where my heart picks up its pace, nerves making my palms sweat. "Boys don't wear makeup," is my son's reply.

I pause in the hallway where they can't see me and close my eyes with a wince. I never would have told them such a thing, but Leo can't know that.

"Some people feel that way," his reply is just as even and patient as all his other interactions with the kids have been. His voice warps a little as he continues, and I crane my neck to peek through the doorway, watching him contort his face as he applies a brush to his skin. It smears a thin layer of creamy-coloured liquid over his skin, then he brushes in gentle circles, spreading and blending the colour over his face while he talks. "But I think boys can wear makeup if they want to."

At his sides, both boys are watching with rapt attention. "Why?" Prez asks.

"Well, it's not hurting anyone if they do, is it? Plus, sometimes it makes them feel good." He pauses. "But some people —girls and boys both— also feel good if they *don't* wear makeup, and that's totally okay, too."

"Do you feel good?" Hudson asks, still transfixed by watching the quick strokes of Leo's brush. He cocks his little head when Leo reaches for a tube of gloss and twists the lid, bringing the soft head of the applicator to his lips.

"Uh-huh," Leo says with his lips stretched out over his teeth. Finished with the tube, he rubs his lips together and surveys his handiwork in the mirror.

I'm not quick enough to move out of sight and we lock eyes

through the reflection. There's a momentary flash of panic in his eyes, and I shake my head. I hope that the smile I shoot him says that I really don't mind that he's wearing makeup, or that he's being open about it with the boys.

"Can I try?" Hudson presses.

Leo glances down at him and then back at me as Prez, not wanting to be left out, declares that he wants to try the makeup, too. Whatever he sees on my face must reassure him, though, because his lips quirk before he smiles back down at the boys and nods. "You can try a little bit of lip gloss today," he answers easily, and moves the tube in question out of Huddy's grabby reach, "but I'll pop it on you. No sense having you two look like a couple of Picassos this early in the morning."

I snort while Prez scrunches up his nose in confusion. "What's Picassos?"

Leo considers the question. "Picasso was an artist who made, hmm, let's just call them *messy* pictures of faces."

The boys giggle and I lean against the doorframe as Leo applies a super-thin layer of gloss to Huddy's lips and then to Prez's. The boys smack their lips, then lick them and make identical grossed-out faces.

"It's sticky," Prez complains.

"It tastes yucky," Hudson adds.

"But it looks pretty," I finally say, causing both boys to turn my way.

"Daddy!" they cry in unison and scamper my way. Prez purses his lips and asks, in a squished voice, "It's really pretty?"

"The prettiest," I insist. "Can I take a picture to show Grandpa?"

They cheer and bounce on their heels.

"Let's go back out into the living room, then." I say, and

Chapter Five - Jack

they're out the door before I've even finished the sentence.

I'm chuckling as I move to follow them, but I catch sight of the bright, approving smile on Leo's face as I do and my breath catches.

I have no idea what that's about, but the boys call my name insistently and the moment is broken.

I tell myself that I'm just relieved the kids and I didn't upset the nanny on his first official morning on the job and the day continues without a hitch.

* * *

Thanks to my boss being incredibly understanding, I arranged to have a few additional days off while Leo got settled in with the boys. I didn't want to be a helicopter parent, but I can admit that I was anxious about leaving them with a complete stranger so soon after their entire lives were upended.

I shouldn't have worried, though. Leo is everything the agency and his supporting references said he'd be. Over the past few days, I've handed him the reins and just lurked in the background as he got to know my kids. He got into a routine with them, learning their favourite foods, what kind of activities they enjoyed the most, and even suggested a few new ideas of his own. He never seemed uncertain, and I liked that. Confidence is a personality trait I appreciate in people, especially people I'm entrusting my kids with.

Today's the last day of my leave from work, and I can't help but feel unnecessary as I sit back and watch Leo packing an insulated bag with sandwiches and snacks. He's got the boys helping him; something which initially made me cringe. I don't have the patience to watch two three-year-olds mutilate food with clumsy coordination, but Leo takes it all in stride. He helps Hudson spread peanut butter over a slice of bread with a butter knife, then shows Preston the easiest way to peel a mandarine with his hands, talking through the steps as they go. He talks to them in the same easy tone that he uses with anyone else: he doesn't condescend or pitch his voice high with excitement. I like that, too.

It hasn't felt weird sharing my home with a stranger, either. That part has been the biggest surprise of all, really. The apartment isn't tiny, but there's only one bathroom shared between the three bedrooms, and the rest of the space is all open-plan, shared living. In the minimal amount of downtime he's had since he got here, I've discovered that Leo is quiet and tidy. He loves to read or listen to audiobooks, and he goes for jogs around the neighbourhood in the early evenings when the sun is starting to set. If not for the amount of time I've spent watching him with the boys, I would barely have noticed that he even lived here. Hell, my neighbours in the apartment block in Surfers were way more disruptive of my peace and quiet and they'd lived in entirely different spaces from me.

"Daddy," the chipmunk-esque voice of one of my kids pulls me out of my musings and I look up from my seat in the living room to find three sets of eyes on me. Hudson huffs impatiently, so I gather that it was him talking.

"Sorry, bud. What's up?"

"What sammich do you want?" he asks slowly, brutalising the word 'sandwich' adorably.

"PB and J," I answer easily, seeing the ingredients on the bench already.

The boys blink and scrunch up their little faces in confusion.

Chapter Five - Jack

"Your daddy means peanut butter and jam," Leo explains.

"Well, jelly," I shrug. "But seeing as you Aussies don't do grape jelly, strawberry jam will have to do."

"Eww," Preston screws up his nose. "You can't put jelly on a sammich! It's all wobbly!"

Leo just launches into an explanation about jelly and jello and how we call things differently here in Australia than America, and I'm just as rapt by the way he describes it to the boys as they are.

Hudson sighs dramatically when Leo's done. "They're silly. Why don't they just call jam 'jam'?"

Okay, so maybe the boys weren't as rapt as I was.

"Well, we'll call it jam," Leo tells him seriously, then he sends me a conspiratorial wink. I grin back, even as he adds, "but putting strawberry jam on a peanut butter sandwich is still sacrilege if you ask me."

"Good thing I didn't," I banter back, still grinning. Then I look to Hudson. "Can you make my sandwich as good as yours?"

He nods enthusiastically. "Can I tries it?"

"Try it," Leo and I correct in unison. We chuckle and then I nod at Hudson. "But, yes, you can have a bite at lunchtime. And you, too." I add for Prez's benefit when he opens his mouth to ask.

"Maybe we should make two of the abominations, then," Leo suggests.

Preston cocks his head. "What's a abod…adom…ablom…"

"Abomination," Leo repeats. Then he breaks it down into syllables, smiling as Preston dutifully repeats them back. "Good boy. An abomination is something gross that shouldn't exist."

"So…Daddy's sammich is gwoss?" Hudson asks sceptically, narrowing his little blue eyes, and I have yet another moment where I wonder if every parent gets struck stupid by just how cute they think their kids are, or if I'm an anomaly.

"I think it is," Leo nods, then boops Hudson's nose with the tip of his finger. "But you can find out for yourself."

"So, what's the feast for again?" I ask as Leo helps the boys start spreading peanut butter over slices of bread. How he's managing to keep an eye on both at the same time is beyond me, but he leans over each one to correct their technique right before disaster strikes each time. I rub the back of my neck with a sheepish smile when he looks up and arches an eyebrow at me. "I wasn't properly caffeinated when you told me."

"We're going to have a picnic at the park," he says, amusement dancing in his brown eyes. "The boys were really well-behaved yesterday, and they ate all their veggies at dinner, so today's reward is to walk down to the playground on the beachfront." He pauses to remove the slices of bread now slathered in peanut butter and puts a fresh slice of bread on the counter in front of each boy, followed by the jar of jam. I cringe a little as the boys jab their butter knives, still streaked with peanut butter, straight into the jar. Leo doesn't seem bothered, despite all of his anti-PB and J propaganda. "I figure they can tire themselves out on the playground, we can eat lunch in front of the beach, then we can come back home for N-A-P time."

I snort. "Is the spelling for my benefit or theirs?"

"A little from column A…" he sasses back, weighing imaginary scales in the air with his hands.

He's cute when he's sassy.

My heart gives a funny thump as the thought filters through

Chapter Five - Jack

my brain, but the moment is lost as quickly as it appeared when Prez's gasp and murmured 'uh-oh' get my full focus.

"What's up, buddy?" I ask him, already rounding the counter to help.

His eyes are tearful as he cranes his neck back to look up at me. "I had a accident." He gestures down to the wet patch spreading across the front of his jeans. "I'm sorry."

My heart twists at the expression on his face. Both boys have told me that their mom got angry if they had accidents, and while I can understand that the whole potty-training thing is frustrating, I never want them to think I'm going to yell about it. I'm not judging Steph, because I don't know the whole story of what she was going through, but I'm still determined to be different for them. But before I can blink, Leo's on it.

"I've got it," he gently pushes me aside and takes Prez's hand. "It's okay, kiddo. Everyone has accidents sometimes. Let's go get changed. Those jeans wouldn't have been great with the sand anyway." He points at the half-completed sandwiches. "Can you finish up here?" Before I can even nod my reply, he places his hand gently between Hudson's shoulder blades. "Huddy, I think you should head to the toilet now, too, and we'll get you in a pair of boardies as well, yeah?"

And just like that, my nanny wrangles the boys out of the kitchen, through the living room and down the hallway, chattering with them as they go. I listen to him talking to the boys happily, even though I can't make out what's being said, and I'm once again struck by how much I appreciate his confidence and take-charge attitude.

It's a little harder to ignore the increased thudding of my heart this time, but I manage.

You Don't Know Jack

* * *

At the end of my first week of returning to work, I am not expecting to walk into my apartment at 9 p.m. to the sight of a perfectly shaped ass wrapped in sleek black lycra, the slender form of its owner bent over a thin yoga mat in the middle of the living room. Unable to recall the last time I was intimate with anyone, my dick immediately takes notice.

Long legs. Pert, round globes. The gentle curve of a spine and the hint of narrow hips. All of it presented in an enticing, feline-like display just for me.

Well, no. Probably not for me. But I'm only human and it is my living room.

Of course, that thought jolts me enough to question why this tempting display is happening in my living room at all. Then it hits me.

This siren in spandex is my kids' nanny.

My kids' very male nanny.

Well, I think to myself, bemused and maybe a tiny bit confused, *that's new.*

Can I put it down to the androgynous nature of the display? Being overtired and stressed-out? Or even the simple fact that I've only had my hand for company for the past couple of months?

Probably not.

I swallow roughly, determined not to overthink it. "Uh," I say after clearing my throat, amusement chasing away my confusion as Leo jumps in surprise, almost toppling over, "hi."

"Jesus," he huffs, straightening his spine as he spins to face me. He splays a pale hand over his chest dramatically. "Wear a bell or something!"

Chapter Five - Jack

His dark blond hair sticks to his forehead with sweat. There's a thin, glimmery sheen on his rosy, pink cheeks and in the divot of his throat beneath his Adam's apple. Thin, pale chest hairs peek out from beneath the scooped neck of the loose singlet he wears and my eyes are drawn to them.

It's funny, but I imagined he'd be waxed or shaved or something. Not that I can recall actually giving the subject of his body hair any thought, but now I am and I can't stop.

"Sorry," I reply belatedly, the silence between us having spanned just a touch too long, "I didn't mean to scare you."

He just shrugs and waves me off. "Nah, it's my bad. I lost track of time. The boys extended bathtime and then wanted two extra bedtime stories and I couldn't say no, so my whole routine was a bit out of whack. Then I didn't hear you come in." He points to his ears where two black earbuds are nestled, presumably previously playing music or yoga instructions or whatever one listens to while they're doing the downward dog.

I can't help the way my lips tug up at the description of his night, though. "Huddy and Prez know just how to use those puppy dog eyes, don't they?"

"Mmmhmm," Leo agrees, now wearing a matching smile. It's soft and full of affection and it makes my insides tumble to know that he genuinely cares about my boys. "I'd like to pretend that I'll learn to be immune to them, but we all know that'd be a lie."

It's not entirely true. I've seen him stand firm just as often as I've watched him give in to the boys' wide-eyed pleading. He picks his battles the same way Con and Dad do with Vicky. He's firm but fair, and only a pushover when there's no reason not to be. It's the way I want to be, too.

You Don't Know Jack

I don't say any of this, though. I just chuckle and bob my head in agreement, then watch as he turns slightly, stooping to roll up his yoga mat. The fabric of his shirt gapes around his huge sleeve holes and I catch a glimpse of his chest. More of that creamy, pale skin and a smattering of fair-coloured hair, and a far-too-cute, tiny, pink nipple, pebbled and hardened. I have the strangest urge to nibble at it.

I cough and avert my gaze.

What the hell is going on with me?

"Anyway," Leo chats in his usual bright and chirpy way, "there's a plate in the fridge for you. It's just sausages and mash, but it's there if you want it."

There's honestly something to be said for coming home after a long shift to a clean kitchen and a meal prepared by someone else. Leo's not paid to cook for me, but he does it anyway. I don't have to force my grateful smile. "Thank you. That's perfect."

Once again, he waves me off dismissively. "I was cooking them for the boys, anyway. Did you know Huddy prefers the honey beef ones while Prez only wants chicken sausages? You've got one of each."

"No, I didn't know that." I could write a book full of all the things I don't know about my sons. "But I'll make a note of it."

"Meh, they'll change their minds within a few weeks. All kids do. Just when you think you've got a handle on their favourite things…bam! You're wrong. They hate them now."

With his yoga mat rolled up, Leo follows me into the kitchen and then bypasses me, pulling my meal from the fridge. I watch as he tears off the cling wrap, balling the plastic up before he slides the plate into the microwave. He leans against the counter and tells me, "Anyway, I took them down to the

Chapter Five - Jack

park again today. Will and Vicky came along, too. It was nice getting to know him a bit better."

I don't know why, but the thought of my manny befriending my dad makes my heart skip a beat in a good way. It's like I want them to like each other, to have more reasons to drag Leo into my personal life. "Dad's pretty great," I admit, knowing that Leo's expecting some sort of response. "This used to be his place, actually." I gesture vaguely at our surroundings. "Until he fell in love with his downstairs neighbour."

Leo laughs and turns as the microwave beeps. "So he said. They're lucky men, Connor and your dad." I don't like the almost melancholy lilt to his voice, but it's gone before I can try to comfort him. "Anyway, it sounds like the wedding's going to be a blast." He pulls the plate from the microwave before he slides it onto the counter in front of me.

"That's what you get when one of the grooms is a party planner."

"Events coordinator," Leo corrects me with a wry twist of his lips.

I laugh, reaching for my fork. I point the tines at him. "I see you've been Connored."

"Is he aware that you've turned his name into a verb?"

"I mean, mine already kind of is. I'm sharing the love."

His laugh, when it's uninhibited and startled from him, is dorky and stupidly cute. It's like a little wheeze and finalised with a short snort. His cheeks turn pink again, as though he's embarrassed, but he still says, "And now I'll never use the phrase 'jack off' again."

"Not without thinking of me, anyway." There's stunned silence after my thoughtless quip and I resist the urge to facepalm. "That's not what I meant."

You Don't Know Jack

If Leo's cheeks were pink before, they're bright red now. He nods so vehemently that it even shifts the lock of hair from his forehead that was previously plastered down by sweat. "Oh, I know."

I have no idea how to smooth over the awkwardness I just created, so I don't bother trying. Instead, I just pretend like I have no shame and I keep talking while I use the side of my fork to cut into one of the sausages on my plate. Who needs knives, anyway? "And you'll think of me when you see some guy and say he's jacked up."

"That's not a verb, though."

With a bite of food in my mouth, I roll my eyes. "You're getting me on a technicality?" I ask with my mouth full, amusement flooding my belly with warmth as he crinkles his nose. "Really?"

"What can I say? I like semantics." The pink hue to his cheeks and neck are starting to fade, the weirdness I'd caused now dissipating. Instead, we're just bantering playfully, and if I tell myself that it's no different from the way I tease my friends, I might just believe it.

The desire I felt for him when I walked inside was an anomaly, that's all. Maybe now that I've got a roommate for the first time in my life (well, one I'm not related to), it's just a delayed curiosity caused by proximity. People who live together get close, right? Isn't that why so many people have 'experimental' phases when they move away for college? It's easy for a close friendship to develop, and then lines between affection as friends and attraction get blurred. Add onto that an unexpected dry spell and ta-da! Projection.

As we settle in for a chat which takes the topic of semantics and somehow moves into movie trivia, the weirdness inside

Chapter Five - Jack

me finally drains away. I'm glad for the company while I eat my meal, and it's nice getting to know Leo as a person and not as my kids' nanny. Even if he does admit that he prefers Star Trek to Star Wars, the nerd.

Everything is back to normal by the time I'm washing my plate and yawning, and I'm glad. Not because the thought of being interested in a guy really bothers me, but because he's my kids' nanny. Being into him would complicate things in all the worst ways, and my boys need stability in their lives.

But my heart still thumps a little bit harder when Leo and I part ways at our respective bedroom doors, and his impish smile is burned into the backs of my eyelids when I try to go to sleep.

I'm not sure what's going on with my brain, but it needs to get with the program sooner rather than later, or I am fucked…and not in the way I'd like.

Chapter Six – Leo

Torture. Living with Jack Bradford is torture.

Oh, he's a nice guy and a considerate roommate. He's friendly, he cooks when he's off shift (and he's damn good at it, too), and he's happy to leave me to my own devices.

But he's also ridiculously hot, and the fact that he's proving to be a hands-on, attentive, doting dad is making my non-existent ovaries go kaboom!

Case in point: I've just come out of my room to find him wrestling with the boys on the living room rug. The couches have been pushed aside and all three of them are laughing and rolling around with wild abandon. It's heartwarming to see. But the fact that Jack is currently shirtless is making my heart pound and other parts of my anatomy are taking notice, too.

It's been a long time since I've hooked up with anyone, but the more I watch the strong, tattooed body on the floor, the more I think I need to go out and get laid before my slowly developing crush on my employer becomes creepy.

Chapter Six - Leo

Clearing my throat, I force what I hope looks like an easy smile and I step into the room from the hallway. Three matching heads of dark hair, tousled from their play fighting, swivel in my direction. Before I know what I'm doing, I raise my phone and snap a picture of the scene.

Honestly, I couldn't help it. Jack's smile is wide, and the boys are beaming from their positions kneeling beside him, trying to use their combined strength to roll his muscled frame over. They're all a little sweaty and pink from their exertions and they look like three peas in a pod. Even though I know he had DNA testing done to confirm his paternity, there's no denying that Jack is the boys' dad. They look just like him.

"You gonna send that to me, or is that for your personal collection?" Jack asks me from where he's still sprawled on the floor, seemingly ignorant of the two small humans pushing at his shoulder and hip.

Hoping that I'm not blushing, I aim for cockiness and shrug. "Why can't I do both?"

"Just gotta crop the boys out of your copy," he pushes the joke further, nodding as though the idea of me wanting to keep his photo for personal reasons is completely acceptable. "Otherwise it's just weird."

I can't help laughing at that. "Because taking photos of my boss isn't weird to begin with?"

"Hey, when your boss looks as good as I do, you can be forgiven."

I shake my head, but a smile still tugs at my lips. "No-one's ever accused you of being humble, huh?"

"Perish the thought."

"Daddy!" Hudson demands, clearly bored with our grown-up bantering. "Prezzie and I still have to win!"

You Don't Know Jack

The boys always win. And if that doesn't add to Jack's hotness, I don't know what does.

Holding my hands up in surrender, I inch past them and head towards the kitchen. "Have you guys eaten yet?" It's still only early and Jack's off work today, so I technically have a day off, too. But I don't mind cooking for all of us, just as Jack doesn't mind including me when he's making family meals, either. It just works.

"Not yet," Jack calls back to me. "I was gonna do bacon and eggs, but then I was challenged to a duel."

And, because he is such a good dad, entertaining and bonding with his kids was more important to him than feeding them. I get it. My heart gets it. My stupid, traitorous cock gets it.

"Well, you can't possibly turn down a challenge like that," I call back towards the lounge. "I'll get brekkie going."

I'm actually grateful for the distraction. I much prefer focusing on scrambling the eggs and sizzling the bacon to daydreaming about doing some wrestling of my own with Jack.

I mean, how unprofessional could I be? For all intents and purposes, he's my employer. He's just had his whole life turned upside down, too. Oh, and he's also straight. Having his needy gay manny lusting after him is a complication he does not need in his life right now. Or ever. Plus, I get the feeling our age gap might be an issue for him, even if it's a lot smaller than the age gap his dad and Connor share.

"Mmm," Jack's deep voice is a rumble that makes me jump as he comes up behind me in the kitchen. "Smells great."

Being so lost in meal prep and cooking, I didn't realise that the sounds of tussling had stopped filtering through from the

Chapter Six - Leo

lounge room. I certainly didn't hear Jack pad across the tiled floor with his bare feet.

"Jesus," I clutch at my chest, feeling my face flush, "don't do that!" I peer around him, frowning. "Where are the boys?"

"I took them to the toilet and then they insisted on dressing themselves. I was sent out here because I was —and I quote— cramping their style." He arches a knowing eyebrow at me. I have to fight back the ungodly urge to lick it. (Seriously. An eyebrow!) "Any idea why my three-year-olds sound like teens from a badly written movie?"

My blush only deepens. I can feel my face turning red under his amused scrutiny. "Uh…no?"

Jack snorts, but his smile turns dopey. It's an expression I've come to think of as his 'dad face'. "It was all kinds of adorable, really."

My heart flip-flops in my chest and I do everything in my power to just laugh the exchange off and tell Jack to set the table. After he does as I've commanded, I toss the big, plastic spoon I've been using to stir the scrambled eggs at him and tell him to dish the meal up while I go in search of the kids.

"It's your day off," he argues at my retreating back.

"I know," I toss over my shoulder.

It doesn't matter that I'm not supposed to be working. I love these kids, and it doesn't feel like a chore to look after them. In fact, the whole setup feels increasingly more domestic with every passing day, which adds to the torture and is also probably kind of dangerous.

I know better than to get so attached. One day, these kids will be old enough for school. Or they'll return to their mother's custody. Or —and this is the possibility that will hurt the most— Jack will find a nice woman to settle down with and she might take over the child-wrangling when he's at work. In any case, I won't be needed any more.

Just the thought of the inevitable future hurts this time around.

I am too attached. Too emotionally involved.

It's only been a month.

But the boys have come out of their shells so much in such a short amount of time that I can't help being this attached. Hudson's feisty little personality is accompanied by a fearlessness and sense of adventure I struggle to quench. And Preston is the most curious little thing I have ever come across. He asks about a thousand questions a day, and I've even had to resort to Googling answers. Now that they're settling in, they're both happy children, and they absolutely adore their daddy (not that I can blame them). They also love their grandpas —as much as Connor whines about being too young for the title— and both boys are super protective of their toddler aunt.

Because I've been here to see this all develop in front of my eyes, I can't help but feel like I'm a part of it.

It's incredibly dangerous thinking.

I shake the thoughts off as I enter the boys' bedroom which is decorated with decals of superheroes. The bedding is all brightly coloured and there are two long, low bookshelves overflowing with kids' books and toys. But, most notably at the moment, there are clothes strewn across the floor and both boys are still naked as they play with toy cars in the middle of the fabric hurricane.

"I see getting dressed is going well," I say, startling them from their play. "Weren't you supposed to put on your clothes?"

Hudson looks up at me, completely unrepentant. "It was

Chapter Six - Leo

too hard. My shirt got stuck. Cars are more fun."

"Cars are a lot of fun," I agree, bending to pick up the myriad shorts, shirts and tiny pairs of undies littering the carpet, "but getting dressed is important. Your brekkie is ready. Aren't your tummies all growly? Mine is! Listen."

Both boys cock their heads and strain to hear. Unable to help myself, I affect a deep voice and growl, "Grrrr, feed me!"

They erupt into giggles. I swear I live for that sound.

Tossing the pile of clothing onto the nearest of the two single beds, I grab the closest boy —who I know to be Preston because a) he wasn't challenging me and b) he's got a little tan coloured birthmark on his left butt cheek, whereas Hudson does not— and laugh as he squirms in an attempt to escape. "Come on, which clothes are you wearing today?"

After some back and forth, and a whole lot more wriggling and protesting, both boys are finally dressed and ready to face the day. When we finally emerge and head into the kitchen/dining area, my hair is plastered to my forehead.

Jack chuckles and arches his eyebrows. "I told you I should have gone."

"Nah," I wave him off, lifting Huddy onto his chair and pushing it in, then moving to do the same with Prez, "I don't have to go to the gym, now. Wrestling naughty children is enough of a workout." I ruffle both boys' already messy dark hair affectionately.

"I not naughty," Hudson protests.

"*I'm*," Jack and I correct him at the same time, then I continue to illustrate, "I'm not naughty."

"Yes, you are," Hudson laughs, completely missing the point.

Jack and I share another grin while he slides two matching plastic plates in front of the boys. He's already cut their bacon up into bite-sized pieces and has cut Huddy's buttered toast into triangles while Prez's dry toast has been cut into squares. The crust is missing from both.

It's perfectly normal for parents to know their kids' preferences, but this simple action only reminds me what a great dad Jack is. Even when the twins are at their most frustrating, he never loses his temper with them.

He's too hot for his own good.

"So, I was wondering," he says as he hands me my plate. Mine is plain white and ceramic, but I note that he's buttered my toast all the way to the edges the way that I personally prefer it. My heart squeezes as I realise it. "I know it's your day off and hanging with your boss is probably the last thing you wanna do, but I've got a spare ticket for the Roar game tonight. Wanna come with?"

I set my plate down on the table and head over to the fridge, pulling out the half-empty bottles of orange and apple juice. Jack's already got glasses for us and plastic cups for the boys set out at our place settings. "Doesn't Connor usually go with you?"

It's actually really cool to see the friendship between Jack and his dad's fiancé. They even play on the same recreational indoor soccer team. I doubt most guys would be that cool with their dad being with someone their own age, but Jack and his twin brother, Wes, seem to be cut from a different cloth.

"Yeah, but Dad's going to some old-man tribute band thing with his buddy, so Con's gotta stay home with the Vickster and the boys."

Having piled bacon and a mound of perfectly scrambled eggs on top of my toast, I use a fork to cut through my open

Chapter Six - Leo

breakfast sandwich. I snort a little at his description of 'old-man tribute band', and then offer: "I could look after them so he can go."

"Dude, no. It's your day off." Jack frowns at me. "Besides, in the past month, I don't think I've seen you go out for anything other than the boys' stuff."

My cheeks heat and I keep my gaze studiously focused on my plate. I buy myself some extra time, cutting off another bite and chewing it thoughtfully.

It's true that my social life is dead on arrival. My ex kept most of my friends in the split and I'm not exactly a social butterfly to begin with. Lately, I've been getting my fill of social interaction from Jack himself, or from Will, seeing as we often take the boys and Vicky down to the park together. In fact, I'd say Will is probably my closest friend nowadays… which is kind of sad when I consider the fact that we only met a month ago, and we really only talk when we're taking the kids out. But it's hard not to bond with the guy when he's a) the twins' grandfather and b) a stay-at-home dad who lives in the apartment directly beneath us.

"I'm an introvert," I eventually respond when it becomes clear that Jack's expecting me to say something. It's not exactly the truth, but it's not wholly a lie, either. Since my breakup, I've become an introvert by circumstance.

"Bull-*er*-irt. Bullshirt." Jack manages to correct his swear in time, cutting his eyes towards the boys who have more breakfast scattered across the table than they've managed to get into their mouths. We've been enforcing the use of cutlery with them, and their hand-eye coordination still needs work. Content that the twins are still focused on their food, Jack looks back at me and points at me with his fork. "You're too chirpy and friendly for that to be true."

I frown. "Are you suggesting introverts aren't friendly?"

He rolls his gorgeous eyes. "Not intentionally, no. I'm saying I think that you, personally, are more social by nature." His expression softens and he leans in towards me until I catch a whiff of his spicy aftershave. Fireworks explode in my brain as the masculine scent registers. For as long as it's been since I went out to socialise, it's been even longer since I went out for other reasons. I'm so distracted by how damn good he smells that I almost miss his softly murmured, "You know I'm not going to be a di-*er*-doofus if you wanna date or whatever, right?"

Now my cheeks flush for a different reason. Because I don't want to 'date or whatever' with a random guy. I want Jack.

Jack, my boss.

Jack, my boss who is straight.

Jack, my boss who is straight and who is only just finding his footing after having his whole life upended.

I sure can pick 'em, huh?

"I know," I hurry to assure him. I cast another quick glance at the boys. They're slowly making their way through their meal, still distracted by the food. "But I had a rough breakup not all that long ago and I'm…" What? Living in a permanent state of self-torture? "…recalibrating." I finish lamely.

Jack's scruffy face contorts with concern and sympathy. "Shi-*uh*-oot, man. I'm sorry. I didn't know."

Why would you have known?

I shake the question from my head and paste on a smile. "It's all good. Really. But, yeah, I've kind of been starting from a clean slate, so…" I shrug. "Finding new friends is a lot harder at our age than it was at theirs." I tilt my chin at the boys. They

Chapter Six - Leo

make new friends on a daily basis, easily playing with other kids out on the playground. My lips tug upwards in what I'm sure is a melancholy kind of smile. I miss those days where you could just ask 'will you be my friend?' and that would be that.

Jack nods. I watch his lips curl into a much brighter smile than my own. "Then it's settled," he says, tucking back into his breakfast with renewed zeal. "You're coming to the game tonight. Some of the guys from work and my indoor team will be there, too. Con and I usually catch the train to Brisbane, because traffic —and parking— near the stadium's a pain in the ass. It means we can have a couple of beers, though. You good with that?"

I feel mildly intimidated by the thought of meeting so many new people at once —especially people who are presumably big, brawny firefighters or sports nuts; people who are Jack's friends— but I must admit that a night watching soccer sounds like fun. Travelling on the train for the hour and a half it takes to get from Varsity Lakes station to Milton Station isn't as appealing, but I'll be travelling with Jack, so I'm sure I won't get bored.

I bob my head. "Okay, sure. Sounds good."

Jack offers up his closed fist for a bump and I laugh when the boys demand fist bumps, too. I have to ignore the way my stomach flips when Jack happily indulges them.

* * *

Suncorp Stadium at Milton is exactly the same as it was the last time I was here. Only, when I was here last, it was to attend a concert, so the grass sports field was not visible beneath the stage or the plastic click-clack flooring that protected it from thousands of people. It's a fairly standard open air stadium, setup-wise. Rectangular in shape, solid concrete construction, 360-degree seating in rows upon rows of solid plastic maroon and yellow flip-down chairs, with a short roof overhanging half of the seating areas for shade and protection from rain, and a big, green sports field in the middle, under the open-air space.

The season passes Jack and Connor hold are for prime seats in the middle of the seating area, about ten rows up and with a fantastic view of the entire field. When we arrive, there's already a group of four men in the seats next to ours. Jack introduces me to them one at a time.

The furthest away is Evan, a guy on Jack's soccer team, who certainly looks like he has the broad shoulders of an athlete. He looks to be in his thirties, with a shaved head and a sexy smile hiding under a short beard. I give him a little wave and then I'm introduced to the next guy down, Brett. He has long brown hair tied back in a low ponytail at his nape. He's also on Jack's soccer team, but his build is less athlete and more 'dad bod'. He has a welcoming smile and kind eyes, and I give him the same awkward little wave.

Third down the line is a guy introduced to me as Smitty. Smitty is stupidly hot. He looks like he just stepped off a catwalk somewhere. Even sitting down, he looks long and lean, effortlessly graceful and comfortable in his very pretty mocha-coloured skin.

"Indoor soccer team?" I guess, and Smitty shakes his head.

"Nah, I can't kick a ball to save my life. I work with this schmuck." He gestures at Jack for emphasis.

I had not picked him as a firefighter, and I feel bad for

Chapter Six - Leo

just assuming that because he's not built like Jack, he's not strong enough or whatever bullshit stereotyping played a subconscious role in my initial assumption. "Ah, I see," I reply awkwardly. "Soccer fan, though?" It's a stupid question, seeing as the guy has a season membership and all.

Nevertheless, he grins. "Yeah, to my dad's ongoing disappointment. He's all about NRL."

I make a face. "Still better than AFL, right?"

"Yeah, man," Smitty laughs and offers his hand for a high-five. "No aerial ping-pong for me."

"Anyway," Jack interrupts us and, am I imagining it, or does he sound a little irritated? "Finally, this guy here is Pete. He's kind of my boss, but I'll forgive him for that."

Pete rolls his eyes and extends his hand for me to shake. His palm is calloused, and his grip is firm. He also looks like he's a bit older than Jack, but maybe only by ten years or so. His dark hair is cropped short, and he has a smattering of freckles over his face and arms. Like the others, he seems easygoing and friendly enough, and I don't feel as uneasy about hanging out with a group of strangers now that I've met them.

I'll admit, I had imagined that they'd all be uber-masculine men, like a walking, talking version of the annual firemen's calendar. Thankfully, they're not intimidating, nor do they seem to mind my somewhat more effeminate self joining them. I should have realised it wouldn't be a problem, considering they hang out with Connor a lot, too. None of them seem to care I'm so much younger than them all, either, even though my twenty-one seems far from their closer-to-forty average.

In fact, if I'm not mistaken, Smitty actually starts flirting with me not long after the game begins. He's even switched seats with Pete so he can lean in to talk and doesn't have to yell.

I can't help but notice that, like Jack, he also smells delicious.

"Are you a big soccer fan?" he asks, his green eyes boring into mine with interest.

I shrug. "To be honest, I'm not huge on sports in general, but I can follow soccer. And a live game is always way more entertaining than watching it on TV."

"God, yes," he replies, putting emphasis on the words in a way that sounds almost sinful. "Doing anything live is usually better than just watching it, though, right?"

When I blink at him, not quite following, he smirks and starts offering examples. "Cooking, concerts," he pauses for a split second then dips his voice low, "sex..."

"So, if you're not huge on sports," Jack cuts in almost forcefully, leaning into our conversation from my other side, "what do you do for fun? I know you like to read."

"I, um, yeah. Reading is my escapism, I guess. Uh, I do yoga and go jogging, which you also know, but that's not exactly for fun." Sighing, I give a shake of my head and curl my lip in a self-deprecating smile. "I'm kinda boring."

"Stop that," Smitty chides me, giving my bicep a nudge with his shoulder. "You're Jack's nanny, right? Your job is probably all the fun and excitement you need."

Warmth spreads through my chest. This guy gets it! My smile is wide and genuine as I agree enthusiastically. "It is. Kids are unpredictable and they keep you on your toes."

"They sure do."

Tilting my head to the side, I ask, "Do you have kids?"

"Nah," he shakes his head. "But I've got a six-year-old brother. My parents' oops baby. They had me in their teens and thought they were all done, but...nope. He's a handful,

Chapter Six - Leo

but I don't think they'd change a thing." Smitty looks past me to Jack. "Will's pretty much in the same boat, isn't he?" Then, for my benefit he adds, "I used to work with Will, too, until he retired last year."

I nod, following the connection. Meanwhile, Jack chuckles and answers, "Yeah, Dad wasn't exactly looking to start a new family from scratch at fifty, but he fell hard for Connor and Vicky, and the rest is history." He sighs and scrubs the back of his neck, the strips of skin on his cheeks above his beard turning pink. "But I can obviously relate to the 'oops baby' thing as well."

"You're not still beating yourself up over that, are you?" Smitty frowns. He points his index finger at Jack, leaning over me to do so. "Condoms fail sometimes, man. It happens. You manned up when it counted. Plus, she didn't do you the kindness of telling you until it suited her. Regardless of how much of a dick you were to her the morning after, that shit's not right."

I swear if I nod any more today, my head is going to fall off. But Smitty's right on all counts. My heart goes out to Jack all over again when I'm reminded that he missed out on three years of those boys' lives. He missed out on the chance to brace his mind and heart for parenthood as best he could. He missed out on that addictive newborn smell, on the tiny squeaking yawns, on the cute squirmy noises and the incomparable feeling of holding that solid warmth to his chest or shoulder. He missed out on first words. First steps. First everythings.

I don't realise that I'm clenching my fists until they start to ache. I surreptitiously flex my fingers and try to shake them out while the conversation goes on around me.

You're getting too invested, I tell myself. *He's your boss. Your straight boss.*

If I repeat it enough times, it will hopefully sink in.

Chapter Seven – Jack

"You wanna tell me what the weird possessive vibe I got from you the other night at the game was all about?" Smitty asks me as we climb out of our PPE gear after attending a false alarm at one of the hotels on the esplanade in Miami.

A sensor had been tripped in the trash chute, setting off the building's alarms. A large number of grumpy tourists had been assembled on the footpath across from the building when we had arrived to assess the situation. The majority had been rumpled and in various states of undress, which isn't unusual, considering the alarm had been tripped just after midnight. Still, having to deal with their complaints while we tried to do our jobs had sucked.

At almost two a.m, after checking every damn floor of that high-rise to make sure it was properly evacuated while the other guys looked for the source of the raised alarm, I am tired and ready for my shift to be over. The last thing I need right now is my nosy-ass colleague and friend grilling me over something I am still trying to process myself.

As soon as Smitty had started flirting with Leo, I'd been overwhelmed by jealousy.

Jealousy. Me. Over a man.

Over my manny.

My cute, smart, so-good-with-my-kids, pretty-sure-my-dad-wants-to-adopt-the-guy manny.

My too-young-for-me manny.

There's so much to unpack there, I don't know where to start.

And of course Smitty noticed. That asshole is too perceptive for his own good. (Then again, I wasn't exactly subtle, was I?)

"I have no idea what you're talking about, dude," I eventually reply, knowing it's a cop-out.

And, because we've been friends for most of the past decade, Smitty doesn't buy it. He leans his long body against the metal lockers and folds his arms, arching one of his groomed eyebrows knowingly. "Pull the other one, Jax. It plays a little ditty called 'Don't Lie To Me, Moron.'"

I can't contain my bark of laughter. "I like that song. Isn't that by the same guy who sang 'Don't You Know When To Back Off'?"

He makes a show of holding his chin between his index finger and his thumb. "Hmm," he answers, "Nope. Doesn't ring a bell. But I think it might be by the guy who wrote 'Are You Having A Big Bi Freakout?' because the notes sound the same."

"Fuck you," I huff, unable to stop the laugh that accompanies my complaint. I push at his shoulder and shake my head. "I'm not freaking out."

"Ah, but you are having bi thoughts?"

Chapter Seven - Jack

I consider lying to him, but I'm not lying when I say I'm not freaking out about that. Just because I've never been attracted to a man before doesn't mean I'm against the idea. It's still namely the fact that he's my kids' nanny that I'm concerned about. He's my employee. He lives with me. There's a conflict of interest here. I don't want to make him uncomfortable or make him feel like he has to reciprocate in order to keep his job and the roof over his head, especially not after what he went through with his family. And he's young. *So* young. I feel like a dirty old man admitting that I think he's hot. I mean, he's only twenty-one. His brain hasn't even stopped developing yet.

"Does it matter if I am?" I settle on half-confirming Smitty's assumption.

And yeah, okay, while I might not be completely freaking out over the fact that I'm attracted to a man, I'm adult enough to admit that it makes me feel like a virgin all over again because I have zero experience in that arena. I understand the mechanics (let's not talk about Dad's super thorough, incredibly disturbing sex ed talks from my teens), but I've never put theory into practise. Not even the women I've been with have been up for a little —*ahem*— backdoor fun.

Plus, what if I suck at…y'know…sucking?

(I'm also very aware that my complete lack of freaking out over the concept of actually *doing* these things is telling, too.)

But I'm getting ahead of myself. The fact of the matter is, I feel guilty for being attracted to Leo because of the power imbalance between us. And the last thing I want to do is drive away the guy who is keeping my kids safe and happy when I'm not at home. He's been so perfect for them.

He's been perfect for me.

You Don't Know Jack

I fight back a groan at that thought. There's no lie there. Leo has slipped into our lives so effortlessly. He doesn't complain when he has to work overnight, he's happy to cook (and he leaves me meals to heat up so I don't miss them), and he loves my boys. Even on his days off, he asks to take them on 'adventures'. He doesn't nag. He doesn't judge my parenting fails. He's patient and kind, and he's so confident in his own skin. He even gets along with my friends. Hell, my dad loves him, too. They've become fast friends.

Even though I don't date and have never felt the compulsion to have a serious relationship with anyone, Leo's the kind of person I could see myself being with long term.

That is the scary part.

I've never met anyone who has made me feel this way.

The fact that he's barely out of his teens makes me wonder if he'd even reciprocate, or whether he would rather sow his own wild oats like I did at his age and for the entirety of my twenties…which brings me right back to convincing myself that it's a moot point because I'm not going to act on these conflicting feelings anyway.

Smitty's eyeing me intensely. "No," he answers me slowly, as though he's reading my mind, "but it matters if your feelings are serious. You're a 'hit it and quit it' kind of guy."

"I was," the words escape me before I can even think about reeling them back, "before the boys showed up. Now I'm a 'befriending my right hand' kind of guy."

My friend snorts. "You've got very little chance of repeating the surprise parenthood thing if you're hooking up with other men. You know that, right?"

"I'm not hooking up with anyone. I don't have the time." I mean, how fucking selfish would it be to ask Leo to work extra

Chapter Seven - Jack

hours just so I can go get my dick wet? And I'm definitely not going to ask Dad or Connor to take the kids while I go to get my rocks off, either. Nope: part of parenting is prioritising my kids over my libido. At least it is for me, personally. Right now, anyway. Maybe when the boys are older, things might change.

"Hey, I can see you spiralling, Jax." That's twice Smitty's used his affectionate nickname for me in a matter of minutes. I really must seem unhinged, because we don't really do touchy-feely talk very often, even if the guy is my best friend outside of my twin brother. Smitty's tone drops into something far gentler than I'm used to hearing from him and he places his hand on my shoulder comfortingly. "You just have to do what's right for you, man. That's all I'm saying. Taking a night off to blow off steam isn't going to hurt those terrors of yours."

"Dad never did," I mutter, thinking back to my childhood. Dad sacrificed his happiness for me and Wes. As far as I know, he didn't date until we were adults and, even then, I'm pretty sure Connor was the first real serious relationship he'd had in a long, long time. He was a great dad —the best dad— and I want to be the same for my boys.

"Oh boy, there's a lot to unpack there, huh?" Smitty chuckles and shakes his head. "Firstly, you're not Will. Secondly, your mum was also in the picture, wasn't she?"

"Well, yeah, but—"

Smitty's index finger is wiggling side to side in front of my face before I can complete my protest. "Uh-uh-uh," he chides. "No buts. Were there days or weeks when you'd be with your mum and not Will?"

I roll my eyes. "Yeah. They eventually shared custody when Mom met Mike and Dad moved out, but—"

"So, both your parents had a chance to see people when you were with the other one, right?"

My lips firm into a tight line and I scrunch up my nose. I hate it when he's right! "That doesn't mean—"

"Except it does," he cuts me off gently. "My parents take time out for date nights, too. And, hey, if you don't wanna ask that hot manny of yours or Will and Con to look after the boys, I'm happy to babysit. I've been looking after Rhett since he was born. How hard could two little munchies be?"

"Ask me that again once you've spent more than a handful of minutes with them," I tease, then pull Smitty in for a quick hug complete with manly back-thumping. "Thanks, man." I don't have any intention of taking him up on it, but I really do appreciate his offer.

He gives me a shit-eating grin as we pull back apart, then he tugs a fresh t-shirt on over his bare chest. Tugging the hem down, he asks, "So…if you're not gonna ask Leo out, can I?"

I don't even have to think about my answer. "Absolutely not."

Don't get me wrong: Smitty's a great guy. But the thought of him putting the moves on my Leo? Nope. Not gonna happen.

He laughs as he climbs into his jeans. "You're going to have to make a move yourself then, man. A guy like Leo won't be available for long."

I want to growl, but my friend is right.

Unfortunately, though, I'm not the right guy to snap Leo up. I just wish I was.

Damn.

* * *

Chapter Seven - Jack

"Hey," the softly spoken greeting has me almost jumping out of my skin as I enter the dark apartment.

Squinting into the room, I ask, "What the hell are you doing up at four in the morning?"

I can barely make out the lump on the couch, but I know it's Leo, especially as he shushes me. "Prez had a nightmare. Night terror? I dunno, something along those lines, anyway. He wouldn't go back to bed, so we camped out here to watch the twinkling lights outside. He only crashed about fifteen minutes ago."

My heart clenches with guilt. I hate that I wasn't here to comfort my boy.

"Don't do that," Leo chides me gently. "I can practically hear you beating yourself up over there. You were at work doing all sorts of heroic fireman stuff."

I think back to the call-out and sigh, scrubbing my hand over my face as I drop heavily into the armchair which sits kitty-corner to the couch. "Tonight's last-minute call-out was a false alarm. Nothing heroic about it."

"But it might not have been," Leo insists firmly. "Your job is heroic whether the call-outs are for actual emergencies or just potential ones."

I swallow roughly.

Have I mentioned how much I like his optimism, too? He's always looking for the bright side or silver linings. He doesn't let anyone put themselves down. It's sweet.

Ugh.

Forcing my eyes to shift away from his, my gaze lands on the dark tufts of soft hair sticking out from the bundle of blankets on Leo's lap. "I'll carry him back to bed," I murmur, leaning forward to get back up again, already biting back a groan at having to move so soon after getting comfortable.

"Leave him. We can nap here for a bit." Leo yawns.

I even think that is cute.

I'm so fucked.

Maybe I should take Smitty up on his babysitting offer after all. Getting laid might help me shake this crush, right? But, even as I consider it, my stomach turns unpleasantly.

I don't want a random hookup. I want Leo.

I am so incredibly fucked.

Chapter Eight – Leo

"So, are you nervous about the big day?" I ask Will as we sit and watch the kids digging in the sand.

We're at Burleigh Beach, having walked down together from home, and the day is absolutely perfect. The sky is clear and blue, with only the odd wispy, white cloud floating by, and there's a refreshing ocean breeze taking away the heat of the day. It's late in the afternoon, so the worst of the sun's heat has been and gone, but the soft, white sand is still hot to the touch in places. We've combatted that by sitting ourselves at the water's edge where the sand is harder and cooler, compacted by the water.

Because my pale skin burns easily, I'm wearing a pale blue long-sleeved rash shirt over my Hawaiian-print board shorts. I've dressed the boys in similar shirts and slathered all three of us with sunscreen, too. And, even though we're not swimming, I've got both the boys wearing Spider-Man float vests, just in case one of them (most likely Hudson) decides to venture farther than he knows he should.

You Don't Know Jack

Will has got Vicky dressed in frilly, pink swimwear and her soft baby skin is also coated in sunscreen. She's wearing a wide-brimmed floppy hat, also in pink to match her outfit. Will himself has opted to go shirtless, leaving his furry, tanned, toned chest and abdomen on display, and the grey in his chest hair and beard glints where the sun catches it. He's most certainly a silver fox if ever I saw one, and I can't help but think that Connor is one lucky guy.

Speaking of…

"The wedding?" Will shakes his head, smiling softly as he considers my question. "No. I can't wait to marry Con."

"How many weeks now, then?" I tease lightly, even as my heart pangs with jealousy. Not over Connor or Will, but over their happiness.

If my ex hadn't been a lying, cheating dickhead, that could have been me. You know, if he'd ever proposed. Which wasn't actually on the cards because he was a lying, cheating dickhead and I'm only twenty-one. But still…

I fight back a sigh. I can admit to myself that I'm lonely. That there's a part of me that wants to find my person. Rationally, I know I'm young. I know that I have a whole lifetime to find love and settle down and have babies and all that other mushy stuff. I mean, hell, look at Will. He was fifty before he found the man he wanted to marry.

I don't want to wait thirty years to find mine, though.

"Six and a half," Will answers me, oblivious to the path my thoughts just took.

"April is so close now," I brace my arms behind me and lean my head back, soaking in the sun's rays. "I can't believe how fast this year is going already."

I took the job working for Jack in late January and already

Chapter Eight - Leo

March is looming over us.

"Time flies when you're having fun." My companion's tone is soft and sage.

Over the sound of the waves crashing, I can hear the boys splashing in the shallow water that ebbs and flows at our feet. Their giggles and squeals light me up and warm me in ways that the sun can't reach. I grin. "Well, Hudson and Preston do provide endless hours of fun."

Will makes a sound of agreement. "Mmm. They're so much like Jack and Wes, it's uncanny."

Lazily turning my face towards him, I take in the wistful twist of his lips beneath his beard. Over the weeks of bringing the kids to the park or the beach together, we've spoken about his past, so I know he was a teen dad. I also know that he adores his sons, even if they weren't planned, though he struggled with their early years. Seeing little doppelgangers of them now must bring back so many memories, and not all of them are necessarily good.

"I can only imagine what kind of terror Jack was at their age," I reply, hoping to keep the conversation light. "He seems to think Hudson's much naughtier than he ever was."

Will laughs at that. "He and Hudson are well-matched, I'd say. And Wes was every bit as calculating and sneaky as Preston is. Together, my boys were practically unstoppable. Just like this pair." He gestures to where the boys are now trying to build a sandcastle in the wet sand, falling back onto their butts and laughing every time a new wave trails up and licks away at their foundations. "They were trouble in the best of ways." After watching the twins a moment longer, he turns back to me, his expression serious. "How's Jack coping? He tells us he's fine, but I know better than most that it's a

You Don't Know Jack

lot. Plus not knowing about them until their mother dropped them off…"

I sigh at the same time he does and try to think of the best way to respond. I don't want to talk about Jack behind his back, but this is his dad. He's asking because he loves his son. As someone who could only dream of having a support system like that, I find myself answering, "It's not really my place to say, but I honestly think he's doing great. Better than I would have, if I were in his shoes." Directing my gaze back to the boys, my lips curl upwards of their own accord. "He's such a great dad. He's patient and kind, he never yells or lets them see his frustration…and they love him so, so much." From out of nowhere, tears sting my sinuses and prickle in my eyes. I bat them away quickly and clear my throat. "They've come out of their shells so much in just the few weeks I've known them, and that's all because of him. He's given them a safe space and now Huddy's no longer having meltdowns anywhere near as often, and Prez isn't anywhere near as shy and timid, either. Plus, I see how much Jack loves them, too. Even if this is all new to him and freaks him out, he's genuinely happy to have them. He lights up with them, you know?"

When I turn back to Will, he's watching me intently. My cheeks burn. I blame it on the sun.

"Good," he eventually says, but his blue-grey eyes bore into mine with a knowing glint that I want so badly to look away from. "And I'm glad he's got you there. You're good for him."

"Them," I adjust, waving my hands at the boys. "I'm there for them. It's my job."

There's a moment of silence that stretches just a little too long for comfort. It feels weighty, and I regret letting my guard down and babbling about how wonderful Jack is. To his dad,

Chapter Eight - Leo

no less!

"Uh-huh," Will eventually says, then thankfully lets the topic drop. He picks his daughter up and shifts her a little further down towards the waterline, and she cheers and splashes as the wash from the next wave travels up over her pudgy toddler legs. "Only a little while longer," he tells her gently, "then we'll get you out of the sun and have a nice bath at home, huh?"

"I want a bath!" Hudson declares, dropping his spade where he stands. He sticks out his bottom lip and quivers it. "Daddy only gots a shower."

"Has. Daddy only has a shower," I correct him. "And you like the shower. We got you those cool crayons to draw on the glass, remember?"

Will winces. From what I understand, the renovated bathroom was his pride and joy when he lived in the apartment. It's because of him that the original layout was replaced by a giant shower spanning the length of one wall, with two rainfall showerheads and a bench seat. I snort and nudge him with my shoulder. "They're b-a-t-h crayons. They wash off easily."

"I miss playin' with my boats," Huddy continues to pout.

Out of the corner of my eye, I watch as the most recent wave picks up his little plastic spade and drags it towards the ocean. Surging to my feet, I race forward and grab it before it can be dragged away completely. Unfortunately, I've run a little farther into the surf than I'd hoped to and another crashing wave comes in and takes out the backs of my knees as I turn to make my way back to our group.

I fall forward, copping a mouthful of saltwater and sand grit as I land in the shallows, a startled 'oomph' escaping me as another wave pushes me forward again, right on the tail of the first one. Then the tide ebbs back and tries its best to pull me with it, but my hands and knees dig into the swirling wet sand I've landed in, still gripping the bright yellow spade. I push to my feet and, waterlogged, trudge back to the water's edge.

Hudson laughs his little arse off while Preston stares at me with wide, startled eyes.

"You okay?" Will asks me through chuckles of his own.

Wiping my eyes with the back of my arm, I nod, grinning despite my embarrassment. "I feel like a drowned cat, but I'll live."

"Now you need a bath," Preston says.

He's not wrong. Even though I plan on rinsing off at the beach shower on the edge of the footpath, I can feel that sand has made its way into places where sand most certainly does not belong, which is always a risk when you're dumped by a wave in the shallows. "Yeah, bud," I reach out to ruffle his hair, already feeling my skin turn tacky with the salt from the sea, "I think we all need to shower when we get home."

"I don't want a shower," Hudson whines again and stomps his foot in the dry sand behind the spot we'd been sitting. Granules of the stuff fly up and stick to his legs. "I want a bath!"

"Grampa," Preston turns his big brown eyes on Will, "can we bath in your house?"

"Can we have a bath," I correct him, then frown. "Or 'can we bathe'. Either way…" I trail off and mutter, "you're not paying any attention, are you?"

Both Prez and Huddy are sending their best pleading expressions Will's way, focused solely on his reply. Just like me and Jack, their grandfather caves under the cuteness assault.

"What kind of grandpa would I be if I said no, hmm?" As they

Chapter Eight - Leo

cheer, he mutters under his breath about being too young to call himself 'Grandpa' and I snigger unhelpfully. Nevertheless, he beams as the two little bodies leap at him for a giant group hug, and I scoop Vicky up out of the way of their flailing limbs.

"Come on, then," he eventually cajoles, "let's head home."

Overjoyed by the prospect of splashing in Will's tub, neither of the boys sulk about having to end their beach fun. I count that as a win.

Jack's tiny clones each cling to one of Will's hands as we force ourselves up the gentle slope of slippery dry sand and I'm more than content to carry Vicky on my hip and the bag of beach toys and baby paraphernalia over my opposite shoulder. Vicky babbles half-words, half baby-speak as we go, and I happily chat with her, distracting myself from the burn in my calf muscles. It's not a long distance to get to the footpath from the water's edge, but somehow the walk always seems to drag.

"You're right, pink is the superior colour," I acknowledge while one pudgy toddler hand smacks at my sticky, clingy rash shirt. "But I don't think that poodle over there should be dyed pink, no. Maybe green, though?"

She giggles and Will looks over his shoulder to grin at me. "Are you two having fun plotting back there?"

"Yep," I reply. "First step of world domination: planning what colours look best on other peoples' pets." I point out a yellow Labrador loping along the sand at its owner's side, leashed because this section of the beach requires it. "What do you say, princess? Purple for the lab?"

She giggles again and says something that sounds vaguely like 'boo'.

I gasp just as my feet meet the scraggly grass by the footpath's edge. "Blue, you say? I hadn't considered it. But a nice bright blue might work very well."

"You're silly, Leo," Preston says, allowing Will to direct him in front of the squared-off space for the outdoor shower. The shower has two taps: one for the showerhead, and one for the tap that sits about knee height. That's the tap Will turns on to help Preston rinse off his sandy lower half.

"Aarrrgh!" Preston complains, "It's cold!"

"Then we'll all rinse off quickly," Will replies easily.

I set Vicky down between Will and Hudson and head back over to the spot where we'd all abandoned our shoes at the top of the beach. I grab the pile of thongs and drop them on top of the rubber mat that serves as the floor of the shower space. Will helps Preston into his bright green pair of flip-flops, securing the elastic band around his heel, then declares him all done. The entire process is repeated with Hudson, then Vicky, and finally Will. It's only me who needs a full-body rinse-off.

Will takes the kids out of the shower's reach and I weather the cold water with as much dignity as I can, sliding my own thongs on once I'm sure that I'm as sand-free as I can possibly be. The sun is still blazing in a cloudless sky and I've forgotten the shock from the shower by the time I've joined Will and the kids on the other side of the footpath. The boys are looking at the nearby playground with hope on their tiny faces, but we usher them in the opposite direction towards the pedestrian crossing that lets us cross the Gold Coast Highway safely. Paranoid about road safety, I clutch both boys' hands tightly for the walk past the mouth of James Street and its eclectic mix of boutique stores and cafes and up the hill towards the street we live on.

Chapter Eight - Leo

At Will's door, he tells me he's got the boys and I'm free to head upstairs to shower. I feel a little guilty, considering I'm technically on the clock, but he waves me off. "I'm their grandfather," he insists. "Take as much time as you want. I could use some bonding time of my own, you know?"

I can't exactly argue with that, so I don't.

I head upstairs, locking the front door behind me once I'm inside. The apartment is eerily silent, and it strikes me that this is the first time I've been truly alone in this space. With the boys guaranteed to be entertained for at least the next half hour, I strip my tacky, damp clothing off and toss it into the laundry hamper on my way to the bathroom, then prepare myself for an indulgent hot shower.

Under the spray of one of the two showerheads, I close my eyes and soap up my body, sighing as I finally start to feel fresh and clean again. My cock hardens when I reach it. The slippery, soapy slide of my hand over my shaft feels so fucking good, I can't stop myself from giving in to temptation and stroking deliberately.

After all, I'm alone in the apartment and, short of a few quick wanks here and there, I haven't properly pleasured myself in longer than I care to admit.

With one last furtive glance towards the bathroom door, which I'd kept open to let out the steam, I give in to temptation and let fantasy wash over me.

In my mind, it's Jack's hand on my dick. My other hand also becomes his, gliding over my chest, teasing my nipples before diverting course, dipping down between my butt cheeks and toying with my hole. With my eyes closed and water sluicing down my body, I widen my stance and tilt my head, imagining Jack's mouth at my neck, sucking sensual kisses into my skin while he fingers me and strokes me off in equal measure.

I whimper as his finger slides in deeper, rocking in and out slowly, readying me for a second one. In my fantasy, his broad upper body presses against my back, his delicious tattoos and tanned skin contrasting with my pale, freckled torso. He practically envelops me with his frame, making me feel safe and treasured, and then he crooks his fingers and stars burst behind my eyelids.

"More," I beg, thrusting my arse harder onto those perfectly probing digits. "Please. More."

"Easy, baby," Fantasy Jack's voice ghosts into my ear, deep and dirty and perfect. "We're going to do this right."

I whimper again, the sound bouncing off the tiles and glass around me. The volume of my own neediness surprises and embarrasses me until I remember that I'm alone in the apartment. I can scream Fantasy Jack's name if I so choose and the only person who will hear it is me.

My rapid heartbeat calms a little with that realisation and I close my eyes again, taking a moment to centre myself back in my daydream.

"I've got you," the decadent whisper I imagine in my ear brings on a full-body shudder. "You feel so good around my fingers, baby. So tight. What's that going to do to my cock, hmm?"

I'm panting now, feeling my orgasm building inside me, like a coil tightening incrementally until the tension becomes too much and it snaps. "J-Jack," I breathe, my cheeks heating up from arousal and not the temperature of the water, "please. Please, I need to come. Make me come."

When the rush of endorphins disappears, I'm probably going to feel guilty for inserting my straight boss into my

Chapter Eight - Leo

masturbatory fantasising. However, for now it's easily the hottest thing I have ever experienced...and I'm including my actual, if limited-to-very-few-partners, sexual experience in that assessment.

The fingers inside me twist and curl, grazing my prostate again. The hand around my slicked-up shaft tightens at the same time pleasure ignites in my veins.

"Oh, God," I practically sob as the telltale tingles of my release start in my balls. "Jack..."

A growled, low, drawn out "Fuuuuuuck" that is *not* my own, nor a figment of my imagination, reverberates off the tiles around me and startles my eyes open again. I meet the wide eyes of Real Life Jack and, to cap off my embarrassment, shoot my load all over the glass that separates us.

Well, I think as my brain reengages, *fuck indeed*.

Chapter Nine – Jack

My favourite shifts are the ones that start in the early hours of the morning and end in the early afternoon. Especially in summer, when I can capitalise on the remaining daylight. But since I met my boys, these shifts have meant even more to me because it means I get to come home and spend those precious daylight hours building a relationship with them.

Now, when I get home early enough, I get to listen to Hudson tell me about the epic (if imaginary) battles he's waged, and Preston repeats all the trivia he's wheedled out of Leo and Google. For their birthday, I'm pretty sure I'm going to get one of those Alexa things so he can ask Google directly. And Hudson? Well, I don't think weaponry is a great idea for a four-year-old, but maybe I can get him one of those battle-robot sets.

These are the thoughts circling my brain as I let myself into the apartment, only to be greeted by suspicious silence.

"Hello?" I call out to no answer.

Chapter Nine – Jack

Hmm.

It's possible Leo's still running them ragged down at the park or on the beach, but I did send a message half an hour ago to let him know that my shift finished on time and I was coming home.

After ditching my keys in the bowl on the side table near the door, I kick off my shoes and tug off my socks, then head towards the hallway. The sound of the shower running relaxes me. Even though I can see the bathroom door has been left open halfway, it makes sense that Leo couldn't hear me call out over the sound of running water. Plus, if he's wrangling the boys in there, he's most likely distracted.

I head towards the door, already grinning with anticipation of finding Leo drenched from the efforts of washing two squirmy, cheeky three-year-olds, but then the sound of his voice, echoing off the tiles, throws me off guard.

He stammers my name and makes a plea I can't quite work out between the semi-closed door and the sound of rushing water, but I hurry forward, wondering if he did hear me get in after all and needs my help with the boys.

That is not what I find.

No, what I find instead has my dick springing to attention within the confines of my jeans while my mouth goes dry and my brain short-circuits.

Leo is soaped up under one of the rainfall showerheads, bent forward slightly, one hand wrapped around his cock and the other seems to be moving rhythmically behind him. His eyes are closed and his skin is flushed pink. His hair has been darkened by the water, both on top of his head and across his chest, as well as on his arms and legs. His perfect, plump, pink lips are parted and his chest heaves.

"Oh, God," he cries, sounding blissed-out and close to the edge. The desperation in his voice and on his face make my cock throb. "Jack…"

He's thinking of me.

He's thinking of me while he brings himself to orgasm.

"*Fuuuuuuck*," I can't contain the way the curse spills from my lips as I watch him.

The sound of my voice, unexpected and uninvited, startles his eyes open. They lock onto mine and he comes hard, painting the glass wall of the shower with stripes of his release, and it's one of the hottest things I've ever seen in my life.

Then, as he comes down from his high, horror takes over his expression and that's about the same time that I notice that I'm still standing inside the bathroom doorway, staring at him like a lion might stare at a gazelle.

"Shit, fuck," I stammer out, belatedly covering my eyes. "I'm sorry. I'm just…I'm just gonna…" I stumble back out into the hallway and look around uselessly, not sure where to go or what to do. My dick says I should head back into the bathroom and finish what Leo unwittingly started, but thankfully there's still enough blood flow to my brain for me to know that would be a stupid idea. Besides, the horror on his face is now seared into my mind and that's enough to calm my arousal further.

I can't imagine being in his shoes right now. Memories of Wes catching me jerking off when we were in high school are bad enough, but to be caught by the person you're thinking about has got to be ten times more embarrassing than that. Not to mention the fact that I'm his boss and I'm pretty sure he thinks I'm straight. Talk about awkward!

Sure enough, when the water shuts off, I can hear him berating himself. My heart goes out to him, and I want so

Chapter Nine – Jack

badly to assure him that he hasn't fucked up as terribly as he seems to believe he has. I'm not offended, or appalled, or upset. If anything, I'm the one who violated his privacy by barging into the bathroom like I did, regardless of the fact that I thought he'd needed my help. I need to apologise to him, not the other way around.

I'm so lost in my thoughts that I jolt in surprise when the bathroom door opens. Leo, wrapped only in a towel, squeaks and swallows roughly. His face is so red it almost looks like it hurts.

"Sorry," he mutters, staring resolutely at my toes. "I just… I'm just gonna get dressed…" I read shame in the set of his shoulders and the way he hangs his head. "I didn't think anyone would be here, so I didn't grab any clothes."

"Sure," I reply, trying to put as much softness and understanding into the word as possible. "I'll be in the living room when you're done. We, um," I rub the back of my neck, "we should talk. About…stuff."

I cringe at my stumbling words and fight the urge to blurt out all of my reassurances as I watch him flinch and nod, defeat written all over him. "Okay," he says quietly. "It won't take me long to pack, and—"

"Whoa! Pack?" I straighten up and push off the wall where I'd been leaning. Without thinking, I hook my index finger beneath his chin and tilt his face up so I can look him in the eye. The moisture in his gaze makes my chest ache. "What are you packing for?"

"I…You…" With the hand not clenching his towel closed, he waves frantically towards the shower. "That."

I can't help it: I snort. "Go get dressed." I shove him in the direction of his bedroom. "You're not going anywhere."

You Don't Know Jack

* * *

When Leo finally creeps back out from his room after taking ten minutes longer than he probably should have, I pat the couch cushion beside me. He looks adorable, with his hair stuck up at odd angles and a small, sheepish smile tugging at his lips. His eyes are wide and dart towards the door as he steps into the room, and I swear I can see him calculating just how quickly he might be able to make his escape.

I chuckle and pat the seat again. "Come on," I urge, "let's talk it out."

"But…" he inches towards the front door, "the boys are with your dad and—"

"And he's fine to keep them for a little longer." I hold up my phone and grin. "I checked. Right now, he's got them all watching *Peppa Pig*. I think he likes it more than they do." When I'd called him, he'd sounded vaguely amused when I told him that I needed to talk to Leo without the boys around, but Dad's mind works in mysterious ways sometimes, and I figured he was already distracted by Daddy Pig's unique brand of ridiculousness.

"Right. Okay." Leo still makes no move to come sit on the couch, pointing towards the kitchen instead. "Have you eaten lunch today? Skipping meals isn't good for you, you know. I can whip you up—"

"Leo. Sit. Now." Dutifully, he stops babbling and finally comes to sit on the couch, leaving a space between us. I smile softly. "Thank you."

Holding his hands in his lap, he fidgets, using the nail of his right thumb to scrape and pick at the thumb on his left hand.

Understanding that I have to lead this conversation, I scoot

Chapter Nine – Jack

towards him and reach out, taking his right hand between both of mine. "I'm sorry for walking in on you," I start to speak, and his surprise is palpable. He flickers his gaze to mine and gapes soundlessly, so I continue. "The door was open, and I thought I heard you asking me to help with the boys or something. When I realised that wasn't the case, I should have backed out of there. So, I'm sorry for invading your privacy. It was wrong, and the last thing I want is to make you feel uncomfortable or unsafe."

"Wait…what?" He blinks at me, completely bewildered. The shock from my apology seems to shake off his embarrassment because, with incredulity, he says, "Let me get this straight. You caught me in your shower, wanking to thoughts of you when I should have been watching your kids, and you're the one apologising to me?"

I can't help it, I laugh. A deep, unstoppable belly laugh that brings tears to my eyes. I release his hand so I can wipe my eyes on the back of one of mine. "Leo, babe, you weren't doing anything wrong. Dad said he pretty much demanded grandpa time, and this is your home now. God knows neither one of us get enough privacy these days. If I'd had the place to myself, I probably would have let off some steam the same way."

Leo squeaks at first, then rallies, sarcastically asking, "What? By thinking about your boss taking you up the arse?" Even though his cheeks are stained pink as he asks me the question, I'm struck by how hot it is to see his backbone returning. His confidence has always been one of my favourite things about him. Seeing him shameful and quiet felt wrong.

"Nah, I don't think of Pete fucking me," I shrug nonchalantly. "He's not my type." Then, despite knowing this is possibly the worst idea of all bad ideas, I shoot my shot and go for broke,

"I prefer the idea of being topped by Mary Poppins types. Especially when they're all firm and bossy...even if they do mock my favourite sandwiches."

My nanny inhales so sharply he chokes on air. "What?"

"Admittedly," now it's my turn to blush, but I feel like I owe him complete honesty. I've seen him at his most vulnerable, now I need to even the playing field. "I've never been with another guy before. But I, um...I want to. With you. You know, if the whole Mary Poppins thing was too vague."

"Did...did I drown earlier? Is this some sort of weird coma hallucination?" Leo pinches his own arm and then yelps. "Nope. That hurt." His chest rising and falling rapidly, he stares at me again, with understandable disbelief written all over his pretty face. "You want to," he swallows roughly, the pink on his cheeks returning again, "have sex. Um, with...with *me?*"

"Yeah, look, like I said, I don't want to make you uncomfortable, and I know that I'm your boss, and a decade older, and then there's the whole 'new dad to twin three-year-olds' mess, but—*oomph*."

I fall back against the armrest of the couch as my lap is suddenly full of one hot nanny. Instinctively, my hands drop to his waist steadying him and holding him in place.

His brown eyes are full of wonder as he looks down at me from his new position. "Really?" he asks, and the question is little more than a whisper.

I nod. "Really."

Despite the enthusiasm with which he pinned me to the couch, Leo is much slower and more tentative when he bends down and brushes his lips over mine. It's the ghost of a kiss, as though he's afraid I'll freak out and change my mind at

Chapter Nine - Jack

any second. I can smell his shower-fresh scent, the newly applied deodorant and a hint of his smoky-sweet cologne, and it drives me wild. Flicking out my tongue, I try to catch his taste for the first time, knowing in my gut that it will be just as addictive to my senses.

From where he's pressed against my lower abdomen, I feel his cock thicken beneath the fabric of his cargo shorts. My mind flashes back to twenty minutes ago, to the scene I accidentally walked in on. I barely got to see him in all his glory but, from what I can recall, every last inch of him is gorgeous.

"Kiss me again," I whisper up at him, my heart thudding with excitement and anticipation. It's the same reaction I've always had to him, and I never want it to stop. "Please, baby."

"Baby," Leo practically exhales the word as he repeats it. His whole expression melts back into that wondrous one he was rocking before, and I will say the new nickname on repeat until my dying day if it means he'll continue to look at me this way. "Wow."

It's on the tip of my tongue to say it again when he dips his face back down and presses his lips to mine a little more firmly than before. It's still a sweet, chaste kiss. A tentative meeting of our mouths. His lips part slightly and mine follow, but I let him set the pace, revelling in being the more passive partner for once. He pulls back very slightly, allowing breath to pass between us, and it's more erotic than it has any right being.

"Is this okay?" he asks me, kissing my lips ever so softly again.

"More than okay."

That's the understatement of the year. Kissing him is a

revelation and we haven't even involved tongues yet. His lips are thinner than I'm used to kissing, his jawline slightly more angular and his nose larger. The skin on his cheeks and jaw are gently stubbled from a day's growth where I'm used to smooth softness. And it's all wonderful. Different —no better, no worse— but completely wonderful.

While we continue to kiss and get used to one another's proximity, our bodies move of their own accord, determined to settle in comfortably. He gasps into my mouth as our erections align and I groan right back.

Any remaining doubt about my newfound interest in men —in him— vanishes at how fucking good his bulge feels next to mine. It's so new and different that it's almost a novel sensation…but it's also so much more than that. It feels *right*. It feels like something I've been missing without even realising it.

Not that I ever felt like being with women was lacking anything, mind you. I still find women attractive, and discovering my equal enjoyment in men (or even just in Leo) doesn't diminish that. But to think that, if I'd been more self-aware, I might have been able to spend time indulging in all these additional pleasures makes me a little annoyed with my past self.

This train of thought is derailed when Leo's tongue darts out to lick at my lips and mine moves to engage with his without any further encouragement needed. The taste of his mouth, minty and fresh, makes me moan happily.

Even with our tongues twisting around one another, we keep things calm and exploratory. I appreciate that, even though my cock is begging me to rush us towards a happy, mutually satisfying ending. But I want to get a feel for the

Chapter Nine - Jack

way he kisses. For the way his mouth moves against mine. For the way he seems to favour teasing my tongue with his before drawing back and then repeating the action over and over again. For the ever so tiny pauses where he sucks at my bottom lip and then parts his lips for me all over again.

"You are the hottest man I've ever kissed," he confesses quietly when we part to breathe.

I pull backwards so I can look at him. His cheeks are flushed and his eyes are closed. He looks and sounds far too innocent to have been making out with me the way he just did. "Wow," he adds and scrunches his nose, "could I sound any lamer?"

My hands are cupping the lush globes of his ass and I squeeze them in admonishment. "Hey. Stop that. You're not lame." His pretty eyes open, but his expression is guarded and sceptical. "You're not," I insist and rock my hardened length against his again. "Feel that?" I relish in the way his blush darkens. "You're the hottest man I've ever kissed, too."

"I'm the only—"

"Semantics," I cut him off dismissively. "You think someone else could make me feel so comfortable for my first time?"

It's terrifying to be so honest about my lack of experience, but I know Leo won't abuse my trust in him. In the couple of months I've gotten to know him, he has proven to be compassionate and kind. Why would this be any different?

His Adam's apple bobs as he swallows roughly. "They probably could, yeah. Someone like Smitty—"

I shudder and gag exaggeratedly. "Dude. He's basically my brother from another mother. That's just…eww."

Even though it looks like he wants to continue arguing with me, the corners of Leo's lips twitch. "Okay, okay! Sorry!" The sparkle in his eyes undermines the apology. "I won't mention

Sm-*mmmph*."

I had to release my hold on his perfectly shaped butt in order to clamp my hand over his mouth. The look I pin him with is firm. "Don't even *think* his name while we're rubbing against each other like this." I roll my hips for illustration, delighting in the way his eyelashes flutter and his eyes roll back with pleasure.

When I'm pretty sure he's got the point, I move my hand away and it finds its way back to the curve of his ass. I squeeze him and pull him into my body at the same time as I roll my hips upwards again, increasing the friction between us.

"God, you feel so good," I can't contain the words. They spill out of my mouth without censor. There's a distinct wet patch growing at the front of my underwear. I'm almost certain that I won't be able to contain my orgasm, either, and that seems ridiculous. I haven't come in my pants since I was fifteen and Trina Morris accidentally brushed my erection when we were making out behind the bleachers at school. Yet here I am.

On top of me, Leo lets out a breathy whine. "I'm going to come," he practically mewls, grinding down while we rock together. "Jack. *Jack*. I'm going to...*nnnngh*."

His hips lose their rhythm and I feel the rush of warmth against my crotch. Between that and watching his expression contort into ecstasy for me (again) is all it takes before my balls draw tight and then empty themselves in an orgasm so much stronger than I'd anticipated. White noise drowns out my hearing for a moment. My arms and legs tremble in the aftermath. I don't even realise that I've lurched upwards and buried my face in the crook of Leo's neck until his scent tickles my nostrils.

"Holy fuck," I exhale in wonder, flopping back down onto

Chapter Nine - Jack

the couch with an exhilarated little sigh.

My underwear is sticky and growing more and more uncomfortable with each passing second, but I don't care. My heart is beating rapidly, and my head feels light and floaty. I can't remember the last time I felt so giddy after coming. And it was *in my pants*. We're both fully clothed and the only real skin-to-skin contact has been between our mouths. Despite that, I would rate this in the top three sexual experiences of my entire life…and, not to brag, I have had some great fun over the years.

"Uh-huh," he agrees, breathing just as heavily as I am. When I force my eyes open, he looks absolutely wrecked and a thrill of pride shoots through me.

I did that.

I mean, okay, he kind of led the whole experience, but it was my name on his lips.

"We should, um, get cleaned up." Leo says softly, pulling me out of my trance. Warning bells start ringing in my head at the set of his shoulders and the fact that he's refusing to look at me as he extricates himself from my lap.

I reach out for him, but he takes a step backwards.

With my stomach dropping, I try, "Babe…"

The endearment gets him to look at me, but I don't like the resignation I find in his gaze, nor do I like the sad shake of his head.

"We shouldn't have done this," he tells me. "I shouldn't have…*y'know*…in the shower, either."

"You think I don't jerk off in the shower?"

His angry red blush returns. It's not the same as the flush of arousal, but I still love the look on him. "You know that's not what I meant. I shouldn't have been thinking of you."

You Don't Know Jack

"Well, I'd much rather you were thinking of me than someone else." I think I surprise us both with the honesty in my words. I'd intended them to be playful, but I really don't like the thought of him wanting anyone else. Especially not after what we just did.

"You're my boss, Jack." Leo sighs heavily and then runs his hand through his already messy hair. "I shouldn't...*we* shouldn't..." After another shake of his head, he seems to collect his thoughts. "It's a conflict of interest for both of us, and I like this job too much to risk making things even weirder between us. I like *you* too much to make things weirder."

I bristle and sit up, grimacing at the tackiness in my pants when I move. "It doesn't have to be weird," I argue. "We can still work together and—"

Leo's scoff cuts me off. He plants his hands on his hips. I try not to stare at the obvious wet patch on the front of his shorts. Try not to think about pulling them down and using my mouth to clean his skin.

"We don't work *together*, Jack. I work *for* you. There's a difference." Before I can protest, he softens his tone. "Just think about it for a moment, okay? I know that you're too good a man to make things uncomfortable if we were to date and break up or whatever, but I don't want to confuse the boys. I also don't want you questioning whether I'm doing things for the money, or because I feel obligated or whatever." His pretty face falls. "But, ultimately, it really is about the boys. Think about trying to explain things to them if they saw us kissing or touching."

"So we'd tell them that you're my special friend or something." I honestly don't see the issue, and I am mildly horrified at his insinuation that I would ever believe him capable of

Chapter Nine – Jack

being with me for money or to keep his job. "We wouldn't be doing anything wrong by dating."

Dating.

That's the first time I've said the word with the desire to actually pursue the activity. Usually, the thought of attempting anything more than a couple of nights of casual sex would give me hives. But Leo is worth more than my usual *wham, bam, thank you, ma'am* (or, in his case, *wham, bam, thank you, man*) style.

The realisation that I have feelings for Leo hits me unexpectedly.

No, one orgasm and a crush isn't enough to have me declaring that I've suddenly fallen in love, but I would say that he has become my friend over the course of the past couple of months. That changes things.

He's not some random guy I picked up off an app to fool around with. He's someone whose feelings mattered to me even before we started making out. He's someone whose happiness I cared about before I even realised that he reciprocates my crush.

And I can't deny that I have developed a crush on him. Getting off with him has only made me want him more.

"Jack," Leo's tone is one that I have used myself so many times over the years. He's trying to let me down gently. "We can't. I wouldn't feel comfortable dating my boss. As it is, I feel bad for…" he pauses and waves his hand over me and the couch, "whatever you want to call what we just did."

I want to tell him we can fix it, but my parents raised me to understand that no means no. Pushing the issue isn't fair on him, no matter how hard my heart is clenching right now.

"It's not that I don't want you," he adds in an attempt to make things better. Oddly enough, it helps.

I snort before I can stop myself, my lips tugging up into a wry grin. "Oh, I think today's events make that clear." It's a bit of an asshole thing to say, knowing that it'll make him squirm and remind him of the line we crossed, but I'm relieved when he laughs lightly and nods.

"Yeah, well, I am only human." There's a moment of silence before he says, "Thank you for today. For not freaking out, I mean. And I am sorry. If things were different…"

"I know."

It sucks that this is where we're going to leave things, but I can't force him to wind up on the same page as me. And I refuse to make him uncomfortable or try and guilt him for the boundaries he has set himself. His inner strength and moral compass have always been elements of his personality which I have valued. Just because they're working against me right now doesn't change that.

As he starts backing away towards the hallway, I say, "Thank you for making my first experience with another man something special."

He closes his eyes and swallows, then nods once before turning and fleeing down the short hallway. I wait until I hear his door close before I head towards my own room, still wishing that things could be different.

Chapter Ten - Leo

My heart thunders in my chest as I leave the living room, ignoring the impulse to look back over my shoulder. I feel like today has been a roller coaster of emotions and experiences. On one hand, I am beyond thrilled that, against all odds, Jack reciprocates my attraction. On the other, I am mortified that he caught me in a compromising position and that I allowed my hormones to override my better judgement.

The skin around my lips still tingles from where his beard rubbed against me as we kissed. I'm almost certain that I've got beard burn.

I wonder if I can convince Jack to pick the boys up from his dad's place. I don't think I could look Will in the eye right now. He'll take one look at my swollen lips and ruddy skin and *know*.

Safely in my bedroom, I take my time getting changed for the third time today. My cheeks burn as I use the back of my cum-stained underwear to wipe myself clean. They burn even hotter when I think of Jack doing the same thing in his room, climbing out of sticky boxer briefs and dampened denim.

These thoughts are dangerous.

I really need to stop thinking about Jack this way. About the feel of his mouth on mine. About the taste of his tongue. About the searing heat of his palms on my hips. About the length and girth of his cock against mine, painfully separated by layers of fabric.

My resolve wavers as the memories invade my senses.

I know I made the right call. I know I did. But it doesn't make me want him any less.

Still, I'm being paid to prioritise his kids. Things have changed enough for them lately. They don't also need to be privy to their daddy exploring his newfound interest in men with their live-in nanny.

God, I wish I had someone I could talk to about the crazy situation I have somehow landed myself in. Unfortunately, I am still pathetically alone.

My closest friend these days is Will and I can't exactly see myself turning up on his doorstep to a) out his son and b) cry on his shoulder about why I've turned the Adonis of a man down after practically molesting him when he told me he was interested in me. Talk about giving a guy mixed signals!

A light knock on my door jolts me from my thoughts and I jump. "Um, yeah?" I ask, feeling ten different kinds of awkward.

"Can I come in?"

I appreciate the hesitation and caution in Jack's voice as he asks. Even though this is his apartment, he values my space and my privacy. Even after I just dry humped him until we both came and then ran away like a scared little mouse.

Chapter Ten - Leo

"Yeah," I answer, "Of course."

I'm obviously worried that I've still made things weird between us. That I let things get way too out of hand before I walked away. Hell, I'd made things weird by fucking myself in the shower to vocal fantasies of him. Even though he didn't seem at all freaked out by it, everything that happened this afternoon is bound to change our dynamic, right?

I just have to do everything in my power to force things back to normal.

The handle turns and the door opens slowly. It's almost comical to watch Jack peek around the door before he finally pushes it open the whole way and steps inside my bedroom properly.

He tucks his hands into the back pockets of the cargo shorts he's changed into and gives me a slightly strained smile. "Before I get the boys, can we finish our talk?"

Yeah, I think to myself sarcastically, *because that worked out so well for us before*. Nevertheless, I nod. I want things to be normal, I remind myself. That means facing the choices we've made head-on.

"Okay," I agree, but I don't say anything further.

He sighs and scrubs his hand over his beard. The action reminds me yet again of how the bristles felt against my skin. Softer than I'd imagined they'd be, smelling faintly of something sweet. I have to give myself a shake to focus on the moment.

"We're cool, right?" he asks me imploringly. His big, blue eyes remind me so much of his kids that my heart gives an ill-timed pang. "Like, we can be grown-ups and act like nothing's changed?"

I nod with more enthusiasm than the question warrants. "Of

course. I mean, as long as I haven't made you uncomfortable or angry or whatever..."

Dark, bushy eyebrows pinch together. "Why would I be angry?"

I shrug and direct my gaze out the window. My bedroom is on the hill-facing side of the building, not the beach-facing side. I'm greeted with leafy, green trees and a couple of rows of tan bricks belonging to the block of flats on the street behind ours, the rest of the building out of view from my window, given how much higher up the hill it sits.

"Leo," Jack prompts.

I exhale and force myself to look him in the eye again. "Because I led you on, got you off, and then told you I wasn't interested? Face it, I'm a cocktease."

His laugh seems to startle us both in the quiet of my bedroom, and it breaks the tension, flooding me with relief. When he steps forward, he grips my shoulder and squeezes, but it's an innocent touch. Friendly and reassuring.

"Firstly," he declares, "you didn't lead me on at all. Secondly, everything we did was consensual. Thirdly, you never said you weren't interested; you gave valid reasons as to why dating would be a bad idea for now. And finally, I'm a big boy and I can handle a little teasing. In fact, I've been known to enjoy it."

Now it's my turn to laugh. "You don't like it when I tease you about your weird American sandwich fetish."

"It's not a fetish and it's not weird," he grumps exaggeratedly. "You're the weird one for not liking them."

"Uh...no, I'm not."

"Yes, you are."

"Am not."

Chapter Ten - Leo

"Are too."

"Not."

"Too."

A burst of laughter escapes me before I can rein it in. "I see you've been learning the art of debate from your boys."

Arching a sinful eyebrow, Jack quirks his lips and his eyes gleam with mischief. He leans in close and, despite our agreement to be normal, my breathing hitches. "You started it," he teases, sounding just as insolent as Hudson.

Not having expected him to double down on the joke, it takes half a moment before another bout of the giggles takes over me.

"Alright," I hold my hands up in surrender when I can breathe again. "Truce?"

I can't read the emotion that flashes over his face, but he grins and nods. "Truce."

Now, if my heart (and cock) could get on board with the plan, that would be great.

* * *

"You know you're welcome at the wedding, right?" Connor asks me over dinner. It's been a month since the day Jack and I crossed a line we shouldn't have, and I think we've bounced back well from it.

Sure, sometimes I catch him looking at me in a way that suggests his thoughts are just as filthy as my own, but he hasn't pushed the issue or behaved any differently to the way he always has, and that has made it a lot easier for me to control my own urges. I've even managed to act normally around his family and friends, which I'm additionally glad for. As far as

I'm aware, he hasn't said anything about his attraction to men to anyone and I'll be damned if I accidentally out him before he's ready. Of course, that means I need to sit through family dinners the way I always have, and today that's proving harder than I thought it would.

How do I explain that I can't go to Connor and Will's wedding because it means having to look at Jack in a suit all night? I'll have to pretend that he's not my walking, talking wet dream, and I'll have to sit on my hands and force myself not to ask him to dance with me at the reception. I've already seen him in the suit he's wearing as one of Will's best men and I know my willpower will not hold for an entire wedding. It just won't. So, it's safer if I don't go.

"I know," I reply, trying to sound chipper and apologetic all at once, "but I'm really just the help, and Jack says his mum wants to look after the boys because she's only gotten to FaceTime with them, so I'll kind of be a fish out of water. I mean, I only know you guys, and I'm not the greatest with social stuff."

"Pfft," Connor waves off my concerns with an eye roll. "Please. You know some of the guys from soccer now, right? And some of Will's friends from work. You can sit with them. Or with Toby. He's bringing Violet as his date. His daughter. She's almost twelve, and she's a riot."

Well, there goes all of my arguments. I turn my hands up at my sides, my palms facing the ceiling in a frozen shrug with my shoulders near my ears. "I mean, the wedding's in two weeks. Do you even have a spot for me? I haven't RSVPd or anything. I'd feel bad putting you guys out."

"You're not," Will assures me, leaning over to wipe remnants of mashed potato from Vicky's chubby cheeks. He smiles across the table at me. "You're a friend now, Leo. And the

Chapter Ten – Leo

boys love you. You're basically family, and Connor's got connections. I'm sure he can finagle an extra place setting and meal with the reception venue."

"You gots to come," Prez tells me, deciding to add his two cents' worth to the conversation now that he's mutilated his meal. The plate of cut-up pieces of grilled chicken with veggies and mash now resembles a massacre, drowned with tomato sauce and mushed together into an unappetising mess. "You gots to meet Granma and have cake. Grampa says it's a *big* cake!"

We all laugh and I already know that I can't turn down Preston's cute pleas. I'm not a monster, after all.

"Well, I do like cake," I tell him and he cheers.

Not wanting to be left out, Hudson asks, "Is it chocolate cake, Grampa? Chocolate cake's my favourite."

"There'll be chocolate cake for you," Connor tells him, smiling softly at the kids who'll be his grandsons through marriage. "I promise."

Jack leans into me to murmur, "Cake-tantrum crisis averted." His voice is playful, but it still sends a shiver up my spine. I force a chuckle, trying not to make more of the interaction than it was.

We promised to keep things normal. I have to act normal.

When I glance across the table, Will's watching me with an arched eyebrow. My chuckle turns into a cough and I cover by grabbing my glass of water and drinking it down in a few gulps. I'm practically gasping for breath when I'm done.

So much for normal, idiot.

"So," Connor prods with blatant amusement when I set the glass down. "You'll be at the wedding, then?"

With all avenues of escape closed to me, I can only paste on a bright smile and nod. "Sure. Thank you for inviting me." This part is easier to say, because I mean it from the bottom of my heart. "It means a lot, actually. That you're treating me like part of the family, I mean. I haven't had that for a while."

"Well, you're stuck with us now," Connor says cheerfully. "Even when the boys are grown up and heading off to uni, I like to think we'll still be friends. I tend to collect the good ones and keep them long-term...and you, my friend, are a good one. I know this because I'm a fabulous judge of character."

Will snorts. "Except for your ex."

Connor rolls his eyes. "Ant wasn't *always* an ar-um-aardvark."

"Aardvark?" Jack repeats flatly *"Really?"*

Connor shrugs. "I blanked."

"What's a arvark?" Preston asks, ever curious.

"An aardvark," I correct him gently, "is an animal. It looks kind of like if a wombat, a pig, and a rabbit had a baby together."

He scrunches up his nose. "Gross."

I shake my head. "Nah, they're kind of cute. I'll show you a picture before bedtime if you brush your teeth properly tonight, okay?"

"And me?" Hudson all but demands.

"And you," I nod, then gesture to his plate. "Now eat up before your dinner gets too cold."

"You're honestly like the Super Nanny," Connor declares in awe when Hudson does as I've asked without complaint. "How can you be so young and yet so good with kids? It's unfair. I basically have to bribe them to do what I want." He shoots a wide-eyed look across to Jack. "Not that I ever bribe your children. Nope. Never."

Chapter Ten - Leo

Jack snorts. "Don't worry, Con. I do it, too. Leo's the only one who can cast some sort of weird spell over them." He nudges my shoulder with his own.

"Uh," I wave my hand wildly around the glass dining table, "didn't anyone hear the part where I bribed them with pictures of aardvarks?"

I'll take 'weirdest things I've ever said' for ten dollars, Alex.

"Whatever," Jack waves me off. "You've also somehow managed to turn bathtime into a bribe, and that just proves that you're magic."

"Bathtime?" Hudson perks up. "Can I have a bath now?"

"See?" Jack says, pointing at his son like the kid has sprouted horns. "Magic."

"Grampa, Grampa," Huddy steamrolls right over his dad's commentary, his dinner well and truly forgotten in his excitement, "Leo gotted us a *way* better bath than yours." He starts pushing his chair back, waving his hand in the universal 'follow me' gesture. "Come see!"

Will arches an eyebrow at me. "What have you done to my bathroom, Martin?"

I roll my eyes. "Like I could afford to renovate someone else's bathroom. It's just an inflatable bathtub. It fits in the shower stall and it has saved us hours of arguments."

"Maaaagic," Jack adds, using jazz hands as he draws out the word.

"Aaaaamazon," I snark back, mocking his tone and gestures with my own.

"Inflatable tub," Will echoes, closing his eyes and wincing. "My beautiful, beautiful bathroom."

Connor smacks Will's bicep with the back of his hand. "Child," he mutters at his soon-to-be husband, but his tone is laced with affection. He turns his gaze back onto me. "That's actually genius."

"It's a bit of a pain to deflate and reinflate, but worth the effort," I admit. "But I can't take credit for it. My Facebook ads kept showing them in increasing frequency the more I argued about shower time with the boys. Targeted advertising at its finest, I'm afraid."

"Yeah, and you still won't tell me how much you paid." Jack grumbles. "You don't have to make purchases like that out of pocket."

"It wasn't expensive," I assure him like I have every time the argument has come up. "And I like spending money on the boys. Plus, it's more for my sanity than it is for their happiness."

Jack snorts. "Liar."

"Grampa!" Hudson hollers from the hallway.

Will sighs and pushes his own seat back. "Coming, bud!" he calls over his shoulder, then gives me another exaggerated side-eye. "Let's go see what kind of devastation you've wrought."

Holding my hands in surrender, I shake my head. "Nuh-uh. I'm staying here where I'm safe." I lean into Preston. "You'll keep me safe, won't you, kiddo?"

He shrugs. "I just wanna see the armvark."

"Aardvark," I correct him, then ruffle his hair.

He rolls his eyes. "Whatever."

Jack and Connor burst into laughter and I can't help but join in even as my heart gives a telltale squeeze.

I love this family so much, it's almost painful. It's almost too easy to imagine myself here under the capacity of Jack's boyfriend instead of as his employee. As a prospective stepdad,

Chapter Ten - Leo

despite how young I am, instead of just the nanny. But I know not to let myself get carried away by my daydreams. I made my choice —the right choice— and now I have to stick with it.

Will's loud 'Oh, dear God!' comes from down the hall and my eyes widen.

"Quick," Jack gives me a little shove, "run! I'll stall him!"

Throwing my head back, I laugh so hard I almost cry.

Then my thoughts shift again and, if I look at Jack now, I probably will cry.

I'm in too deep and I know it.

Fuck.

Chapter Eleven – Jack

Mom's hugs are unlike anything else in the world. She doesn't even speak before she crosses the threshold of my apartment and throws her arms around me, squeezing my midsection tightly. I bury my nose into the dark hair on the top of her head and draw in comfort I didn't know I desperately needed.

This is the first time I've seen her in person in a couple of years. Having to introduce her grandsons to her via FaceTime had sucked hard, and it had taken a lot of convincing to keep her in California for the extra few months before she was due to fly out here for Dad's wedding. She's been getting to know the boys through weekly calls, but even they know she's champing at the bit to meet them in person. Still, before asking about them, her first port of call was to hug me, and it means more than I can say.

I'm a little jealous that Wes has had the chance to spend extra time with her because he picked her up from Brisbane International Airport yesterday, and she and her family

Chapter Eleven — Jack

crashed in his and Vanna's house last night, but it's not enough for me to whine about. Now she, Mike and their daughters, my half-sisters, are staying in the hotel where the wedding is being held, and they've come over to meet the boys face-to-face.

"How are you doing, baby? And I mean really, Jack." She pins me with an expectant stare as she pulls back.

"Mom?" my eldest half-sister, Dana, peers around from behind our mother. She looks so much like Mom these days it's uncanny. Her dark eyes meet mine with humour as she asks, "Can we all come inside while you interrogate he who doesn't understand condoms?"

She's just shy of twenty and that knowledge makes me a little uncomfortable when I realise that she's barely a year younger than the man I've been crushing on for months now. I flip her off half-heartedly, then pull Mom aside so the rest of the group can muscle into my apartment.

"Can you not mention condoms around my impressionable three-year-olds?" I ask her with a hint of irritation. I love my sisters, but she and I have always been like oil and water. "Also, I used 'em. They didn't work. Hence the three-year-olds."

"Jack," Dad says in warning, bringing up the back of the group, because of course Wes stopped in at his apartment first. "Which one of you is the adult here?"

I wince, but not because I'm being told off like I'm a kid. It's because I only just made the connection between Dana's age and Leo's, and if Dad thinks Dana's still a kid, what would he think if he knew what Leo and I did on the couch he's just dropped onto?

Dana pushes onto her tiptoes and grazes a kiss over my bearded jaw. "I've missed you, big bro."

You Don't Know Jack

My irritation melts away. "Yeah, I've missed you too, runt."

Her younger sister, Roxy, has already sat herself down on the playmat in front of the couch, avidly playing with Vicky, who seems to adore all the new attention she's getting. "Hey, Rox, I've missed you too," I say with exaggerated bemusement. She just waves back at me dismissively.

Mom sighs and shakes her head, touching my bicep to refocus my attention. "Seriously, how are you? And where are my boys?"

This I can answer honestly, and it's only because of Leo. I don't care what he says: he's played a vital role in the routines and life I've now built. "I'm great. Really, Mom. The first month was hard, but…I'm good. I can't imagine not having the boys now. And they'll be out in a minute. Leo's getting them changed. Prez had an accident, and then Huddy peed himself in solidarity…" I laugh as I say it, shaking my head at the absurdity of the statement. "It was a thing." And, as always, Leo had been totally calm about dealing with it when the knock at the door had sounded.

"Potty-training's going well, then?" Mom asks with sarcasm. She reaches up to poke me in the chest with her manicured index finger. The bright red gloss glints in the sunlight streaming in through the living room window. "*Someone* used to refuse to use the potty to poop."

I roll my eyes and sigh, "Damn Wes."

From the vicinity of the kitchen, my brother cackles. "Nuh-uh. That was all you!"

"Don't get too high and mighty, mister," Mom calls back in his direction. "Or I'll remind you who used to deliberately pee on the rug and blame it on the dog."

"The dog that didn't exist," Dad adds, shaking his head as

Chapter Eleven — Jack

though he couldn't believe how dumb we were as kids. "I don't miss those days."

"Doggy?" Prez's voice interrupts before I can remind him that he's got a one-year-old who will be potty-training soon enough. I look over my shoulder to catch Leo ushering my freshly dressed kids down the hallway. "Did Grampa say doggy?"

"Now look what you've done," I tell my dad before I turn to grab Hudson. As much as they've come out of their shells, meeting strangers can still be hit-or-miss for them, so I'd rather ease him into it with a cuddle.

Leo hoists Preston up and props him on his hip, too, without needing me to ask.

"Anyway, guys, I want you to meet Grandma, Grandpa Mike, and your Aunts Dana and Roxy." I point out each person as I say their names. "You've met them all on FaceTime, but they've come to visit in real life. How cool is that?"

Preston turns pink and hides his face in the crook of Leo's neck. Hudson just narrows his eyes in suspicion. "Gramma?" he asks, tilting his head.

As predicted, my mother's eyes fill with tears at meeting her grandsons in person for the first time. She doesn't reach for either of them, though, even though I can tell she's itching to cuddle the life out of them.

"You look *just* like your Daddy when he was little," she tells Hudson. "And Prezzie looks just like his Uncle Wes."

Hudson rolls his eyes. I blame Leo for that habit. "We is twins, Gramma," he says as though she's unaware of the fact. "We look the same."

"You *are* twins," Leo corrects, coming to stand by my side. "And so are Daddy and Uncle Wes."

You Don't Know Jack

Hudson doesn't buy it. "But Daddy is a different shape. Uncle Wes is skinny. Daddy is wide. And Uncle Wes gots no beard."

"I'm not *wide*, I'm muscled," I grumble and Leo snorts.

"Here," Mom says, pulling a familiar-looking photo album from her handbag like a magician, "I can show you."

Prez perks up and peers over at the prospect of pictures, wriggling in Leo's arms until he's set down to investigate properly. Then, because the photos have caught his brother's attention, Huddy follows suit. But it's Leo who seems the most curious, leaning in close with the boys, grinning from ear to ear as my mom shows photos of me and Wes at the boys' age, naked and attempting to maim each other with plastic swords.

"I see nothing's changed," Leo deadpans, causing Vanna to chortle while Wes and I splutter. Leo's cheeks turn pink. "Not what I meant! I just meant that you're still childish. Geez," he pinches the bridge of his nose. "This just illustrates my point."

Everyone's laughing by now, even the boys — though they're not in on the joke. I want so badly to reach out and pull Leo to my side and kiss the top of his head, but I know I can't. We made a deal.

Mom leads the boys over to the couch and they sit next to each other between my parents, sharing the photo album between them, their tiny dark heads bent together as Mom and Dad tell them stories to go with the photos. Leo pulls out his phone and takes a photo of the moment, and that brings a lump to my throat.

How am I supposed to keep my feelings platonic around him when he does thoughtful things like that?

Chapter Eleven – Jack

* * *

"So, your manny's cute," Dana says, dropping into the empty chair beside me. It's late into the reception at Dad and Connor's wedding.

The ceremony was perfect, complete with Vicky stealing the show as she tottered down the aisle and then veered off course, and the reception has met all of Connor's expectations and then some. For the amount of time he's spent planning the wedding, I should hope that he was happy with the end product.

I give my sister the side-eye. "He's gay, Danish," I revert back to her old nickname just to annoy her, "so you're barking up the wrong tree."

She shrugs and lifts her glass of wine to her lips, sipping at it with a satisfied sigh. "Have I mentioned how cool it is that I can legally drink here? Like an actual adult. Which I am."

Dragging my eyes away from the dance floor where Leo is dancing with Dad's friend, Toby, and his daughter, Violet, I wonder if her statement was meant to be as pointed as it sounded, or if I'm just being hypersensitive. "You are, yes," I agree cautiously.

My sister swirls her remaining wine with a flourish of her wrist and tips the glass in the direction of the dance floor. "And so is he."

I hope my face is impassive because I'm pretty sure I just had a heart attack. "I beg your pardon?"

Dana laughs wickedly. "God, you've spent too much time here. You're picking up their way of talking." She affects a terrible Australian accent, sounding more British than anything. "I beg your pardon," she mocks, then laughs again.

I squint at her glass. "How many of those have you had?"

"Don't change the subject," she says primly, then beckons someone else over.

I don't need to turn around to recognise Wes as he steps up and takes his previously abandoned seat at my other side. Tonight was the first time he's sat separately from his girlfriend, what with the two of us being part of the wedding party and all. It was nice having him to myself again, even if it was just for the meal, which has long since been finished.

"What's up?" he asks, stealing my beer from in front of me and taking a long drag from it.

"Twenty-one's not too young for someone your age to date, right?" Dana prompts while I choke on air.

Wes pats my back and gapes at her. "You're not dating someone our age, are you, Danish? Mom might be okay with that, but Mike will lose his shit."

She rolls her eyes. "No, not me. And I'm not twenty-one yet. Thanks for forgetting my age, dumbass."

"So I was rounding up," Wes shrugs. "And if we're not talking about you, who are we talking about?"

I try to kick Dana's shin under the table, but she seems to expect it and twists her legs out of the way.

She shoots Wes a coy smile. "Oh...just a new single dad who's pining over his kids' nanny, and whose nanny totally reciprocates on the pining front."

I want to kill her. I don't know how she worked it out when Leo and I have barely even spoken tonight (which is a crime in and of itself, because he looks hotter than ever in his suit with a full face of glam makeup that makes his pretty eyes pop), but she's not wrong.

In addition to that, she's just outed me to Wes, arguably the

Chapter Eleven — Jack

person I should have spoken to as soon as I started having all sorts of complicated feelings because he and I have been there for each other literally since before we were born. And I would have talked to him eventually if I'd been able to catch him on his own. But it wouldn't have been at Dad's wedding, and it would have been when I felt like I had my thoughts sorted out.

Wes is silent for a long moment, then his tone is steely when he does speak. I've only ever seen him in court once, but the way he spoke then, delivering a speech to the judge, was very much like the way he's speaking now. "Damn it, Dana, you should walk away."

Her mirthful expression slips. "But…"

"You don't just out someone like that," he says, still calm, but clearly pissed. "Walk away."

I shake my head, defending her as she pales and her eyes water. "Wes, it's fine. She didn't know…"

"Bullshit," he scoffs. "She's not a kid, Jack."

It's ironic that he's arguing the same point she was trying to make earlier.

Her voice is wobbly as she pushes her chair back and squeezes my shoulder. "Shit, Jack. I'm sorry. I thought…I mean, it's *Wes*. He knows *everything* about you. And if I worked it out…" She stops and sighs shakily. "I was just trying to do the sibling teasing thing."

"It's fine," I repeat, even as Wes huffs dramatically on my other side.

"It's really not."

"Wes," I finally snap at him. "Stop."

The thing is, I understand exactly where Dana's coming from. There was a time where Wes and I were inseparable.

You Don't Know Jack

Before Vanna, he would have been able to read me like a book. And all Dana wanted to do was get in on the sibling bonding shit that we would usually banter about. She wanted to be part of the grown-up jokes with her big brothers when her only other sibling relationship is a teenaged girl going through whatever hormonal changes teen girls go through. But even though Wes and I do still give each other shit, we're not in each other's pockets anymore…only Dana wouldn't have known that because she's even more distanced from us than we are from each other.

"I really am sorry," she says meaningfully, and I reach for her hand to squeeze it.

"I know. And it's okay. I promise."

Dana nods and then wanders back over to her dad and sister, and I don't turn back to face Wes until I'm certain she's not too upset.

"Where are the boys?" Wes asks me, fiddling with the neck of my half-empty beer bottle.

"Mom took them up to their suite. She's insisting on having them stay with her and Mike tonight, and it was after their bedtime." I'd argued that I was responsible for them and that she shouldn't miss out on the reception because of my kids, but she'd just laughed and said that once Dad and Connor left, she'd seen all the real fun of the event anyway.

"Good. Then you're free to come with me." Wes doesn't bother checking if I'm good with that, he just hauls me out of my seat and tugs me along by my bicep. We leave the reception hall and head out onto the balcony overlooking the ocean. From where we're standing, the breeze is cool and salty. It's dark out, but under the light of the moon, the white foam from the ocean hitting the sand in gentle bursts shimmers silver. It's

Chapter Eleven — Jack

a clear night, and stars twinkle at us from the inky-coloured sky.

Music from inside filters towards us, muted by the double-paned glass of the wall and door, and the sound of pedestrians and traffic floats up from the street. It's relaxing. Or it would be, if I wasn't tensing for the conversation I'm about to have with my twin.

He stands quietly at my side, his back to the ocean, leaning against the balcony's balustrade. I face forward, gripping the cool metal railing under my palms, bracing myself physically as well as mentally.

"I'm sorry Dana did that," Wes eventually says softly. There's no censure in his voice, and no demand to know why I hadn't told him. He doesn't sound hurt or even affronted. "She took your choice from you."

"She didn't realise…" I start, but Wes's scoff stops me.

"That doesn't matter. Did you initiate the conversation? Bring the topic up at all?" I'm already shaking my head before he finishes asking the questions. "Exactly," he says. "She shouldn't have done that. I know that she just wanted to mess around, but it was pretty obvious that you were keeping your feelings to yourself and she should have respected that."

"Well, she's learned her lesson now, I guess." I reply with a sigh. "She was just excited, Wes. She's watched us mess around and hang shit on each other for years and she just wanted to feel like she was part of that."

"She—"

"—should know better than to tease about someone's sexuality, yeah. But I don't think she gave that part a second's thought. I bet she would have done the same damn thing if Leo was a woman and she'd caught me checking them out."

You Don't Know Jack

It's the first time I've acknowledged it out loud to anyone but Smitty and it feels like a weight has been lifted from my shoulders. I smile wryly. "I thought I was doing a good job of keeping it under wraps, but apparently not."

"I never would have picked it." Wes slumps a little at that. Out of the corner of my eye, I watch him turn to stare at me. "Have we really gotten so far apart that I missed it? I used to be able to read you like a book."

My eyes water a little at the resignation in his tone. It's hard to explain the twin bond to people who aren't twins, but I've felt increasingly incomplete with the more distance we've managed to put between ourselves. Swallowing roughly, all I can do is shrug. "People change, Wes. You grew up faster than I did."

"Bullshit," he seethes. "You're a fucking dad, Jack, and instead of freaking out, you've taken to it like a duck to water. Not to mention the years you've spent keeping an eye on Dad, making sure he was taking care of himself..." Wes stops to take a breath and calm himself. "You're more mature than I am in a lot of ways."

"Wes..."

Shaking his head, my twin continues sadly, "I wanted to be my own person, you know? That's why I moved a couple of hours away. It's why I settled down with Vanna so quickly. I mean, I love her, but I know it was all fast, and I know you resented that. Resented her. But it was all me, Jack. Not her. In the beginning, anytime she suggested that I organise a guys' weekend or spend some one-on-one time with you, I baulked. I wanted an identity separate to 'Jack's twin brother' and then time flew by and it was just normal to always bring Vanna along. After that, I felt like I couldn't go back to the way things

Chapter Eleven – Jack

were anymore."

The morose information dump takes me completely by surprise. I had no idea Wes felt that way, and the guilt that I hadn't known him as well as I'd thought I did stings like a bitch.

"I feel like shit, Jack," he says while I'm still reeling from his confession. "Dana's right: once upon a time, I *did* know everything about you before everyone else. And now I feel like I barely know you, and that's all on me."

"Oh, fuck off," I finally cut in, refusing to let him be the martyr here. "I could have forced the issue, too, you know. I whined and bitched about losing you to Vanna, but I could have manned the fuck up and talked to you about it."

We stand in silence for a long while after that, both of us processing. Eventually, he leans over and bumps my shoulder with his.

"So…Leo, huh?"

I groan, but I'm smiling at the gentle teasing tone he's used. "Fucking came as a surprise to me, too," I acknowledge. "Like, wouldn't I have liked guys before now? I work with enough buff men that someone should have caught my eye."

Wes snorts. "I hate to break it to you, but Leo's not what I'd call buff. Maybe your type is twinkier." He finally turns around to face the ocean at my side, chuckling, "I mean, Dad seems to like them slim and marginally effeminate, too, so—"

"Eww," I cut him off and ram him with my shoulder. He stumbles sideways before he regains his footing. "Don't suggest that Dad and I share a type. That's just weird. And gross. And did I mention weird?"

Laughing, he rams me back, but I don't budge. "All I'm saying is maybe you haven't come across as many men who tick the right boxes is all. Plus, with the number of women you get throwing themselves at you, I'm guessing you never had the time to really look."

I roll my eyes. "They don't *throw* themselves at me."

"Let's agree to disagree on that front." After another beat, he goes on, "But, seriously, you might not have even realised you were checking other guys out. Did you ever think 'that guy's attractive' and then keep going with your day?"

"Well, yeah, but it was never in a 'I'd suck him off' kind of way. More like…" I search for the right way to describe it, "just acknowledging an attractive person in my proximity."

Wes snorts again. "Dude, I've *never* looked at another man and thought 'hmm, he's hot' in a platonic way. Or in any way."

"Yeah, well, it never really felt like I was checking other men out," I try again to explain. "But I guess, like you said, it was always in passing. Like, okay," I feel my cheeks heat, "I might have noticed that Smitty has a fantastic ass once or twice, but…I never really felt like doing something with that information."

"Until Leo."

I nod. "Until Leo."

There's more silence, then, "Have you tried talking to him?"

I look over my shoulder to make sure we're still alone on the balcony. "We, uh, fooled around a little."

"Holy shit. Really? When? Did you kiss him?" He stops and huffs at his own question. "Of course you did. Did you like it?"

Snickering, I shrug. "You sound like Roxy, you know that?"

"Fuck off, this is huge. You've never wanted to go back for seconds with anyone."

"Gross," I shudder, "He's not a buffet, Wes. He's a person."

Chapter Eleven — Jack

After a low whistle, Wes sounds awed when he observes, "You're actually serious about him. You're not just attracted: you care about him."

I can't look at him now. I'm ashamed of the way I've treated women in the past. They all had feelings, too, and I treated them like objects for my pleasure. Between Steph reminding me of what an asshole I was, and discovering that I honestly care about Leo's feelings, it's hard not to feel guilty for my past behaviour. He deserves better than me.

Clearing my throat, I force myself to nod. "Yeah, well, it doesn't matter. He asked me to back off and I'm respecting that."

"Shit. Is it the age thing? Because Con and Dad have a bigger age gap and they're making it work. Granted, Con was older than you are now when he met Dad, but—"

"No, that's not it." I stare out into the darkness, catching glimpses of silvery ripples of ocean under the moon's light. "I'm his boss. He's not comfortable crossing that line. There were a bunch of other reasons, but that's ultimately the biggest one."

Wes seems to slump in defeat and he groans. "I can't say he doesn't have a point. But that sucks for you, man. I'm sorry."

"It's okay," I assure him, feeling the honesty in the words. "I don't want to make him feel uncomfortable, and he's a damn good nanny: I'm not running him off if I can help it."

"Yeah, well, I've spent time with your kids. The guy's a saint if he can wrangle them."

I bring the arm closest to him up and punch him hard in his bicep. He yelps. "You had that coming. That's your nephews you're dissing."

He just chortles. "Dissing? Who uses the word *dissing*?"

"I'll have you know I am hip and with it."

He snorts. "Face it, Jack. We're getting old. Like," he checks his shiny gold watch, "it's just past ten p.m. and I'm having issues staying awake out here. There was a time where a Red Bull and vodka would get me through until the morning, and then I'd still go to class."

"Red Bull and vodka? And *you're* the straight one?"

"Fuck off with your drink shaming. It tastes better than beer."

It's good to feel like we're getting back on track, bantering and bickering like we always used to. Coming out to him, however unintentionally, feels like a weight has been lifted from my shoulders. Or maybe it's the fact that we finally cleared the air about the whole Vanna thing. Either way, I feel ten times lighter now.

"Come on," Wes gives me another nudge, "let's head back inside before Vanna sends a search party."

As I push back from the railing, I keep my snarky thoughts about his girlfriend to myself.

Hey; maybe I have matured after all.

Chapter Twelve – Leo

"You've got it bad for Will's son, don't you?" Toby asks me as he sits back in his dining chair, his daughter now asleep in his lap. Her legs dangle on either side of his, the toes of her shoes barely brushing the carpet, and she's buried her face in the crook of his neck, looking more like a wiped-out toddler than the eleven-year-old girl she is.

Toby doesn't seem in any rush to dislodge her. Her dark hair contrasts with his blond mane, which is currently tied back from his face in a neat ponytail at the nape of his neck. They both have the same tanned skin, though, but his eyes are bright blue where hers are hazel. Earlier tonight, he explained that he and his late husband had flipped a coin on which of them would be the donor for their surrogate, and he's now relieved to still have a piece of the man who died unexpectedly a few years ago.

I can't imagine what he's gone through, to be honest, and it's amazing that he's so cheerful when he's lost so much.

Still, if he could be a little less nosy, that would be nice.

"I don't know what you're talking about," I answer him, reaching for my drink. I jut my chin towards Violet. "I'm feeling like I could do the same thing right now. You guys danced me ragged."

Toby's smile turns wicked, enhancing his deep-set laugh lines in sun-weathered skin. "You could go climb into Jack's lap and take a nap."

I groan. "You're not going to drop it, are you?"

"Nope." He's not at all repentant. "You two have been giving each other ridiculously pining looks all night, so I don't think he'd mind."

"We have not," I protest, sounding so much like Huddy and Prez that I want to cringe. I've even got the whine down pat. "It's not like that. He's my boss."

"Uh-huh," Toby shifts and reaches for his beer, causing Violet's head to loll on his shoulder. After taking a sip from his glass, he sets it back down and resettles his daughter with care. "If you two were trying to be inconspicuous, you probably shouldn't have been so obvious with how you've avoided each other all night. I could cut the tension with a knife."

Scrunching up my nose, I consider my arguments. I can't play the 'Jack's straight' card because even though he hasn't announced that he's bi, or bi-curious, or whatever label he's most comfortable with, I know I'd be lying and I don't lie. I can't say that there's nothing between us, either, because that would also be a lie. Same for the tension that's been building ever since I set eyes on Jack in his suit and his pale pink dress shirt. *Ugh*.

I fidget, fingering a corner of a linen napkin which is overhanging the edge of the table.

In the end, I sigh. "We agreed that it would be a bad idea

Chapter Twelve — Leo

to act on our attraction to each other," I eventually admit, choosing my words carefully. "He's my employer and I live under his roof, and I don't want the boys getting confused about my role. Plus, he's never been with a guy before, and he's just gone through some crazy major life changes…I just don't think it's a good idea to leap into anything with him right now."

Toby mulls this over for a moment, his expression turning serious. "You're more mature than half the men my age I've met recently," he tells me, sounding resigned. "Even though I want to say 'screw it; go for it', I think you're right not to. Damn it," he huffs. "I hate being wrong."

"You weren't wrong, though," I remind him with a laugh. "If circumstances were different, I'd be climbing him like a tree."

Toby laughs, then shushes himself when Violet grizzles and raises her head, moving it to his opposite shoulder before she settles back into sleep again. "If I was ten years younger, I'd be tempted, too."

"*Eww*! Aren't you his dad's best friend? How can you think things like that about Will's kid?"

"Okay, one: by the time I met Will, his boys were already *thirty*. Two: I did just say 'if I was ten years younger'. And C—"

"Don't you mean three?" I cock my head, smirking cheekily. "Aren't you supposed to be a teacher?"

Toby glares at me. "C," he repeats deliberately, even though his lips are twitching, "there's a whole romance trope dedicated to dad's best friend. You're just saying it's gross because you *liiiike* him."

I am so glad that Connor and Will sat me at this table because Toby has been a hoot. Chuckling and shaking my head, I accuse, "You've been spending way too much time with primary school kids."

"Says the nanny who just whined like a toddler not three minutes ago."

I reach for my drink again and raise it in a marginally patronising toast, before taking a sip. "Touché."

Toby's eyes focus on something over my head and he smirks. "Well, hello, Jack," he greets, and I want to kick him in the shin for being so obvious. He makes it worse by adding, "We were just talking about you."

I glower and mouth 'I will end you' before pasting a far-too-false smile on my face and turning to greet Jack as he comes to a stop a couple of feet away from me. "Ignore him," I tell my employer. "What's up?"

"I'm about to get an Uber home. Did you want to come with, or are you heading back with Toby?"

Toby, I discovered earlier, only lives about a fifteen-minute walk from our place.

Huh.

Our place.

I know that I have every right to live there as part of my employment contract, and that room and board are factored into my take-away wage every month, but it still feels strange to think of Jack's apartment as my home, too. Or maybe I'm just overthinking.

"Or," Jack continues when I don't immediately respond, "Tobes, do you and Vi want to get an Uber with us?"

I turn back around to watch Toby nod and drain the last of his beer. "Sounds like a plan to me," he says, pushing to his feet with Violet still sleeping on his shoulder. He hefts her up higher, making the act of carrying her seem far easier than it

Chapter Twelve – Leo

should. "Vi's wiped anyway, and it looks like the party's fading out now that your dad and Con have gone off to—"

"*Lalalalala,*" Jack clamps his hands over his ears as he singsongs, "I can't hear you."

Toby chuckles. "I was going to say 'enjoy their brief honeymoon', but if your mind wants to take it further, that's on you."

"Ugh. I've changed my mind. Your sick ass is uninvited." Jack snarks back at him and then holds out a hand to me. "Come on, babe. Up you get."

My cheeks flush at the endearment, and I hope that the layers of foundation, concealer and highlighter I'm wearing tonight hide the worst of it. Even though Toby knows that there's something between us, I still try to cover for Jack anyway as I take his hand and let him haul me up from my seat. "I see you've hit the beers hard tonight, then."

He frowns. "No, I'm still pretty sober. Why would you…*oh.*" It's his turn to blush. "Shit. I, um…"

"Don't go making shit up on my account," Toby interrupts him, "I guessed earlier, but I won't say anything. Not my circus, not my monkeys."

Jack snorts and gestures for Toby to lead the way out of the reception hall. "Whatever. Just get moving, Tobes, before I decide it's easier to leave you and your munchkin behind."

* * *

The drive back to Burleigh from Surfers is quick and uneventful. At this time of night, we're going against traffic, and the Gold Coast Highway —which is more of a suburban road lined with shops and restaurants than its title would lead you to believe— gets us home within twenty-five minutes. It would have been earlier, had we not stopped to drop Toby and Violet off at their house, but it wasn't as though we were in any rush to get home.

"It seems so quiet without the boys," I muse as Jack lets me enter the apartment first, toeing off my shiny, black dress shoes at the door. I feel my lips quirk as Jack bends to pick them up and put them on the shoe rack before he does the same with his own.

At some point during the ride, he loosened his tie and rolled the pale pink sleeves of his shirt to his elbows, his jacket long since removed from his person. It's a phenomenal look for him, emphasising his toned muscles and delicious tattoos.

"Is it weird that I can't really remember what life was like before them?" Jack asks rhetorically, leaning against the wall next to the shoe rack, giving me a smile that makes my knees feel as though the bone has been replaced by jelly. "And if I didn't have them, I wouldn't have met you."

My mouth goes dry and my resolve wavers. "Jack..." Even I can hear how half-hearted the reprimand sounds.

"Have you got any idea how hard it was to keep my hands off you tonight?"

His low —dare I call it sultry?— tone sets my heart racing.

He continues, "That suit should be illegal, Leo. The way your ass looks in those pants..." he trails off and shakes his head with a dry chuckle. "No wonder people can tell I'm into you. I couldn't stop watching you. When you danced with Smitty..." More trailing off, this time accompanied by a sexy-as-fuck growl. "I don't get jealous, Leo, but I was jealous of him."

I've gravitated closer and I'm reaching out to smooth my

Chapter Twelve — Leo

hands over his broad, firm chest to soothe him before I realise it. "You have nothing to be jealous of, Jack. Smitty's sweet, but…"

He dips his head, his voice a gravelly whisper as he prompts, "But what?"

"But…he's not you."

He lets loose another growly sound that goes straight to my dick, even as I feel the vibrations through his chest against my palms. "I need to kiss you. Please say I can kiss you."

The last vestiges of my control flee me. I nod, then hold up my index finger in front of his lips before he can surge forward to act on his desire. *Our* desire. "But only tonight. After tonight? We have to go back to normal again. Can you do that?"

Beneath the thin cotton of his shirt, I can feel his heart thumping just as rapidly as mine. His chest rises and falls as he takes a deep, calming breath, then releases it slowly. "If that's the only way I get to have you, I'd rather that than nothing at all."

How am I supposed to respond to something like that? Lost for words, I push up on my toes to close the distance between our mouths, practically melting into the kiss as our lips finally connect.

It takes barely a couple of moments for the kiss to deepen, and I open up willingly for him. Jack's tongue tastes like the breath mint he popped into his mouth while we were in the Uber: refreshing and a little bit spicy. His hands tug my shirt free of my suit pants and slip beneath the material at my back, sweeping over my heated flesh, exploring and mapping my body beneath his palms.

My hands, meanwhile, are balled into fists against his

shoulder blades, tightly bunching and gripping the once-pristine dress shirt he wears so well. Just like last time, I can't help thinking that he kisses like a dream, knowing just when to apply pressure and when to pull back and slow us back down.

"Bed?" he suggests, barely separating our mouths to do so. The word is gravelly with lust, but I can hear the slightest touch of hesitation in his voice.

"You sure?" I whisper back. "We can fool around on the couch for a bit instead, like last time."

His hands travel down the slope of my spine and then cup my bum, squeezing me over the fabric of my suit pants. "Is that what you want?"

With reluctance, I let go of his shirt and put a little space between us so I can look him in the eye. His face is flushed, and his eyes are dark with arousal. "I know this is new to you," I reply gently. "I don't want to rush you into anything you're not ready for."

"I'm the one who suggested bed, babe," his lips quirk, and he takes one of my hands, guiding it to his clothed erection. He feels as hard as steel beneath the thick black fabric of his trousers. I swallow roughly as he continues, "That's how ready I am for you."

He's going to be the death of me.

"Your place or mine?" I tease playfully, curling my fingers around his bulge, trying to ignore the voice in my head screaming 'Bad idea, Leo!' and 'You're only going to get more attached if you fuck him' and, my personal favourite, 'Have you learned *nothing* from all the cheesy romance books you read?'

That voice doesn't know what it's talking about. I can do

Chapter Twelve – Leo

friends with benefits, I'm sure of it. Instead, I relish in the way Jack throws his head back and arches into my touch, groaning low in the back of his throat.

"I honestly don't care if we stay right here," he answers me, his voice gravelly with desire, "but we need to be naked, like, five minutes ago."

With reluctance, I tear myself away from him and start towards the hallway, unbuttoning my shirt as I go. When I get to my doorway, I hesitate, looking over my shoulder towards Jack who is hot on my heels.

"My bed's bigger," he tells me with a cocky grin, jerking his head towards the closed door at the end of the hallway.

"Sure. But does your bedside table contain lube and condoms?"

Jack chuckles. "Does the pope shit in the woods?"

I snort. Of course he'd be into malaphors. Rolling my eyes with blatant affection, I toss my jacket into my room, watching as it lands in a heap a foot from the bed, and then I turn back to him. "Lead the way, then, Your Excellency."

I delight in his loud laughter, squeaking as he wraps his arm around my waist and pulls me in roughly for another divine kiss. I gasp for breath when our mouths separate again, releasing a quiet 'oomph' as I'm gently shoved back against the wall.

"Jack, what—?" I start, then almost swallow my tongue as he sinks to his knees on the carpeted hallway floor in front of me, his fingers deftly unbuckling my belt.

'What happened to taking this to the bedroom?' I want to ask, but I can't form words, too distracted and far too turned on by his actions. It feels surreal, watching the big, broad firefighter work to release my now suddenly aching cock from its fabric prison.

It's only as he pops the button above my fly and starts to lower the zipper that I remember what I'm wearing beneath my suit.

"Jack, I should warn you—"

Too late.

"Holy shit," he breathes, then sits back on his heels, looking up at me with eyes full of surprise. "What…you…when…"

Biting my lip, I shrug helplessly and gesture down at the lace he's found. It's impossible not to notice it, considering the fact that my cock is attempting to push its way through the thin scrap of fabric which has bulged obscenely out from the open placket of my trousers, and my precum has made the lace shiny and wet.

I can feel my face burning. "I, um, I feel sexy in them. I've never worn them *for* anyone before. Only for myself." If I'd known that we'd be stripping each other down tonight, I never would have put the pretty, black g-string on.

"Fuck," he brings his right hand up to tentatively fondle me, smoothing the pad of his thumb over the silky-smooth material. "Fuck," he repeats again, this time lower and more drawn out.

I think I've broken him.

I'm about to open my mouth to call everything off, to admit that this was all a mistake and to beg him to forget that his prissy male nanny has a thing for lingerie, when he pulls his hand away, then leans forward and sucks at my erection through the lace.

This time, it's me who says "Fuck." Loudly. I complete the sentiment by unintentionally banging my head against the wall as I tilt it back, squeezing my eyes shut in an attempt to

Chapter Twelve — Leo

prevent myself from coming too soon. "Jack," I mutter, doing my best not to rock my hips. I'm beyond conscious that this is his first time doing anything at all with another man's dick and I don't want to rush him, even though my body is screaming for more. "Jack, Jesus, fuck."

(Why, yes, I am extremely eloquent when I'm turned on. Can you tell?)

My eyes roll back when I feel his fingers carefully tugging the front of my panties down, helping my cock to spring free completely. The brush of his work-calloused skin against my rock-hard flesh is intoxicating and I can't help raising my hips into it, encouraging more stimulation.

Jack lets out a sound that's somewhere between a shaky exhale and a nervous chuckle. Opening my eyes, I look down at him, meeting his darkened gaze.

"I've never…" he starts, his hand wrapping around my cock and slowly stroking, even as he peers up at me with the most vulnerable expression I've ever seen on his face. I don't like the way my heart squeezes at the sight.

One-night stand, I remind myself forcefully. *Don't go falling for him.*

I just know I'm going to be a walking, talking cliché when all this is said and done because, in real life, men like Jack don't wind up with men like me. If I fall for him, not only will he break my heart, but I'll be out of a job as well.

But, even though I know I can't let that happen, I'm powerless to the sweetness of the ridiculously hot man at my feet.

"I know, honey," I tell him, the endearment slipping out before I can contain it, "but, trust me, I don't think you can do anything wrong at this point. I almost came from you touching me."

"Yeah?" A bit of certainty seems to return to him, sparking mischief in his expression.

"Mmhmm," I nod. "But you don't have to do anything you're not ready fo—*oh, Jesus Christ.*" My knees almost buckle at the wet heat and suction of his mouth descending on my cock without further preamble. He takes about half of my length and wraps his hand around the base, taking a handful of seconds to get himself into a rhythm that works for him.

There's nothing tentative in the way he squeezes and strokes my shaft while he bobs his head up and down. His movements are purposeful, and his pleasure-fuelled moans reassure me that he's enjoying the experience, which is good because I am losing myself in how good he's making me feel.

Eventually, he seems to become more confident, and he brings his other hand up to fondle my balls. It's been way too long since the last time I received this kind of attention. His touch sends bolts of electricity through my veins, lighting a fire in their wake.

"Oh, God," I breathe heavily, feeling my balls drawing up. "I'm going to come."

Jack pulls off my dick with a wet 'pop'. I whine in complaint and look back down at him. His lips are slightly swollen, pink and slicked with saliva. He wipes them and his chin on the back of his hand and grins up at me with an air of smug satisfaction. "You can't come yet," he tells me, fluidly rising off his knees until he's looming over me and rubbing his bulge into my abdomen. He bends his mouth to my ear and murmurs, "I want you to fuck me first."

Chapter Thirteen – Jack

Leo gapes at me for so long that I get worried.
"Oh God," I breathe, "I didn't even ask if you top. I just—*blargh*." I make a vomiting gesture with my hand, feeling completely stupid.

"No, I...I mean, I *do*, but..." my gorgeous manny stammers and then gives himself a shake. "Come on. We're not talking about this in the hallway." He quickly stuffs his dick back into those brain-melting panties and secures the button of his suit pants, not bothering with the fly. Then he takes my hand and leads me the few feet down the carpeted hall to my door, pushing it open before guiding me inside.

Once we're seated on the edge of the mattress, Leo cocks his head at me, a small smile playing around his lips, the gloss he'd been wearing long gone now. As pretty as he is with the makeup, he's even more beautiful without it, but I'll take him any and every way he'll let me. "You're constantly surprising me, Jack. You know that, right?"

"Why? Because a guy who looks like me can't be interested

in bottoming?" The words are a little more defensive than I had intended them to be.

I've been watching a *lot* of gay porn, and I can't deny that I have been drawn to videos of guys built like me taking another man's cock. And if I so happen to get *really* turned on by the ones featuring toppy twinks, well, there isn't anything wrong with that, right? It doesn't mean I don't want to try it both ways —or every which way possible— but ever since I saw the first video, it's been all I can think about.

Leo scoffs, yanking me from my thoughts. The tenderness in his touch when he places his hand on my tattooed forearm and squeezes soothes my frayed nerves. "No, honey. I was more surprised that you didn't just assume that my effeminate, makeup-loving, lace-covered butt only bottoms." He sighs. "But I should really know you better than that by now, hmm? I mean, the day you caught me..." his cheeks flame, "well, *y'know*. Anyway, you said something about thinking about me topping you then. It just never fully clicked until now."

Swallowing roughly, I nod. "Yeah. I, uh, I've been thinking about it for a while." I hate feeling like this. Inexperienced. Virginal. Vulnerable. I'm not the lanky, acne-ridden teenager who came in his pants the first time he even got close to rounding third base with a girl anymore, but this feels similar in all the worst ways.

At least Leo seemed to enjoy my first ever given blow job, not that I took him all the way to the finish line. I'm not above admitting that I've read a lot of advice online about giving them. Even though I know what I personally enjoy, knowing not to attempt taking all of him in on my first go was a helpful tip. The last thing I wanted to do was embarrass myself, not that I think Leo would have made me feel bad if I did.

Chapter Thirteen – Jack

"Well then," his tone is seductive, almost a purr. It goes straight to my dick, encouraging it back to full hardness, "if we've only got tonight, we'd better give you a night to remember, hmm?"

Have I mentioned that his confidence turns me on? Maybe once or twice?

Bobbing my head with enthusiasm, I can't help grinning as he holds my face in his hands and kisses me fiercely. His tongue tangles with mine in long, probing strokes. Then he pulls back and gives me a soft nudge. "Lie back and let me take care of you, Jack."

Put a freaking fork in me; I am done.

Who knew that such sweet words could light such an intense desire in me? It's kind of ironic, really, because I know Dad often calls me a mother hen…but here I am, desperate to let someone else take the reins and look after me, albeit in a completely different context.

Before I recline fully back onto my pillow, Leo helps me out of my shirt and then tosses it aside. Then he pushes me to lie down and reaches for my belt buckle, whipping the leather through the loops before undoing my pants. I raise my hips at his silent request, mesmerised by his focus and his lust-blown gaze. My pants and underwear go sailing off the side of the bed as well, but I pay them no mind.

Leo licks his lips and tangles his fingers into my chest hair, then smooths them over the ink hiding beneath it. My breathing hitches as he maps out my pecs with his hands, then swoops lower over my abs. I don't have a six pack, but I'm solid and stocky from a lot of physical activity, and the way Leo bites his lip tells me that he likes what he sees.

He gets down to the prominent V directing him to my dick

before he meets my eyes again. "Can I touch your cock?"

It practically lurches towards him when he asks, dribbling with excitement at just the suggestion. I chuckle, trying not to feel self-conscious. "Please." I can't contain my strangled groan when his hand wraps around my base and then strokes me with long, firm movements, twisting at the head on each upstroke. I close my eyes to enjoy the sensation, even though I want to watch every second and commit it to memory.

"Tell me what you like," he all but demands, his voice dipping into a lower register than I've ever heard from him.

I open my eyes to find him staring at me intently. "This...this is good. Maybe...*ungh*...squeeze the base a bit? Fuck, yeah, like that."

I look down the length of my body to watch his hand work, trying not to let the embarrassingly needy sounds building inside my chest out. My precum slicks the way for him, and I marvel at just how much I'm leaking. It's been a while since I've been with anyone, but I honestly can't remember being brought so close to the edge so quickly. The dry spell has to be a part of that, but is it also that Leo is someone I care about? Regardless of gender, *that's* what feels so different right now. I've never been so intimate with someone I cared for.

It's kind of scary having my heart involved.

I'm not falling in love with him or anything, but just acknowledging that he means *something* to me means acknowledging that he has the power to hurt me in ways I've never been hurt before.

The familiar *snick* of the lube clicking open brings my attention back to the moment. Whatever fear of intimacy was building inside me makes way for trepidation of a whole different kind.

Chapter Thirteen — Jack

Leo releases my cock and looks up at me, rubbing his left palm over the inside of my right thigh. It trembles beneath his touch.

"Hey," he soothes, "relax, honey. I'm going to make you feel good, okay?"

My throat constricts and I try to swallow and nod.

His eyes narrow. "If you want to stop—"

"No!" I surprise us both with my vehemence, my shout far too loud in the quiet of my bedroom. Blushing, I lower my voice. "No," I repeat, "I'm just…"

"Anxious? Nervous? Embarrassed?" He's still rubbing gentle circles into the inside of my thigh. "I felt all of that my first time, too. I mean, I won't lie: it's going to feel weird at first." He cocks his head. "Want me to get naked, too?"

I chuckle and feel some of the tension in my body loosen. "Yeah, well, it's not a hole I've really thought of as an entry point before…and yes, please. Naked is good. Perfect even."

Leo nods, his plump lips drawing into a knowing smile. I watch as he removes his clothes and tosses them in the same direction as mine before he reaches for the lube again and squirts some on his fingers. I don't know whether to focus on his long, slender cock, his miles of smooth skin speckled by fine pale hair, or the fingers he's just slicked up.

"Have you played with yourself?" he asks sensuously as he takes up position between my spread legs again, resting back on his heels. If I thought I'd feel less vulnerable with the both of us naked, I was dead wrong. Now I'm just much more aware of what's about to happen.

My breathing hitches as a slick finger runs down my taint. His other hand moves back to sweep over the inside of my thigh, his fingers reaching out to tease at the base of my cock, which has started to soften a little. I try to will it to wake back up.

"Jack?" Leo prompts.

"Hmm?"

"Eyes on me, honey. Now, have you played with yourself?" The cool, slick finger is now circling my rim.

I think of the toys I've got hidden at the back of my closet and my skin flushes. But I can't lie to him. I nod.

"Good boy," he praises and my heart rate increases. "Just your fingers?"

Shaking my head, I admit, "I…I bought a small plug, and a…*oh!*" I'm unable to prevent myself from squeezing my eyes shut as his finger finally breaches me, taking advantage of my distraction.

When I fingered myself, the angle felt awkward, and I felt decidedly unsexy. But this? I have no control over the angle or the depth or even how many fingers he chooses to use, but I know I can trust him to go slow. To do exactly what he promised and take care of me. *That* is sexy.

"Relax," he urges. "Breathe. That's it. Now, exhale and bear down."

I grip the sheets on either side of my hips, tangling my fingers so tightly into them that I'm half expecting that they will tear. His single, solitary finger has slipped in deep, curling and searching for my prostate. There's no stretch at this point, but I can feel a strange sense of fullness that isn't quite pleasurable. Then he finds what he was searching for and my hips arch clear off the mattress as stars explode behind my eyelids. "Oh *fuck!*"

"Mmm, we'll get there," his voice is light and teasing, and that eases a little more of my nerves. "Think you can take

Chapter Thirteen — Jack

another finger?"

I nod, not trusting my voice at the moment.

His finger slides out of me, then returns again, the thickness of two slick digits resting at my rim for only a moment before breaching that first ring of muscle. This time, it does burn with the stretch, and I tense up.

"Breathe," Leo reminds me, breaking through my intense internal mantra of 'get it out, get it out'. "Relax and bear down, remember?"

Determined, I exhale slowly through my mouth and do as instructed. The full feeling is definitely closer to the 'wrong' side of the spectrum of sensation, uncomfortable and intrusive, but if he could just nudge that magical spot again, I know I could start getting used to it. Enjoying it, even.

"You can move," I tell him once I've gotten used to the feeling of his fingers inside me.

"Who's in charge here, hmm?" he replies, but there's laughter in his voice and his fingers do start rocking back and forth in small increments.

When he curls them just right and rubs over my prostate again, pleasure overrides any lingering feelings of discomfort.

"More," I demand, arching my hips, feeling my cock surging back to life now that my body is starting to understand what all the fuss is about, "Leo, princess, please, more."

Leo complies and I become a pleading puddle of bliss, losing myself to the now pleasant burn of his fingers scissoring me open. By the time he's got three inside me, Leo is stretched out over me and his lips are on mine. He kisses me in rhythm with his fingers, his tongue fucking my mouth while he plays with my ass. I can feel his cock at my exposed hip, dribbling his excitement over my skin, and all of a sudden I *know* I'm ready to have it inside me.

"Fuck me," I beg into his mouth. It thrills me to hear his breathing hitch. I get braver and release the sheets from my death grip, curling my fingers around his sticky cock instead. "Put this beautiful dick of yours inside me, Leo. I'm ready."

He dips down to press our mouths together again, but it's not a filthy, desperate kiss like the others we've been sharing. It's softer and sweeter. It makes my heart squeeze and the backs of my eyes prickle. It's not the sort of kiss I've ever experienced with a one-night stand before, and I doubt I ever will again.

When he pulls back, he murmurs, "Just say the word and I'll stop, Jack. There's no shame in changing your mind."

I want to tell him there's no fucking way I'm changing my mind, but instead I nod.

Then he's rolling a condom on and telling me to roll over.

"It'll be easier for your first time," he says, and I believe him because it sounds like he's speaking from experience. Plus, almost every single article I've read online has said the same thing.

There's a part of me that wants to say 'fuck it, I can handle it', just so I can kiss him and watch his face as he sinks into my body, but I chicken out and do as he's said instead.

I'm back to feeling vulnerable and exposed when I'm on my hands and knees on the mattress, facing away from Leo. I can hear him fussing with the lube again, then feel the pressure of his latex-covered cock at my hole. I clench up.

One of his hands smooths over the base of my spine. "Breathe, honey. Relax. That's it…"

I press my face into my pillow and cry out as he starts to push in. It boggles my mind that I was able to take three of

Chapter Thirteen — Jack

his fingers, but that slender cock is stretching me in ways I never could have imagined.

Leo coaxes me through it, not rushing, murmuring encouragement and reminders to bear down. At some point, the pressure seems to relent and even though I'm feeling fuller than I've ever felt, it feels good.

It feels more than good.

It feels fucking phenomenal.

I can tell when he bottoms out, his lightly furred balls meeting my flesh, and we both seem to melt into the moment.

"You good?" he sounds strained, but he pets my hip and leans over me to kiss my shoulder blade. "Because you feel incredible, honey. Your arse is perfect."

I'll be honest, I've never loved the way Aussies say ass, but when Leo says it? I'd happily listen to him on repeat.

I chuckle and he groans and grips my hips tightly. "Careful," he warns, "or it's going to be over a lot quicker than either of us would like."

Despite being the bottom in this equation, I feel powerful at hearing his confession. I'm still controlling his pleasure, even though he's the one fucking me. It's a heady, addictive thought.

"I need you to move," I tell him, and he grunts his answer.

"We're taking this slow," he tells me through panted breaths. "Not just for your sake, but for mine as well."

I nod, but I push back onto him instinctually. We both groan at the feeling, and I yelp as he smacks my ass in reprimand. The sting is strangely enjoyable.

"Slow," he reminds me. Fuck, his confidence drives me wild.

By the time I've thought of a comeback, he's started to move, sliding back and then back into me with long, leisurely strokes.

His hand wraps around beneath my hip and he tugs at my cock at the same pace. Tendrils of pleasure tickle my nerve endings and my gut tightens with every gentle thrust into my body.

How have I not been doing this my entire adult life? If I had a time machine, I'd go back and give my younger self a stern talking to. But building a time machine can wait. There are orgasms to be had.

I lose myself to our movement, falling into pace with him. I relish the feel of his body over mine, over his heavy breathing and the way the hand on my hip grips and flexes every time he's fully sheathed. When he shifts his angle and hits my prostate again on his next slow, steady slide in, I shout in surprise, an incomprehensible sound of wonder and bliss.

He draws that sound out of me again and again, striking that spot inside me on every subsequent roll of his hips.

My balls tighten and the tension in my gut feels ready to snap.

"Gonna…" I start to warn him, but I'm spurting and swearing out my release before I can finish the two-word sentence.

"Fuck," he repeats sentiments I've barely finished saying, his hips snapping into mine with a more frenetic energy than before.

I can feel the way my ass is clenching around him and, now that I've come, I don't know how much longer I can handle having him in me. I feel oversensitised, my body tingling and twitching from the strength of my orgasm.

"Fuck," he repeats, then draws the word out long and low, "*fuck*." His hips still and I swear I can feel him filling the latex inside me, his cock pulsing as he comes too.

Wincing as he pulls out carefully, I flop onto my back, careful to avoid the wet spot. "That was awesome," I tell him with a

Chapter Thirteen — Jack

lazy smile, watching the perfect curve of his ass as he pads towards the door, presumably to dispose of the condom.

He shoots me a grin over his shoulder. "It was, wasn't it?"

I roll onto my side, propping my head up on my hand, wondering if he's going to come back to my room or head directly to his. Even though I agreed that this would just be a one-night thing, I'm not ready for it to end.

Relief washes over me when Leo reappears in the doorway with a damp washcloth in hand. It has *Sesame Street* characters on it. "For the bed," he says, then crosses the room to deftly dab at the puddle of cum on the comforter. Once he's satisfied that he's cleaned it up, he tosses the cloth aside and lifts the sheets, sliding in beneath them, still naked.

I scramble to do the same, my efforts far less graceful.

The silence between us feels heavy with expectation, but not quite what I would consider awkward. Nevertheless, I clear my throat.

"Seriously," I speak quietly, unsure as to why I feel the need to practically whisper in the empty apartment, "thank you for tonight."

I have the strangest urge to reach out for him and curl around his long, lean body. That's new. I've never been a post-coital snuggler before.

"So," he rolls onto his side to face me. It feels nice. Pillow talk. I've never really had this, either. Leo clears his throat. "I know you said it was awesome, but was that just the orgasm talking?"

I snort and give in to the urge to reach for him. "C'mere," I say, tugging him until his head is tucked comfortably under my chin. It's easier talking about this stuff if I don't have to look him in the eye. "It was awesome. Every bit of it. I'm *definitely* bi," I chuckle, as if there had been any doubt. "And…I'm glad my first time was with you."

I both hear and feel his sharp intake of breath. "Jack…"

"Hey now, I'm not making any huge declarations here," I cut him off before he can remind me of our deal. My stomach twists uncomfortably. I ignore it. "I'm just saying that I'm glad it was with someone I trust. A friend. You took your time, made it good for me…" Jesus, I sound like a teenager, all insecure and shit. I shake my head, feeling my cheeks heat, even though he can't see my face. "So…yeah. Thank you."

There's silence again for a long moment before he quietly replies, "I'm glad I was your first guy, too."

Chapter Fourteen – Leo

It's hell enforcing the 'one night only' rule with Jack, but I manage to do it. He's taken the week off work to spend time with his mum, sisters, and stepdad. That leaves me with a week of very little to do but get stuck in my own thoughts, because his mum insists on taking the boys with them for every outing and very gently explains that, with all the family around, I'm not really needed.

It's a stark reminder of my real place in Jack's life. I'm the nanny, nothing more.

After that night spent together, though, I desperately wish I could be more…but while I'm working for him, that is a no good, terrible, very bad idea.

(Why, yes, I have been reading to the boys at night, why do you ask?)

"What's on the agenda today?" Jack asks me, shaking me out of my thoughts. I look up from where I've been pushing my overnight oats around with my spoon and I blink. He's slinging a backpack over his shoulder and has the twins practically bouncing out of their skin on either side of him.

"Daddy's gonna take us to Movie World," Huddy declares before I can respond to Jack's question.

I grin at him. "That sounds super exciting. Are you going to meet Bugs Bunny?"

"I wanna see Scooby Doo," Prez tells me. "Huddy wants to see Batman."

I rack my brain for the last time I visited the theme park. "Well, I'm pretty sure you'll see both in the parade." A flicker of memory hits me about some of the random props on display. "And I'm pretty sure you guys can pose for photos on a Batbike, too."

Jack snorts. "Batcycle is the word you're looking for. Or, depending on the bike, Batblade…or Batpod."

I arch an eyebrow at him. "You're a superhero nerd I take it?"

"Ain't nothin' nerdy about me, prin—" his eyes widen as he stops himself. "Leo."

My mouth goes dry. The affectionate endearment which he almost let slip has my heart all aflutter. Nobody else has ever called me 'princess', and I never thought I'd like it. But he said it so sweetly the night we slept together and now I *want* to hear him say it again.

And again.

And *again*.

Fuck, I've got it bad.

Stupid Leo, you knew this would happen and yet you went ahead and crossed the line anyway.

My inner voice is a bitch, but it's only speaking the truth.

Clearing my throat, I shake my head and force a teasing smile. "Nope. I'm onto you, Bradford. I bet you geek out over

Chapter Fourteen — Leo

all the superhero movies."

He scrunches his nose. "Marvel maybe. The DC ones have been a bit of a letdown."

"And yet, you know *all* the Bat...things."

Jack chuckles. "I do know all the Bat-things, yeah. There are these things called comic books; I don't know if you've heard of 'em."

"No, I haven't, please tell me more," I drawl with a liberal dose of sarcasm. "And you say you're not a superhero nerd."

"Daddy," Huddy whines and tugs at Jack's hand, "when we going?"

"We *are* going now," Jack tells him with a sigh, then looks back over at me. "Did you wanna tag along today?"

For the briefest of moments, I imagine going on some of the adrenaline-pumping coasters, gripping his hand for comfort. The fantasy almost has me saying yes. But then I remember his mum kindly telling me that there are more than enough of them to wrangle the boys, and I don't want to be a third wheel, or fifth wheel, or whatever odd number wheel I'd actually be.

Shaking my head, I decline the offer. "I've got a few errands to run today. Take lots of photos for me, though. And, hey, if they love it," my mouth adds when the dejection on his face proves too much to handle, "we can always take them back another time...or we could go to another theme park?"

"I'm going to hold you to that," he says, allowing the boys to tug him towards the front door. Then they're all gone, and I'm left in the eerily silent apartment, much like I have been all week.

Maybe I *should* log in to Grindr or, better still, try to make some new friends somehow. That would probably go a long way towards making me feel less pathetic and mopey...and less attached to my employer.

After washing away my half-eaten breakfast, I sit myself on the couch and start Googling.

* * *

At lunchtime, a knock at the door startles me from my ongoing research. I'm surprised when I glance at the clock in the top left-hand corner of my screen, and I'm a little ashamed to admit that I've spent the past few hours sitting on the couch, engrossed in my lame search titled 'how to make friends as an adult'.

So far, the results have suggested joining various hobby teams and clubs, or a vaguely sketchy app which is probably just used for hookups anyway. The local library hosts a book club, though, and that's probably my best bet for finding like-minded company.

The knock sounds again, and I haul my arse off the couch with a groan, protesting my stiff muscles. I'm going to have to force myself to go for a walk and do some yoga to balance out my hours of inactivity. Crossing the few paces between the couch and the door, I smooth my hands over my clothes to try and sort out any wrinkles and then swing the door open.

The woman on the other side blinks at me. I blink back.

She's conventionally pretty, for a woman. She's about my height, with curves in all the right places, brown hair which has been cut to her shoulders, and a face which seems almost familiar, not that I could tell you why.

"Uh," she says before looking down at her phone screen. She looks back up at me and scrunches her nose. "Does Jack live here? Jack Bradford?"

Chapter Fourteen — Leo

I nod. "He's my boss. He's out for the day." I check the time on my phone screen, confirming that it is only just past noon. "He probably won't be back until five-ish."

Her shoulders slump. "Damn it. I knew I should have called." A bitter laugh escapes her as she shakes her head. "Old habits and all that, right?" Then she stops and narrows her gaze at me. "I'm sorry, did you say boss?"

"Yeah..." I nod slowly.

"But," she sounds and looks thoroughly perplexed, "he's a fireman."

"He is, yes." I nod again.

"So...if he's your boss...?" The question in her tone is unmistakable, but I don't owe her any answers. I just arch an eyebrow at her. She blushes. "Shit, sorry, I didn't even introduce myself. I'm Steph. Steph Baker. Jack's my...well, I guess 'baby daddy' fits best." She sounds self-deprecating and a little defeated now.

"Oh! You're the boys' mum," I blurt before my brain can tell me it's a bad idea.

For as long as I've been working for Jack, I've never met the elusive Steph, though I know that the boys FaceTime with her once a week. I make myself scarce for those calls, knowing that it's awkward enough for Jack without me loitering. The boys often chatter about whatever it is they talked about with "Mummy", but she has remained a mystery to me. Until now.

Eyeing me with caution, Steph bobs her head. "I am."

Stepping back, I open the door wide. As far as I know, she and Jack are in as much of an amicable relationship as they could possibly be, given the circumstances. And, because she lives a few hours' drive south, I'm not going to make her wait outside for the boys to return. "Come on in, I'll make you a cuppa. Tea or coffee? Have you eaten lunch?"

Steph crosses the threshold and toes off her slip-on black flats at the door, nudging them with her foot towards the shoe rack. "Um, tea's fine. And, yeah, I grabbed a bite on my way here. Thank you, though…?"

"Oh. Whoops." I thwack my forehead with my open palm, then stick my hand out towards her. "Leo. Leo Martin. I'm Jack's nanny."

Her eyes go wide as she shakes my hand. "Nanny? But aren't you a bit, um…"

I swear to God, if she says 'male'…

"…young?" she finishes warily.

I let out the breath I was holding and shrug. I'd much prefer to defend my seeming inexperience over my gender. "I'm in my twenties. I'm fully trained. Got my blue card, CPR and first aid certs…you name it, I've got it." The smile I offer her is full of understanding. "There are plenty of people younger than me in childcare these days."

"Yes," she drawls, but there's nothing cruel in her tone or grin, "they're called *toddlers*."

Sputtering, I laugh and shake my head. "That's not what I meant! I meant employed in childcare."

"I know," the cheeky look she sends over her shoulder as she makes her way over to the couches reminds me of Hudson's, "but I couldn't resist."

I was fully prepared to judge this woman, I realise as I snort with amusement. I was ready to let jealousy get the better of me, to paint her as a villain in Jack's life. But so far, she's been nothing but pleasant and I realise how unfair my gut reaction was.

Clearing my throat, I head back towards the kitchen. "How

Chapter Fourteen — Leo

do you take your tea?"

"White, please. No sugar."

I glance over from the kitchen bench while she sits, noticing the way she's looking around, taking in the details of the space. It has changed a lot even since I've come to live here. The artwork Will had once displayed on the walls is long gone, replaced by canvas prints of Hudson and Preston, and a few family photos which include Jack, Wes, Will, Vicky, and Connor. I'm expecting photos of the boys and their grandmother and Jack's half-sisters to join them.

The paint on the walls is no longer as flawless as it was when I first moved in, either. There are dings and dents along the bottom where toy cars and blocks have gone crashing into them. Smudges from sticky hands show around thigh height, despite my attempts to scrub them off. And then there's the impromptu artwork on the hallway wall from the time Hudson got his little hands onto a ballpoint pen.

It's no longer a showroom, but a home.

"I've gotta say, this is a huge improvement on Jack's last place," Steph muses, having caught me looking at her.

I shrug. "I never saw his old apartment. He hired me after he moved here."

She nods. "You're not missing much."

The kettle clicks as the power shuts off and I pour the boiled water over two tea bags, one in each of our mugs. Then I add two spoons of sugar to mine before I grab the milk from the fridge. Not knowing quite how milky she likes her tea, I aim for about the same as my own, leaving the liquid in our cups a light caramel colour. I carry them over to the couch and choose to sit on the armchair so as not to crowd my unexpected guest.

You Don't Know Jack

We sip at our drinks in silence for a little while before Steph speaks again. "Are they happy?"

I blink. "Hmm?"

"The boys. Are they happy?" Her brown eyes glisten with unshed tears.

I swallow, unsure how to proceed here. She's their mother, sure, but Jack has custody. Jack is my employer. I don't owe her any information about her children, and I don't know if Jack would want me to be too chatty. But then, he does make sure that the boys FaceTime with her weekly, and I presume he talks to her, too.

I decide to err on the side of caution anyway. Holding my cup between my palms, I nod. "They are, yes. But I can't really give you much more information. You're not my employer, and—"

"I get it," she cuts me off and swallows roughly. "But thank you. That's all I wanted to know."

"You're not going to demand custody again, are you?" I blame fear for the question tumbling out of my mouth before I can think better of it. I wince. "I mean, it's not my place to ask that, I know. I just...I care about the boys. I'm sorry. Forget I asked."

Steph's shaking her head before I can even finish my ramble, a soft, melancholy smile tugging at her lips. "I'm not, no. Kind of the opposite." I watch the tea in her cup slosh around, licking at the porcelain rim, and it takes me a moment to understand that it's because her hands are trembling. "I, um, I wanted to see them in person again. Hug them one last time before—"

"Oh, God, things aren't that bad, are they? Please don't do anything rash. There are helplines and...and..." I trail off at

Chapter Fourteen — Leo

the look of wide-eyed horror on her pretty face. My own face heats. "And you weren't talking about…*that*."

"No, but…thank you. That was sweet. Weird, but sweet. And," she takes a deep breath, "a reminder that things could be worse." This time her smile isn't quite as sad, but it doesn't reach her eyes. "No, I've gotten a job, but it's in Melbourne. I'm going to have to move there, and I could only find a place to flatshare, so I couldn't take the boys with me even if I wanted to. Not," she adds hurriedly, "that I don't want to be with them. But," she raises her chin and looks around at all the photos, her lower lip trembling, "this is a way more stable environment than I could give them, and I don't want to uproot their lives again. I've done enough of that."

My heart hurts for her. I couldn't imagine being in her shoes. Clearing my throat, I ask, "When do you start?"

"Next Monday. It gives me just over a week to get my stuff packed and make the drive down from Mum and Dad's. Coming here was impulsive, I know. But I hoped that Jack might let me crash on the couch and spend the weekend with him and the boys." Her voice breaks. "Y'know, live out the fantasy of being a family one last time." Letting go of the cup with one of her hands, she swipes at her eyes and sniffles, laughing softly. "Not with Jack. Just with the boys."

I frown. "I'm sure Jack will take them down to visit you," I tell her, knowing that he would do anything to make sure his sons want for nothing. "He's not a monster."

"No, I know. He's actually been really great about this whole thing." Hanging her head, Steph sighs. "I feel so bad for keeping them from him for so long…"

"The way he tells it," I'm blurting again without thought, "he put you in a pretty shitty position and didn't make it easy for you to get in touch. Besides," I add when she opens her mouth, presumably to protest, "you can't change the past. Don't keep on beating yourself up about it."

I think about the choices I've made lately and realise that I should be taking my own advice. I don't regret sleeping with Jack, but I know I shouldn't have done it. However, it's in the past and I can't undo it. It's time to stop berating myself for giving in to temptation and move on with life.

If only I could get my heart to agree.

Chapter Fifteen – Jack

With two sleeping boys propped against my shoulders, I near the door to the apartment and freeze at the sound of feminine laughter coming from inside. It's the last thing I expect to hear, and I'm instantly curious about who —and what— I'll be walking in on.

It's an awkward manoeuvre to lean back and shift Prez in my hold just enough to support him with my forearm and still turn the door handle, but I manage without waking either of the boys. Pushing the door open, I step inside and stop short at the sight of the woman on my couch.

"Steph," I blink, unconsciously tightening my hold on my sons.

Our sons.

It wasn't all that long ago when I watched Dad and Connor go through a painful custody battle with Vicky's biological father, and I won't deny that the first thought running through my mind is that Steph's here to take my kids back. To take them away from me.

She stands and brushes cookie crumbs from her jeans, smiling awkwardly. "Hey," she greets me, lowering her chin. "Sorry for just turning up." Her head cocks to the side and I watch her gaze roam over the two lumps of dead weight I'm carrying. She sounds choked up when she says, "God, they look so much bigger than I remember."

"I think they've gone through a bit of a growth spurt, yeah," Leo agrees, making his way over from the armchair. He takes Preston from me and I heave a sigh of relief. Each of the boys only weighs about forty pounds (roughly eighteen kilograms if I'm being forced to use the metric system), but I've carried them both up from the car and it's starting to wear on me.

"Bed early? Or wake them up for dinner? It's your call," Leo looks at me expectantly.

I fidget a little under his and Steph's combined gazes, confessing, "I got them Happy Meals on the drive home. They were good all day, and I figured they'd pass out on the drive."

My nanny's grin spreads across his cute face as he nods in understanding. "It's not like they get takeaway often. You'll be Super Dad for weeks."

"Especially when you see the toys that came with the meals," I smirk. "It's superhero month or something."

"They're into superheros now?" Steph asks before Leo can respond again. I nod.

"Huddy got a Spider-Man toy, and Prez got a Black Panther one. You'd think I'd bought them a pony or something, the way they reacted."

"Puppy," Leo interjects as he starts to make his way towards the boys' room. "They'd lose their minds if you gave in and got them a puppy."

"I'm not getting a puppy," I follow him with Steph on my

Chapter Fifteen — Jack

heels.

"It was worth a shot," he sighs, but I can hear the laughter in his voice. It makes my heart squeeze and I wish for the billionth time that we could be more than an employer and his nanny. More than just friends.

I haven't been able to get the night of Dad's wedding out of my head. It's only been a week, but the things Leo made me feel...

I shake my head free of that train of thought.

I made him a promise after all. I've never once had a problem with one-night stands before. I've never once itched with desperation to experience more with a person. Given enough time, I am certain these strange new feelings will pass.

They have to.

I'm not going to allow them to ruin the friendship we have, or the working relationship we share either. We made a deal and I am sticking with it.

My attachment to Leo, if I can call it that, is probably only because of how new this all is to me. I'm not going to sit and catalogue the differences between being with a man over being with a woman, because I genuinely enjoy both equally, but being with a man is just different enough that perhaps it is kind of a novelty...even if thinking about it that way trivialises my feelings to some degree.

Ugh. And now I'm trying to downplay my feelings just to escape them.

Nobody's ever accused me of being smart, I guess.

Leo and I place the boys down on their respective beds and wrangle them out of their day clothes and into their nighttime pull-ups and boxers, leaving them in the t-shirts they're already wearing. Neither of them does more than stir, wiped out from the excitement and activity of the day. I tuck Huddy in, then Prez, brushing back their dark hair to press matching kisses on each of their foreheads. My heart flips over when Leo does the same.

Even though this is a job for him, I know that he loves my boys. The issue is: why does that do things to my insides?

I'm so lost in my renewed denial of my intense feelings for my too-young-for-me nanny that the sound of Steph's sniffles makes me jump.

I'd completely forgotten that she was even here!

I turn to face her, feeling a pang of empathy at the longing gaze she directs at our sons. "You're so good for them," she murmurs, her voice thick. "Better than I ever was."

I'm not having this conversation where the boys could wake up and overhear it. I shake my head, then gesture for her to follow me back into the living room. Leo slips out of the room ahead of us and hightails it into his bedroom. I want to ask him to come back, to give me silent moral support, but I know that's not fair.

Even if we are friends, it's still not his place or his job to hold my hand through whatever new life-changing curveball Steph's about to throw my way. And I *know* that she is. Why else would she turn up unannounced? I've decided that's her whole thing.

When we're sitting across from each other in the living room, with her on the couch and me on one of Dad's old armchairs, she says, "Before you ask, I'm not here to demand them back."

Relief washes over me like a tidal wave. "Okay...?" I don't want to be rude and just blurt out 'Then why are you here?' but it's a close call. I just arch an eyebrow at her.

Chapter Fifteen – Jack

She wipes at her eyes with the side of her thumb. "I just…I wanted to see them. I know we get to FaceTime weekly, but…"

"It's not the same," I finish for her, offering her empathy and understanding.

Even if parenthood was never on my radar, now that I know my kids, I couldn't imagine not seeing their cute little faces every day. Not having custody would hurt me terribly, and I once again spare a thought for what Dad and Connor went through not all that long ago. I also stop to think about just how bad things must have been for Steph for her to seek me out and give me custody in the first place.

"I meant it just now," Steph's quiet reply is shaky. I look up from where I've been picking at my cuticles to meet her watery gaze. She smiles softly and tucks her hair behind her ear. She's looking less wan now, I realise. Less exhausted. Even though she looks healthier, she radiates melancholy. "You've been so good for them. I was barely keeping my head above water and you—"

"Have a larger support network," I acknowledge, cutting her off. "I can afford to pay for help," I wince a little at describing Leo as 'paid help', but it's technically what he is, "and I have my Dad and his husband living downstairs. You were doing it all on your own. Plus, they're a lot more independent now than they would have been for those first few years. Stop being so hard on yourself."

I can't help thinking about my mom and the position she might have been in if Dad hadn't stepped up, or if her parents had been less supportive. She would have struggled as much as Steph did.

To think that I am somewhat responsible (if not almost entirely responsible) for the situation Steph was in makes me squirm with guilt. My parents raised me better than that. And I don't mean getting her pregnant: life happens. But to have treated her so poorly —to have literally blocked her attempts to contact me— was reprehensible. I can't go back in time to change that, but I can do everything in my power to make amends now, and to raise our sons to know that the way I behaved was not at all acceptable.

Steph's brown eyes practically bore into mine. After a long beat and a shaky inhale, she says, "You've changed."

I want to argue with her. I want to tell her that she doesn't know the first thing about me. She *literally* doesn't know Jack. However, even as I open my mouth to make that terrible pun out loud, I shut it again because, whether she knew me or not, she's not wrong.

I have changed.

In the months since learning about the boys, I've had to change my priorities. I still don't think I was doing anything inherently wrong by casually sleeping around, but the desire to do so is gone. I'd much rather spend my nights at home on the couch, snuggled between my kids, watching cartoons and listening to Leo singing to himself in the next room.

And...*shit*.

There I go again: picturing him in my life for the long-term. That can't be healthy.

But, that aside, I'm *not* the same guy I was six months ago. I'm more serious about life in general. I focus more on the future than whatever's happening in the moment. I think about the way I talk to people and try to model positive behaviours for my kids. This new version of me, should I go back to casual sex, won't ever treat my partners with the kind of disrespect I showed Steph.

Chapter Fifteen – Jack

New Me is not the kind of guy who will block a one-night stand's number just because avoiding awkward conversations is easier than facing them. I mean, hell, New Me had a one-night stand with my male nanny and our friendship and working relationship is still great. No avoidance, no running away, no miscommunication: we're good.

New Me is much more mature…even if I can't stop my thoughts from circling back to Leo.

Damn it.

"I'm sorry," Steph's apology has me blinking with confusion. "What?"

"I didn't mean to imply…I mean, I didn't really know you, did I?"

It's funny how, even though I only just had that same thought, my first instinct is to refute her. A wry, self-deprecating smile curves my lips. "Well, I think it's fair to say that, even if what you knew of me wasn't my best self, it was still who I was back then." I sigh. "And I have changed. I never would have thought I was immature before, but being a dad has made me grow up a whole lot."

"Hopefully not too much," she chuckles and swipes at her eyes again. "It's fun being a big kid sometimes, too."

My mind goes back over the day I've just had with the boys, going on rides and taking photos with people dressed up as superheroes and cartoon characters. I grin. "Yeah, it is." Silence descends between us again and I eventually bite the bullet and, crossing my right ankle over my left knee, ask, "So, if it's not that you want to renegotiate custody, what brings you by unannounced? Not that you're not welcome to see the boys whenever. I know I was an ass when we made 'em, but I'd never keep them from you. You know that, right?"

Steph nods and her eyes well up again. "You've been so great about everything since I dumped them on you…"

It's all I can do to smother a groan of irritation. "I don't like thinking about it like that. They're my children. My responsibility. I would have been there from the start if things were different. Maybe life would have been easier for you, too. Who knows? Just…stop talking about them like they're a burden on me, on either of us." Guilt pangs through me as she winces. "Sorry."

"No, you're right. They're not a burden or whatever. I love them. I love them so much." Her voice wobbles and the tears which had been gathering in her eyes spill down her cheeks.

I recoil a bit. Crying women freak me out.

Guess I haven't grown up quite as much as I thought.

"Uh…" I start, all of a sudden stuck for words.

Steph just sits on my couch and cries her way through explaining the real reason she made the trip here. I listen as she tells me about the job she's been offered, and my heart sinks a little when she says that it's in Melbourne. I'd been worried that she wanted to take the boys back, but now I'm worried that they'll never really get to see her.

As someone who grew up with close access to both his parents, I'm concerned that they'll be missing out with her so far away. I was eighteen when I moved across the world with Dad, hours and hours away from my mom, and even though it was something I had wanted to do, it was still a huge adjustment for me. Our boys are still so little, just a few weeks shy of their fourth birthdays, and I wonder how they'll cope when their mom is more than just a few hours' drive away. Not that they've seen her in person since she moved in with her parents, but that was always going to be a temporary

Chapter Fifteen – Jack

situation. Some part of me had assumed that, even though I'd gotten sole custody, we might revisit that arrangement after she got a new job and got herself settled.

I guess this is still following that plan, just not quite the way I'd imagined.

"...I'll keep an eye out for any jobs here or in Brissie," she's saying when I tune back in, "but I'm all set to move my stuff down to Melbourne and I can't afford to keep going back and forth."

"And there's no guarantee that you'll find something up here, while the one down there is a sure thing," I bob my head, hoping to imply that I understand. I know her parents have been pressuring her to get back on her feet and out from under theirs, and they made no secret of their disdain for me when they realised that I had the space to accommodate her here and had never bothered to offer.

The thing is, by the time I'd worked out that she could have just moved into the spare bedroom here and looked after the boys instead of me hiring a nanny, I'd already gone ahead and moved Leo in. I'd already set the boys into a routine and it was one that worked for me, too.

Maybe it was selfish of me, but the idea of doing what my parents had done —platonically raising our kids under the same roof— only set my teeth on edge. I've never really stopped to consider why.

Perhaps some part of me just assumed Steph might get the wrong idea, maybe even pine away at the possibility of us going from platonic co-parents to a nuclear family unit. It's not a concept I want to encourage, not even now that I am settled into life as a dad.

What does it say about me that I prefer the idea of sharing

that kind of life with Leo more than with my kids' other biological parent? (Well, other than the fact that I'm clearly much more interested in men than I ever thought I would be.)

Maybe I am still kind of a dick.

But, at the same time, as much as Hudson and Preston are my responsibility, Steph's shitty life choices are not. She had known where I was the entire time she was pregnant, and for the first three years of our sons' lives. She had chosen not to reach out. Yeah, I had made it difficult and uncomfortable, but not impossible. She could have turned up on my doorstep at any point before she reached rock bottom, but she didn't. That, as much as I felt guilty thinking it, was on her.

So, yeah, I could have offered for her to live with me once Dad and Wes graciously helped make this apartment my own, but it didn't make me a terrible person for not wanting to. It didn't make me a terrible person for resenting her for keeping the boys from me for the first three years of their lives. It didn't make me a terrible person for only stepping up to help them and not her. Not entirely, anyway. Maybe a bigger man might have swallowed his pride and moved her in, but I hadn't wanted to.

My feelings about her haven't changed since our one and only night together, either. I have no intention of leading her on, nor do I want her living with me and warding off any other potential relationships.

Huh.

It's funny how my stance on a relationship with her hasn't changed, but I'm no longer terrified of the 'c' word.

Commitment.

Not marriage-level commitment, obviously, but something long-term with the right partner.

Chapter Fifteen – Jack

Someone sweet and funny. Someone who loves the boys as much as I do. Someone who doesn't cling and who isn't demanding or whiny. Someone mature, with their head on straight and who is unafraid to take charge and set boundaries.

Someone like Leo.

Damn it.

Refusing to give in to thoughts of last weekend, I force myself to focus on the conversation at hand. Steph's doing her best to smile through tears and my guilt flares all over again. Sure, I can resent her for the choices she made, but I understand them, too. Empathy for her situation overtakes me again and I promise her that we will work out a schedule so I can take the boys to see her every few months. She brightens at that, sitting up straighter.

"You will?" Steph asks, then, without waiting for my confirmation, smiles softly. "Leo said you probably would." She cocks her head. "He seems nice. An, um, interesting choice for a nanny."

There's nothing nasty or cruel in her tone, but my hackles raise at the words anyway. Leaning back in my seat, I fold my arms across my chest, noticing the way her eyes drift to my biceps and down the lines of my tattoos along my forearms. Clearing my throat, I arch an eyebrow and demand, "What's that supposed to mean?"

She blinks and her eyes widen with surprise. As much as Huddy and Prez look like me, I see them both in her stunned, innocent expression. Another pang of remorse hits me. Maybe I shouldn't have been quite so defensive.

Then she explains, "I just meant…y'know…he's a guy." She scrunches her nose. "Aren't twenty-something-year-old guys who are into kids usually a bit creepy?"

So, the problem with having kids with a one-night stand is that the vetting process for the other parent of your children is minimal. If I'd known she held beliefs like these, I might not have slept with her at all. But then, our conversations on the app and in the bar hadn't been overly philosophical.

I frown. "But twenty-something-year-old women loving kids aren't?"

Steph holds up her hands in the universal gesture of surrender. "Whoa, no. I'm not trying to suggest *he's* creepy. He's lovely. I'm just saying most guys his age —hell, most guys in general— aren't usually drawn to childcare is all."

That is a painful generalisation and one I know Leo isn't a fan of. I grunt.

Steph tries to backpedal. It makes things worse. "I mean, he's obviously gay, though, right? So it makes sense that he's into a more feminine sort of job."

"Wanna repeat that to my dad?"

"Your…I don't understand."

I sigh and pinch the bridge of my nose. "Dad's gay. And, before he retired, he was a firefighter. A big, tough, brawny firefighter."

'Like me', I almost add, followed by, *'and it turns out I also like being fucked by a man, too, so…'*

But I don't. I keep those thoughts to myself. Not because I don't want to hurt her feelings or make her uncomfortable, but because it's none of her damn business.

"I swear, all I do is make a fool of myself around you," Steph huffs, running her hand through her hair and tugging at it. "I'm not…I don't…*ugh*. I swear, I'm not a bigot or anything. I really was just observing that there aren't many guys Leo's age in childcare, and probably even fewer as live-in nannies.

Chapter Fifteen – Jack

It was a totally innocent comment."

"Mmhmm." I know I don't sound convinced (because I'm not).

"Jack, I swear, I'm not homophobic or anything. I was legit just making conversation."

"Yeah, well, that kind of thinking is offensive, okay? I have too many people in my life who would be hurt by stuff like that." That's not to say they haven't heard it all before, but it's beside the point. I certainly don't want any of my queer or fluid friends and family thinking I'm okay with ignorance of any kind, even if it wasn't said with malice. "Plus," I gentle my tone, "I don't want the boys growing up saying stuff like that, either."

"I'm sorry," she apologises, and she does sound genuine. "You're right. I need to do better. Especially for the boys. I mean, what if one of them is—" she catches my renewed raised eyebrow and closes with "—interested in boys, too?"

I nod. "Exactly. Plus their grandpa is married to another man…and what if I were to start dating a guy?"

I didn't actually mean to ask that last question. But, now that it's out there, I'm not taking it back. If anything, I like to think it's a sign of how comfortable and confident I am in myself now. I am bi. Pan. Something in that vicinity. The label doesn't really matter to me right now. I like women *and* men.

I want us to raise our boys to be welcoming of relationships —of *people*— of all types. I also want to raise them to trust that we, as their parents, will support them under any circumstances, too. Well, unless they grow up to become serial killers. Then we might need to discuss their priorities.

In the stunned silence that follows, I make sure to hold her gaze. She needs to understand that I'm serious and that there's a lot riding on her reaction.

Thankfully, Steph just chuckles a little nervously before she says, "Wow. I didn't see that coming. But you're right, Jack. I said some dumb shit and I didn't think how it would sound. I was just surprised that you didn't hire some pretty, young thing, is all." Then she pauses and it's like I can see the light bulb flaring to life over her head. "Oh my God," she breathes, her voice going all squeaky before a knowing smirk tugs her lips upwards and she points her index finger at me, "you *so* did, though!"

I splutter, because I hadn't even seen a photo of Leo before we met. I just went with the candidate the agency and Connor agreed was best suited. But my choked sounds only seem to make my former one-night stand laugh harder.

"And I said you'd changed," she teases, waggling her finger at me. The response is playful and her eyes are sparkling with mirth, so I find it hard to take offence. Plus, it's nice to be back on even ground, the air around us no longer charged or awkward.

I want to get along with Steph, for the boys' sake. The relief I feel at her complete lack of judgment or bitterness now, while she's teasing me about my crush on Leo, is a welcome sensation. So, I play along, scoffing and rolling my eyes.

"He's ten years younger than me," I remind her, refusing to deny the fact that I think Leo is hot as sin. I can acknowledge that I have eyes, right? "And he's fucking amazing with the boys. No way am I doing anything to fuck that up."

Steph's still giggling as she sits back and nods at me. "Yeah, fair call. Sexually harassing the nanny is a surefire way to get you banned from hiring any new ones, too."

Chapter Fifteen – Jack

I hadn't actually thought of that. It makes sense that, if shit went south with Leo, he could report me to his agency. I'd probably end up on some sort of list. That thought gives me palpitations.

He's right, I realise with sinking clarity. *We can't get involved.*

I was lucky to have been allowed one night with him, really. Luckier still that it didn't fuck things up for us professionally, too.

As Steph and I settle in to talk through the plan once she moves to Melbourne, I can't help focusing on this most recent revelation.

Why does knowing that I have to move on make my stomach turn over?

Chapter Sixteen – Leo

"No, really, you can sleep in my bed. I put fresh sheets on and everything." I insist, having wandered out into the living room at nine o'clock with the intention of making myself a quick snack for the dinner I'd missed, only to discover that Jack's unexpected guest was still here.

At that point, she had realised the time and then groaned at how late it would be by the time she drove back to her parents' place. Then there was the fact that she hadn't actually gotten to interact with her kids, the entire reason she'd driven here to begin with, and I'd been opening my mouth to suggest she just stay the night without even considering what Jack might want...or where she would be sleeping. Having been the one to put the idea out there, I decided it was my responsibility to take the couch for the night.

Steph then protested, not wanting to put me out. And so here we are.

She bounces on the firm couch cushion and then gives me a

Chapter Sixteen — Leo

dubious look. "I don't think it's sleep-comfy."

I shrug. "It's one night. I'll survive."

Steph turns to Jack, the ends of her brown hair flicking with the sudden movement. "Tell him it's your home and he's not being paid enough to sleep on the couch for a night. If anything," her lips quirk, "*you* should be offering *your* bed and *you* should be taking the couch."

I snort. "He won't fit on the couch." Leaning against the wall framing half of the archway between the living room and the kitchen/dining area, I add, "Which is why I offered. Really, it's no big deal."

"I mean, there's one other option," she wrinkles her nose as she looks between me and Jack, as though she anticipates we'll fight her on it.

"Oh?" I ask. "And that is?"

Biting her lip, she suggests, "You guys could share for a night, right? I mean, Jack crashes at the station on shared bunks, right? And you…um…" Her cheeks turn pink. "Not that I'm suggesting…I just realised how inappropriate and rude it was for me to just presume…"

"That I'm used to sleeping with other men?" I can't help taunting a little. She's clearly flustered and already seems to regret saying anything, so I'm not going to give her a hard time for long. I hold my expectant, haughty stare for a few tense seconds before I crack up, laughing and breaking the tension that has started to build. "It's fine, hon. I'm only teasing. I have no issues sleeping beside another man."

Normally, anyway. The fact that it's Jack and I've slept with him in the biblical sense, on the other hand…

Well, she can't know that, and I can't let him know that it affected me when I was the one to insist that we go back to our normal dynamic.

Still, Steph gives me a cheeky wink that makes me wonder if my attraction to my employer is written all over my face before she turns back to Jack and demands, "Are you okay with that idea, then?"

It's obvious to me that he doesn't want her to know about last weekend. Jack's jaw tightens beneath his beard, and I swear his eyes are telling her to shut the fuck up, but the smile he bestows on her is easy and his shrug is convincingly nonchalant. "Sure. It's just one night," he chooses that moment to look in my direction. "We can manage one night, right, Leo?"

Is that a challenge, or am I reading way too much into his words?

I nod back dumbly.

Steph claps her hands together. "Then that's settled. And, I don't know about you, but," she pauses to yawn widely, "I'm beat."

* * *

"I don't bite, you know," Jack murmurs into the darkness. I can practically hear the smirk in his voice when he adds, "Well, not unless you ask me to."

After getting Steph settled in my room, I'd grabbed my essentials, had brushed my teeth and, after a few deep, calming breaths, had made my way into Jack's bedroom, quietly shutting the door behind myself.

He'd been sitting up against the padded headboard, scrolling on his phone as though he didn't have a care in the world. As if this wasn't going to be awkward considering what we had done in this bed only just a week ago. Then he'd smiled

Chapter Sixteen — Leo

as I'd climbed under the sheets on the other side of the mattress, waited for me to get comfortable, then had leaned over and switched off his bedside lamp, plunging the room into darkness.

Of course, it seems like neither one of us can actually sleep if his teasing words are anything to go by.

Rolling onto my side to face him, I eye the lines of his profile. With the blinds closed and the lamp turned off, my eyes can only really pick out the slope of his nose and the vague scruff of his bearded chin with him lying on his back, his gaze directed towards the ceiling.

I sigh. "I can still go crash on the couch."

I can hear the soft sound of fabric moving as Jack shifts onto his side to face me. "Don't be stupid," he whispers back, "there's nothing wrong with sharing the bed."

"Mm." My response is nothing more than a noncommittal hum.

He chuckles softly, but I still feel the brush of air from his breath. "Yeah, okay," he acknowledges without me having to prompt him, "it's a little weird, right? I mean, seeing as the last time you were here with me..."

I'm glad for the lack of light in the room as my cheeks grow hot. I shouldn't feel relieved that his thoughts went to the same place that mine did, but I do. It's nice to know that he's not unaffected by the situation we've found ourselves in, even if we promised that last weekend would be a one-off occurrence.

"*Jack*," I was hoping to sound chiding, but his name leaves my lips in a quiet, plaintive whine.

The mattress wobbles as he shuffles closer. My breathing hitches.

"I know we shouldn't," he speaks so quietly that I'm almost convinced that I imagined the words, and I jump a little when his warm, solid palm lands on my hip, searing my skin through the thin sheets as he squeezes, "but one night wasn't nearly enough."

Closing my eyes, I grasp at all the reasons why this is a Very Bad Idea[tm]. Boss. Age gap. Kids.

But, when my lips part, I surprise even myself by saying, "This *has* to be the last time. And we have to be quiet."

Leonard Xavier Martin, this is the most reckless, irresponsible, monumentally stupid thing you have ever done.

The voice inside my head is berating me louder than it ever has before.

I know, I think back at it. *I know, but I can't help myself.*

It doesn't get another chance to protest, though, because Jack has shaken off his stunned stupor. He closes the space between us and kisses me like he's been stuck in the desert and I'm the first sip of water he's seen in days. I melt into it, allowing his tongue to tease my lips apart, licking inside my mouth, making the fine hairs on my arms stand to attention.

Heart hammering in my chest, I run my palms over the exposed skin of his shoulders. I curse the darkness, wishing I could see his shirtless body, to trace the lines of his tattoos with the pads of my fingertips and also my tongue. Then our cocks connect, rubbing up against each other with the unconscious movement of our hips, and I gasp into Jack's mouth.

I feel his lips pull into a grin against my own. "Yeah, and that's how good it feels with our pants still on," he playfully says before his whisper turns low and gravelly, "now imagine if they were off."

Chapter Sixteen — Leo

This feels like my last chance to put an end to this madness, even though I know he will stop immediately at any point if I tell him to. However, instead of listening to the voice of reason in my head, I find myself scrambling to tug at the waistband of his satin boxer shorts.

"Off sounds good," I whisper back at him. "Really, really good."

"Uh-huh," he agrees.

It's a mad scramble to remove our sleep pants and underwear without making too much sound, but we manage.

"I miss the panties," Jack laments as he reaches between us to wrap his big, warm, calloused palm around my already hard-as-steel shaft, "but this makes up for it."

I bite my lip and try not to groan too loudly. His hand feels superior to my own, even though he's stroking me dry, and I close my eyes and lean into the touch. I do, however, let out a small whine of disappointment when he releases me, then I suck in a sharp breath when the mattress creaks as Jack knee-walks over to the edge of the bed so he can paw through his bedside table drawer.

Even the soft clattering of items being sifted through sounds too loud in the darkness.

"Shh," I hiss at him, terrified the noise is going to give us away, despite my room being two doors down. I'm not worried about the boys waking up — unless they have nightmares or wet the bed, they're usually very deep sleepers.

"You're being paranoid," Jack mutters back at me, then lets out a short, sharp sound of victory. "Gotcha." He turns around, still on his knees, and explains, "Found the lube." He pauses. "No condoms, though. We, um, we used the last of them last weekend."

You Don't Know Jack

It makes sense that he hasn't had a chance to replenish his stash, given that he has spent the past week with his family.

Uncharacteristically, Jack babbles into the silence between us when I don't immediately reply. "It's just...we agreed one night only, so I didn't think I needed to..."

Wow, I swallow roughly. *Did he really not consider sleeping with anyone else?*

It's not that I imagined he would immediately log into Grindr or Tinder or whatever, but his candid confession has shaken me a little.

I clear my throat. "It's okay," I reply quietly, wishing I could see his face properly. "It's probably better if we don't...if there's no, uh, penetrative..." Jesus, my cheeks are on fire. "I just mean, y'know, the bed squeaks and...yeah." I clear my throat again, then wince when I consider how loud it sounds. "The lube's good, though. We'll need that."

"Yeah?" He asks, sounding so unsure. My heart squeezes in my chest.

"Here," I lie down on my side, facing the darkened window, "lie down beside me like you were before. Press up nice and close."

The mattress complains and bounces as he follows my instructions, and his breathing grows heavy against my neck as he slides his currently half-hard erection against the curve of my butt. Turning my head, I encourage a slow, sloppy kiss, almost sighing as I feel him relax into it while his cock slowly swells back to life.

"Now," I breathe, remembering that I had a plan in mind, "we're just going to reposition a bit," I wriggle up a couple of inches and turn my hips further into the mattress, "and you're going to slick up that gorgeous dick of yours and then fuck

Chapter Sixteen — Leo

me between my thighs."

Jack, bless him, doesn't question any of what I've said. I hear the lube cap snap open, listening for the squirt of liquid and then the click of the lid shutting again. I clench my legs together as tightly as possible and exhale in pleasure as his big, broad body is plastered against my back, his slick cock slipping between my butt cheeks and then, after some additional manoeuvring, between my thighs.

"*Oh,*" Jack says with wonder after experimentally rocking his hips a few times, finding an angle that works for him.

"Shh," I remind him, barely remembering to stay quiet a moment later when a long, slow thrust brings the head of his cock in contact with the back of my balls.

His chest is practically fused to my back, and the tickle of chest hairs against my hairless skin is exquisite, but it's the breathy pants against my ear that have me teetering close to orgasm within minutes, not to mention just how amazing it feels to be pinned down by someone so much bigger and, let's face it, brawnier than me.

The friction between my thighs is also delicious. This usually isn't my preferred way to get off, but in the darkness of Jack's bedroom, the silence only broken by our heavy breathing and shaky, stifled sounds of pleasure, it feels fucking amazing.

Jack's movements are slow and measured now that he's gotten into a rhythm and has found his confidence. His cock is big and thick and, on the angle we've managed and the way he's arching his hips on every downstroke, it occasionally brushes my rim on its slow drag between the lower curve of my cheeks. The sensation is almost enough to have me begging him to fuck me, regardless of the lack of condoms or privacy.

Added to that is the feel of his beard at my neck, somehow both soft and coarse all at once. His lips ghost over my skin and his breathing, still heavy, starts to turn ragged.

"How…how does this feel so good?" he asks, and his muted voice is strained and almost a growl. His face moves and he presses his forehead, sweaty despite how unhurried our movements have been, into the crook of my neck. "Fuck, princess, I'm so close."

My heart stutters over the endearment, especially because it sounds so damn affectionate.

"T-touch my cock," I demand, not wanting to look too closely into those feelings. "Stroke it in time with your thrusts. Make —*oh God, yes*— m-make me come with you." I tilt my head back, lost in ecstasy as he does exactly as I've asked.

"This…" Jack murmurs into the skin of my shoulder, peppering kisses over whatever surface he can reach, "this is…" There's a choked, thick quality to his voice that mirrors the tightness in my chest, and I can't deal with that. Not now.

Boss.

Age gap.

Kids.

He's too good for me.

I clench my thighs impossibly tighter, distracting him from whatever thoughts or words he was trying to form. Tears gather in the corners of my eyes, and I curse myself for suggesting we do something so intimate while knowing that my heart was already so far gone for him.

"*Princess*," he groans my new nickname with feeling as his hips jerk and warm, sticky wetness coats the inside of my thighs, the backs of my balls and the inside of my crack.

Chapter Sixteen — Leo

It pushes me over the edge in more than one way, and I try to muffle my sob as I erupt over his hand. It takes everything in my power to control my shaking shoulders, hoping that he'll write off the trembling and hitching breaths as post-orgasmic tremors.

Suddenly, I'm thankful for the darkness.

Jack kisses my shoulders and the back of my neck again as he slowly pulls his softening cock back. "I'll grab some wipes," he whispers, thankfully oblivious to my tears. "I'll be right back."

I nod mutely, then take advantage of his distraction as he rolls away, scrubbing at my face with my palm before giving in and wiping my eyes on the pillowcase beneath me. I'll write the dampness off as sweat if I have to.

I can hear him rummaging through his bedside table again, and then the mattress dips and shifts, signalling his return. Taking long, steadying breaths, I shift onto my back and the cool touch of a wet wipe meets my thigh. I swallow convulsively as Jack wipes me clean with obvious tenderness, and I rail against the instinct to shove him away and tell him that one-night stands should never feel this sweet or caring.

Is it really still a one-night stand at this point? This is our third intimate encounter. It's a habit at this point.

One I have to break.

Chapter Seventeen – Jack

Leo is uncharacteristically tense and quiet in the aftermath of...*shit.* I was about to call it our lovemaking. Honestly, though, that's what it felt like: making love. I've had slow, dirty fucks before but what we just did? It was different. Mind-blowingly, life-changingly different.

I wasn't even inside him, nor was he inside me, and yet I can count on one hand the number of times I've felt that kind of emotion during sex and I'll still have a few fingers remaining.

It's scary. I don't do emotions with sex. Not usually. But with Leo, it feels good. Right. Like a missing puzzle piece, or the final connection of an energy circuit clicking into place, lighting up a bulb.

Did Leo feel it, too? Is that why he's suddenly locked up and silent? Is he as scared about it as I am? Or has he worked out that I'm developing feelings when we promised that we wouldn't complicate things? Is he just trying to work out how to let me down gently?

Chapter Seventeen — Jack

Ugh.

This is why I never do feelings. They confuse me and make things difficult and messy.

And painful.

Just the thought of Leo not being on the same page as I am hurts. It's even more of a foreign feeling than discovering my attraction to men. And this feeling? This is the one that I will fight. This is the one I'll freak out over if I give it enough real estate in my brain. Not the fact that I'm bi. Not the fact that I've slept with a man and have enjoyed it. No: I will freak out over the fact that he has the capacity to break my heart.

I've never been in love.

I know *how* to love, obviously. I love my parents and my siblings. I love my kids, and I love my friends. Hell, I'm pretty sure I love half the guys I work with, platonically speaking.

But I have never loved anyone romantically.

However, if someone asked me to define how I thought it would feel? I'd probably tell them that it's eerily similar to the way I'm starting to feel about Leo.

I care about Leo. Seeing him smile makes my stomach flip. I'm excited to come home to talk to him. I want to hear about his day, including his snarky thoughts about some of the parents he's come across at the local playgrounds. I'm filled with fondness and affection any time we drop onto the couch to watch whatever mindless shows are on TV once the boys are in bed, knowing that his commentary will be hilariously catty and sometimes silly. There are also the meals he leaves me when I'm on a late shift, or the hundred other thoughtful things he does —but isn't employed to do— just because it makes my life easier. Oh, and let's not forget his yoga ritual! Cold showers have become a necessity for me for that reason alone.

Then there's the fear that grips me when I think about how much it would hurt if he left. I can't even lie and say that I'm worried about how the boys would take the upheaval: it's all about me. I've come to rely on his presence in my life and in my home. I live for our chats, for our banter, and now for our secret kisses…and then some.

I'm attached to him more deeply than I'm ready to admit to myself and yet I can't stop myself from falling.

One night only, I promised him. It was only a week ago that I made that promise and already I've broken it. But, God help me, how was I supposed to resist him? He was in my bed, for fuck's sake. I'm only human, and he seemed to want it, too.

Seemed to.

My brain snags on those words, bringing me back to the realisation that Leo's tense and unhappy.

"Princess?" I ask into the darkness, straining my hearing to confirm that he's still awake. His breathing hitches and my heart squeezes at the sound. "Leo?"

Quietly clearing his throat, he replies, "Hmm?"

"Are you…" I pause, then recalibrate, "are *we* okay?"

I've never asked a question like that in my life. It feels strange, and I feel more vulnerable than I did last weekend, when I was exposed and presenting my hole to him for the first time.

I don't like the silence that descends after my question. He shouldn't need time to think if everything was alright, should he?

"We're fine," he eventually says and I'm not at all convinced.

The fear of being hurt tightens my throat, but the fear of Leo being upset because of something I have done makes me

Chapter Seventeen — Jack

forge on with the uncomfortable conversation.

I roll onto my side and squint at his face, trying to make out his expression. It's not pitch black in here, but the blinds are block-out blinds so I can sleep during the day when I've been on night shift. Right now, I'm cursing their existence. I wish I could read him or get a bead on what he's thinking.

"It's just…you don't sound fine," I say, wanting to reach out to lay a comforting hand on him, but holding myself back. I get the feeling my touch wouldn't be welcome, and my stomach turns over at the thought. "Talk to me, Leo."

There's another extended silence between us and I'm almost certain that he's going to ignore me when he whispers, "We can't do this again. Ever. It was—"

"Don't say it was a mistake," I interrupt him a bit too loudly, my chest tight. He shushes me and I lower my volume as my heart hammers in my chest. "Please," I beg quietly. "Don't say that."

Begging. A new low for me. I don't think I've ever begged anyone for anything in my life. Well, other than begging to come, but that's different.

"Not a mistake," Leo eventually says, and hope rises inside me before crashing as he adds, "but it was more than we should have done. I'm your kids' nanny, Jack. I'm not…" He stops short, then sighs heavily. "I like you too much to let us ruin our friendship and working relationship any more than we already have."

And there it is: the hurt I was expecting. Granted, he softened the blow by telling me that he likes me, but the rejection stings all the same.

It hits me, as I try to rally with a smile and some sort of quip to break the tension, that *this* is what I've put a number of women through over the years. Not all of them, no, but I can't say that every woman I ever slept with was completely content with our initial agreement to bang and part ways, either. Just look at Steph and how badly I fucked that up! Now that the shoe is on the other foot, I'm tempted to run into the guest room —Leo's room— and apologise for hurting her.

Ugh.

It's not like I tried to hurt her, though. Well, not until I blocked her. That was a dick move. The let-down, though? It was as gentle as it could have been. It's not my fault she'd set her sights on more and…oh. *Oh.*

This isn't Leo's fault.

I knew that. Of course I did. But getting it to sink into my thick skull is a whole different matter entirely.

"I get it," I tell him, feeling the truth and the weight of those words. "I'm sorry if I pushed you too far. I like you, too." The confession hangs heavy in the darkness between us. I force a light chuckle. "And finding another nanny to handle my hellions would be too much work, so…"

He snorts, and I find I can breathe easier again.

It's going to be okay. Sure, it's not the resolution I would have wanted for us, but I'd rather have his friendship than nothing.

* * *

It takes a few months before Leo and I are back to 'normal'. In that time, I've gone back to work, the boys have turned four, and Dad and Connor have been spending way more time in my apartment than I ever thought I would have been comfortable with in my life pre-kids. Dad's even started inviting Leo to

Chapter Seventeen – Jack

join him and Toby on their old-man social nights, which is weird to me, but it didn't escape my notice that Leo brightened up a lot since he started hanging out with them.

Once I noticed that, I remembered my original plan to get him involved with my social circle. It's obvious that the guy could use some friends, after all. So, I started inviting him to replace Connor at the soccer games more often. Con didn't mind; his party planning company has been getting busier since he posted all of the photos from his wedding online, so he's taken advantage of the additional free time to work on it.

So, after three months, things are back to the way they should be and, aside from the fact that I still want to sink to my knees in front of him at any given opportunity, I'm happy.

Which is why I'm totally blindsided on an otherwise unassuming Saturday afternoon.

Leo and I have just left the elevator and are walking towards my apartment, each of us carrying a sleeping four-year-old, when the door opens unexpectedly and Dad steps out to greet us. His smile is apologetic and then warms when it lands on the boys, before turning into more of a grimace again when I lock eyes with him.

"How was the game?" he asks me. Leo brought the boys to watch me play on the firehouse's basketball team against a local team of paramedics. They sat on the sidelines and cheered and clapped, even though the paramedic team wiped the floor with us.

I've always been better at sports involving kicking or hitting things anyway.

But that's not what I'm focusing on right now. Instead, I narrow my gaze at my father, then glance towards the door

You Don't Know Jack

to my apartment. "What's going on, Dad?"

"I just want to start by assuring you that I had no idea, okay?" He says, which doesn't help me in the least.

"Dad..." My brain races to think about what the issue might be. Something wrong with the apartment, maybe?

"It's not *bad*," he runs his hand through the dark hair on his head, and I note that there are more silvery flecks appearing in it of late. Soon, it'll match his grey beard. "Just...try not to freak out."

"Oh, God, please don't tell me I have more kids," I blurt my greatest fear without realising it, and Leo snorts beside me.

"You've already got a nanny," he nudges me with his shoulder, "I promise not to charge extra if there is another surprise kid. I might buy you some condoms, though."

"Shut up," I groan, feeling my cheeks heat. "I swear I always use them."

"Boys," Dad cuts in with amusement, "it's not another kid. I would have called if that was the case." He sighs. "It's your mother."

Instantly, I'm concerned. "Mom? What's wrong with Mom?"

"Nothing's wrong with your mother, she's—"

The door swings open behind him, cutting him off, and Mom steps out, smacking his bicep. "You didn't spoil the surprise, I hope." Then she turns to me and beams. "Jackie!"

I'm too busy gaping at her to complain about the nickname. She used it a lot when I was little, then stopped in my teens because I asked her to. However, any time she feels the mom-guilts, she reverts to it.

"M-mom?" I stammer, almost dropping a still-snoozing Prez. "What are you doing here?" I put her on a plane back to

Chapter Seventeen — Jack

America three months ago. It doesn't compute to see her here now.

She grins at me and gestures for me to enter my own home. "Come on, I'll explain once the angels are down for their nap and we can sit and chat comfortably."

I share a look with Leo and then cross the threshold, heading to the boys' room to lay Prez in his bed while Leo gets Huddy settled in the other bed.

"I'll get everyone coffees while you catch up with your mum," he says as we enter the lounge room, and then Dad hurries off after him. I watch them in the kitchen as I settle myself on the couch, and then I turn my attention to Mom.

"So?" I prompt.

She bites her lip for a moment, then offers me a sheepish smile. "So, um, when you first called to tell me about the boys, I realised that I didn't want to miss seeing them grow up."

"Okay…"

"So I had a talk with Mike and the girls and we started looking into what it might take to move over here."

I blink at her. "What? Permanently?"

She nods.

I slump back against the couch cushions, my heart racing. "Holy shit."

"Language," she chides, and I roll my eyes.

"I wanted it to be a surprise," Mom continues and she leans forward in her seat, her eyes sparkling with excitement. "I didn't know how long the process would take, or if we'd even be successful, so I didn't want to get anyone's hopes up."

"But now you're here," I say, clearly the master of observation. Nothing slips past me!

Mom nods. "Now I'm here. We all are."

You Don't Know Jack

I think about how much moving to a different continent changed my life, and I was eighteen at the time. My youngest sister is still in high school, so this will be huge for her. "Wow."

"Yeah," Mom agrees, grinning. "Mike's company helped transfer him to one of their sister locations here, and we've bought a house in Mudgeeraba, not too far from that shopping mall you took us to when we were here, and—"

"Holy shit," I repeat my earlier sentiments as the news sinks in. "You're for real." I cock my head. "Does Wes know?"

Her gaze flicks sideways. *Yeah*, I think a little bitterly, *he knew about this. So much for twins sharing everything.*

"Well, we had some questions about the legalities..." she explains, knowing that I hate being left out of the loop.

I sigh and wave my hand in the air between us dismissively. "I get it." Even though I'm still a little annoyed, I smile back at her. "This is kind of huge."

"I'm so excited to live so nearby. Learning to drive on the wrong side of the road and on the wrong side of the car is going to take some getting used to, but we'll manage. And," she claps her hands together as Dad and Leo start walking towards us, each carrying two steaming mugs. I turn my head to widen my eyes at him in an unspoken 'Can you believe this?' while she keeps talking. "I'll be able to watch the boys for you while you're at work, so there's no need to pay for a nanny anymore."

Her words don't really register at first, but I can pinpoint the moment Leo processes them. His face falls and the mugs slip from his shock-slackened grip to the floating timber floor. Porcelain shatters and coffee spills and splatters everywhere.

"Shit," he hisses as Mom and I leap to our feet. Leo drops to his knees to try and pick up the broken mug shards, hissing

Chapter Seventeen — Jack

as he comes into contact with the still hot liquid.

"Stop," Dad tells him, having already retreated to set down his mugs. He grabs a roll of paper towels out from under my kitchen sink and squats at Leo's side, while I direct Mom to grab the mop and bucket from the utility closet in the hallway.

Leo's hands tremble as he ignores Dad and keeps trying to pick up the broken pieces of porcelain. "I'm so clumsy," he mutters, staring resolutely at the mess, and I hate how tight and wobbly his voice is. "It's hard to find good help th-these days." He stammers over the flat delivery of his joke, seemingly linking the sentiment to Mom's bombshell.

"Leo…" Dad reaches out to touch my nanny's shoulder and squeeze, and that pushes him over the edge.

Leo surges to his feet, heedless of the wet patches on the knees of his jeans. "I…I'm sorry, I can't…" Not bothering to finish his sentence, he hurries past me and towards his room, swerving out of Mom's way as she returns through the archway that leads towards the bedrooms and bathroom before he ducks out of sight completely.

I want to follow him. I want to hold him in my arms and comfort him. I want to reassure him that even if Mom does look after the boys, I'm not kicking him out of the apartment. In fact, this might actually be good for us. If he's no longer my employee, there might be a chance that we can date, right?

As if he can read my mind, Dad clears his throat and gives me a disapproving frown.

He can't know, can he? Even though he and Leo have become close friends, there's no way Leo would have told him about our fooling around.

"I've got this," Dad tells me, then glares at Mom as she approaches. They usually get along so well, it's weird to see that expression on his face when he speaks to her. "Really, Jen? In front of Leo?"

She has the grace to appear chagrined and apologetic. "I wasn't thinking. I was just excited to tell Jack my plan and…" Trailing off, she pouts at me. "I'm so sorry, Jack. It was a bit heartless to just announce that I'm taking his job right in front of him."

"You think?" I pause to take a calming breath. "You can't just decide who is looking after my kids for me, Mom. I know it's coming from a place of love," I add when she moves to protest, "but it's still my decision. They're my boys. I have sole custody." Henry helped see to that, and Steph didn't fight me on it. In return, I'll be taking them to Melbourne to visit her once every three months. We have a trip scheduled for next month, in fact. "So, you know, as exciting as it is that you've moved here, I'm going to need you to let me parent at my own speed, okay?"

Mom hesitates, glancing back over her shoulder. "Should I…?"

I shake my head. "You clean this up. I'll go fix it."

Except, when I knock on Leo's door and his sad voice tells me that it's open, I realise it's not going to be that easy.

Chapter Eighteen – Leo

"What are you doing?" Jack asks as he steps inside my room, his gaze zeroing in on the open suitcase on the bed.

Not bothering to pause in rolling up a pair of jeans Marie Kondo style, I chuckle mirthlessly. "What does it look like?"

"You can't just leave," he argues, and I want to believe that the note of desperation in his voice isn't just a figment of my imagination. "Even if she does start looking after the boys, this is your home."

I scrunch up my nose and drop the rolled-up jeans into the suitcase. "That's a bit weird, isn't it? I'm *nobody* to you."

"Bullshit. You're my—" Jack stops abruptly, then lamely finishes, "friend."

Rolling my eyes, I reach for my yoga leggings and start to roll them tightly. I squeeze the soft, stretchy material within an inch of its life, holding onto anger so I don't burst into tears. "Nice save," I mutter bitterly, "but it's still weird. If I'm not your nanny, there's no point for me to live here. And," I force myself to look up at him, to meet his incredulous and hurt stare head-on, "you'd be an idiot not to take your mum up on her offer. You'll save thousands of dollars, plus she'll get to spend time with her grandkids."

"But…"

I shake my head, roughly repeating the clothes-rolling technique on a pair of cargo shorts. Taking my aggression and frustration out on the fabric is preferable to the alternative options, namely crying and screaming about how unfair the situation is.

I didn't feel this torn up over my breakup with my ex, not even when I walked in on him cheating on me. But this hurts. It hurts because I love Hudson and Preston. It hurts because this feels like home. It hurts because I've fallen head over heels in love with Jack, despite all of my attempts to keep my feelings for my employer platonic.

Jack has done everything I asked of him since the last time we slept together. He respected my wishes and has done everything in his power over the past few months to make sure that our friendship and working relationship remained unaffected by our *tryst*. He's encouraged me to hang out with his soccer friends, even though he still grimaces whenever Smitty flirts with me, and he makes an effort to invite me along on any excursions with the kids. We've fallen into a comfortable routine without any flirting or even reminders of the few times we slept together.

And still I fell hard for him.

How could I not?

Not only is he attractive, but he's also a good man. He's considerate, sweet, and hardworking. He's a great dad, a reliable friend, and he's been a fantastic boss.

Chapter Eighteen – Leo

I'm going to miss him so much.

This is why my heart is aching and why my throat is getting tight. I knew I wouldn't get to stay forever, but I wasn't expecting everything to come crashing down around me so soon. Still, even though he's offered to let me stay, I have to leave. It's like ripping off a bandaid. If I do it fast, the pain won't be as drawn out.

Jack steps closer, crowding my personal space. His expression is wretched. "Princess, please…"

Ouch.

It's been three months since the last time he called me that, and to hear it now is just unfair.

"I can't stay here," I repeat, wondering which of us I'm trying to convince the most. "It would be weird, Jack. And confusing for the boys." A lump lodges in my throat. I have no right to ask the next question that tumbles from my lips, but I do it anyway. "Can I still see them on your days off work?" At least I don't lower myself to asking 'can I still see you?' despite the temptation to do so being there.

"We're still friends," he insists. "Of course you can still hang out with us. And with the guys at the games. Oh, and don't forget Dad: he and Toby have decided you're an honorary old guy."

This time when I chuckle, there's more humour in it.

"They're not that old," I dispute in the same way I've done ever since I started hanging out with Will and Toby. We go down to the local Mexican restaurant once a month to eat, drink, and just talk shit. It's been nice having friends again, regardless of their age. Besides, Toby and I are both tragically single, and it's nice to have another gay guy with whom I can lament the slim pickings on Grindr right now.

The tension in Jack's broad shoulders loosens a little as he smiles tentatively. He's still in my personal space as he softly adds, "Then there's me. Don't forget me."

After living with him for half a year, you'd think it wouldn't surprise me when he's so vulnerable, but it still throws me for a loop. This big, brawny fireman is braver than I am on almost every level, including matters of the heart.

"Jack…" I breathe his name, my heart hammering in my chest.

"If…if you're leaving," he ignores me and swallows roughly, searching my eyes with those piercing blue ones of his, "I won't be your boss anymore."

I want so badly to fall into his arms and agree that, yes, the hurdle preventing a romantic relationship between us is gone so we can date or whatever…but I hold myself back. I'm feeling too raw to be making an impulsive decision like that.

"I need time," I tell him, feeling guilty as his face falls. "This… this sucks, Jack. I'm not in the right mental space to start anything new." Especially not with the man whose home I'm opting to flee from.

Even though I don't say that last bit out loud, he seems to hear the sentiment anyway. Backing off, he nods stiffly. "At least stay until you can find a new place."

"I can't."

If I do that, I'll never be able to bring myself to leave. At least I've got a pretty good chunk of savings set aside. Half a year of not paying for rent or groceries and having no social life to speak of has made it very easy to set most of my income aside. I suppose a part of me knew that my life here was only temporary.

Jack finally throws his hands into the air, his handsome face

Chapter Eighteen — Leo

twisted into a scowl. "Fine. Whatever. I tried."

I know that he's only lashing out because he's hurting, but I wince and look away. "I'm sorry."

"Yeah, well, so am I," he huffs, before turning on his heel and stalking back through the door.

My heart officially breaks when I hear the latch click into place, and I finally let my tears fall.

* * *

"You're all settled in at your new place?" Will asks me over the top of his glass of sangria. He narrows his eyes. "You still haven't given me your address."

That's because I'm once again living in a seedy motel while I scour real estate listings and ads looking for a housemate on Gumtree, Australia's answer to Craigslist. I know if I say as much out loud, Will would demand that I pack my shit back up and move into his and Connor's place. However, their apartment doesn't have a guest room, because the room that would be the guest room is actually their home gym, and Will uses it daily. I don't want to crash on their couch and make a nuisance of myself, especially not when they're technically still in the honeymoon period of their marriage, and the fact that it's directly below Jack's apartment is also a turn-off.

I'll take the crappy motel with a roach problem over any of that, thanks.

Miraculously, Toby arrives before I can find a convincing enough lie to put Will off asking again. I stand up to hug my friend, exchanging air kisses on each side of his face. He gives my arms a squeeze before letting me slip back into my seat while he takes his own.

"How've you been?" he asks me as Sophie, the cute teenage server, brings him his usual beer. He grins at her when she sets it on top of the brightly coloured tablecloth in front of him. "Thanks Soph."

"You'd better give me a tip this time," she sasses at him, throwing a long, dark braid over her shoulder.

"Oh, I've got a tip for you," he goads. "Stay in school."

Sophie sighs heavily and rolls her eyes. "At least I can depend on Will tipping well."

"He's American," Toby waves her argument off, "he doesn't understand that Australian employers actually pay their staff a liveable wage." Sophie arches her eyebrow at him and he snorts. "Well. Okay. I'll admit with the climbing costs of living that's debatable, but you're still in high school. You'll survive."

"I'm so spitting in your burrito," she mutters darkly, then pokes her tongue out at him when he flips her the bird.

I laugh and shake my head. Will and Toby love to take turns snarking with our usual waitress. It's apparently their thing, and Sophie seems to love it. And, contrary to his words, Toby does usually tip her well, even though he's right that it's not common practise here in Australia.

"So," Toby leans back in his timber chair and sips at his beer, releasing a hiss of satisfaction after he swallows, "how've you been?"

"You already asked that," I answer playfully.

"And you didn't answer," Will observes.

Toby nods then aims his index finger at me. "We're onto you, kid. So, spill. It's been, what? Three weeks since you moved out of Jack's place?"

"Two," I sigh, knowing that it could be worse, but that every single day away from Jack and the boys has stung like

Chapter Eighteen – Leo

a motherfucker. "And I'm *fine*," I stress the word. "I've got my second interview with a daycare centre in Broadbeach on Wednesday, in fact."

It's not the same as nannying, but maybe that's not a bad thing. I'm less likely to repeat the mistake of getting too attached to the kids or their hot, single, surprisingly bi firefighter dads…

Stop it! The little voice in my head sighs. *It was never going to work. You're twenty-one, he's in his thirties. He has kids to prioritise. And, in two weeks, he hasn't even sent one text asking how you are. If he'd really wanted to date you, wouldn't he have reached out by now?*

I hate it when my inner voice of reason makes a valid point.

I get lost in the conversation debating the pros and cons of a daycare centre job vs nannying vs teaching like Toby. By the time he's whinging about one of his students' dads giving him grief, I'm laughing and able to forget my woes, if only for the evening.

"You know that Vi and I also have a guest room, right?" Toby asks me as we're settling up the bill. I lean against the dark wood of the counter inside the restaurant while he hovers his phone over the card reader. It beeps as the transaction goes through. "And I can charge you room and board if it'll make you feel better taking me up on the offer." The skin around his eyes crinkles with his warm smile. If he'd been fifteen years younger, I would definitely find the whole surfer vibe hot. Thankfully, he's too old to be my type, so living with him wouldn't come with the risk of falling for him.

For fuck's sake, my brain practically sighs. *Well done, Leo. You made it almost forty minutes this time.*

Still, his offer is tempting. He's a friend, his house is much nicer than the gross motel room I'm staying in, and if I'm paying him, I won't feel like a charity case. I mean, it's no different to renting a room off Gumtree, is it? At least I can trust that Toby isn't going to turn out to be a serial killer or the kind of person who listens to *easy listening* radio, right?

Will has paid his share of the bill by the time I've finished mulling the offer over, and as I swipe my card over the EFTPOS machine, I nod at Toby. "As long as you're sure—" I start, and he cuts me off before I can finish.

"Yes!" He pumps his fist into the air and even jumps a little, his mop of blond hair flopping with the excited motion. "Vi's gonna be ecstatic. She keeps asking when she'll get to hang out with you again. You really won her over at the wedding. I think she's got a bit of a crush, to be honest."

I scrunch up my nose. "She's only twelve…and barking up a very gay tree. Also, she's only twelve."

Toby laughs and we fall into step, walking through the arcade towards the car park. Even though it's brightly lit, he and Will insisted that they'd walk with me, overprotective dad-types, the both of them.

"You mentioned that," he snickers. "Don't you remember being twelve? I think I had crushes on almost every guy that gave me the time of day." His lips quirk and a look of reminiscence seems to pass over his face. "It was harder to admit that stuff back then, but my mum was super cool about it when I accidentally swooned over the Woolies cashier once. Made coming out to her a lot easier than I thought it would be."

I snort, ignoring the lingering pang of my parents' much less accepting response to my coming out. "The Woolies cashier?" I echo with amusement. "Really?"

Chapter Eighteen – Leo

"I was twelve and he was hot. He would have been at least sixteen. Snuck me a free Chupa Chup when Mum wasn't looking."

Will shakes his head and claps Toby on the back, a teasing smirk playing around his lips. I totally beat him to the punchline, though.

Waggling my finger at Toby, I accuse, "And what did you think about while you were sucking on that lollipop, I wonder?"

His grin says it all. I throw my head back and laugh.

And, for the first time in two weeks, I feel like things might be okay after all.

Chapter Nineteen – Jack

"You're going to sit your ass down and tell me what's going on with you and Leo," Dad says as he pushes past me and into my apartment.

"Hi Dad," I chirp sarcastically as I close the door. "What a nice surprise. Sure, come on in. Take a seat. Make yourself at home."

He sets Vicky down on the play mat before he plonks himself down on the couch, glaring at me while I resolutely avoid his gaze. I focus on my stepsister instead, watching as she toddles over to the basket of toys and topples it to its side so the collection of toy trucks and plushies spills out onto the mat. The boys are out with Mom today, even though it's my day off work, so she has the whole lot to herself.

Unsurprisingly, she grabs a Batmobile and a Duplo Batman toy.

"That's my girl," I praise, and Dad clears his throat.

"*Jack*," his tone is the same one he used when Wes and I were kids and we were pushing boundaries. Not angry, not yet. But

Chapter Nineteen — Jack

it's a warning, nonetheless. He points at the armchair. "Sit."

Vicky squeals as she mashes Batman against the hood of the Batmobile, the plastic surfaces clacking together obnoxiously.

Poor Batman.

"Now," Dad redirects my focus, "I'll ask again. What happened between you and Leo?"

"What makes you think something happened?"

Yeah, because countering his question with another question isn't going to raise his suspicions more, idiot.

He arches a salt-and-pepper eyebrow. "The fact that he practically flinched every time Toby or I mentioned your name last night, maybe. Or maybe, just maybe, it's that you can't look me in the eye right now."

"Dad," I sigh and rub the back of my neck as Batman gets run over by his own car, "we didn't fight or anything, if that's what you're asking. And, y'know, I'm a grown-ass man, so—"

"Language," he scolds, and gestures towards Vicky, who isn't paying us any attention.

I scowl at him. "You said it not thirty seconds ago!"

"My kid, my rules," he shrugs. "And you're also my kid, so grown-up or not, I worry about you. And about my friends. And about whatever's gone wrong between you and my friends."

Jesus Christ.

"Nothing's gone wrong," I argue. "He just…he asked for space after the mess with Mom and I'm giving it to him." There. I didn't lie.

Dad sits back and cocks his head to the side. "I knew he had a bit of a thing for you," he says slowly, and I struggle not to choke on air with how blunt he's being. "And don't pretend like you were oblivious to it."

I can feel my cheeks heating. "I wasn't."

"Please tell me you didn't make him feel...I don't know, uncomfortable because he was into you."

My heart sinks and I gape at my father. "Really? You really think I'd do that? I don't have a homophobic bone in my body, Dad. You know that." It actually hurts that he might think otherwise.

He shakes his head in denial, appearing contrite. "That's not how I meant the question to sound. After how you said you treated Steph when she wanted more from you..."

I sigh. "Okay. That's...well, that's understandable." I wish it wasn't the case, but I can see why he'd assume I would potentially treat Leo badly with my history. "But that's not it. Far from it, actually." And if those words come out a little bitter, well, I can't quite help it. The one time I actually want to be with someone, they don't want the same. Some might call that karma.

Batman goes sailing through the air between us and lands with a clatter on the other side of the mat. Vicky toddles after him, babbling happily. Dad spares her an affectionate glance before he looks back at me.

"So...?"

I've been waiting to talk the mess in my head out with someone, but coming out to Dad feels kind of huge. Still, Wes knows, and so does Dana. Then, of course, Steph does, too. I might as well take the last step and tell everyone important to me. Besides, if anyone's going to be chill about it, it'll be Dad, so starting with him should be the easiest.

I swallow roughly. "So," I drag the word out and bite my lower lip, "Leo and I...we might have, um, hooked up a couple of times." I wince. "Three. Three times."

Chapter Nineteen — Jack

"Hooked up?" Dad echoes, his expression contorted with confusion before understanding dawns and it's his turn to gape at me. "You…"

"I'm bi, Dad."

A sense of relief I was not expecting to feel crashes over me. It's not like I've been deliberately trying to hide my sexuality or anything. I just wasn't being particularly open and honest about the most recent changes in my life. It's not like me to keep things from Dad. We're too close for that.

"Oh, God, you didn't feel pressured into telling me that just now, did you?" He asks me, pulling me out of my thoughts. His eyes are all shiny and he looks horrified. "Because I feel really honoured that you're telling me, but if you felt like you *had* to just to get me off your back—"

"No, no," I move from my chair to drop into the spot beside him, "you didn't. I was ready. I've been ready for a while, I think. I just…I didn't know how to bring it up, I guess."

To be honest, a silly part of me had imagined walking into his and Connor's apartment for a family dinner with Leo's hand clutched in mine. Cheesy and melodramatic, sure, but it would have been fun. Except, Leo asked me to give him space, so it's probably not going to happen any time soon.

"Dada!" Vicky demands, smacking the Batmobile on Dad's knee. I wince in sympathy as he rubs at the spot and halts her attempt to repeat the action with his free hand. "Baaman! Baaman!"

"Yes, that's Batman," he acknowledges, and she smiles a partially toothed smile back at him. "Why don't you build him his castle out of blocks?"

"Wayne Manor," I correct him, sharing an exasperated look with Vicky. "We'll teach him one day, won't we, Vickster?"

She babbles a series of disconnected sounds at me and then toddles off to smash Batman into a pile of block-shaped rubble.

Still rubbing his likely bruised knee, Dad turns back to me. "I'm gonna hug you now," he declares, then follows through on his words, wrapping his arms around me. I hug him back, getting all choked up when he says, "I'm proud of you and love you as you are, no matter what, Jack."

"Even if I told Wes first?" I joke as I pull back, but Dad doesn't laugh.

"Who you tell and when is your right, not theirs."

I pull him in for another hug, unable to help myself. "I love you, too, Dad."

"I know," he pats my back before he draws away and arches an eyebrow. "Now, about hooking up with Leo…"

I groan and cover my face with my hands. *"I know.* I know I shouldn't have. But he was…well, he was *Leo*, y'know? He's just so awesome and I just…" I make the sound of my brain exploding and mime the action at the same time. My hand falls limply into my lap and my shoulders slump. "I've never really felt like that about anyone before. Like it wasn't just hooking up. Like I wanted it to be more."

"And he didn't?"

"I think he did, but I was his boss, and he didn't want to confuse the boys, and then…"

"Then things got messy when your mom turned up and he left."

I nod. "Exactly! He asked me for space, and I've been giving it to him, but…how will I know when it's okay to reach out again? Or do I wait for him to reach out to me?" My fingers thread through my hair and tug at the longer strands on top as I groan, "This is why I don't do relationships."

Chapter Nineteen — Jack

"Have you considered texting him? Just to let him know that you haven't completely forgotten that he exists, and that you're ready to talk whenever he is?"

"I…" the Batmobile smashes into my knee and I yelp, having been far too distracted by the conversation to focus on Vicky's activities or whereabouts. "Shii…errt. Shirt, that hurt." I rub at the sore spot and look down at my stepsister, who is now waving Batman and a Ninja Turtle (the purple one? Donatello?) at me happily. "Warn a guy, sweetheart."

She babbles and I can only understand the words 'Batman' and 'poop'. It doesn't take a genius to sniff the air and work out that it is *not* Batman in need of a change. I snort and look at Dad. "Pretty sure this is all for you."

He heaves an exaggerated, put-upon sigh and pushes to his feet, picking up his ever-present diaper bag before he lunges for his kid. She's ahead of the game, though, and she squeals and giggles and then runs for the dining area, where she then chooses to hide under the table.

Even though I'm sad about having missed the boys' early years, there are certain things I'm glad to have avoided, the scene playing out in front of me being one of those things. I wince as Vicky screeches once she's caught, and she thrashes in a bid to escape Dad's clutches.

He takes her into the spare room to change her and I don't bother following. I'm too busy lost in thought, mulling over his earlier words.

Does Leo really think I've forgotten about him?

* * *

A few days later, I'm pulling on my soccer boots for our

bimonthly indoor social game. Connor's been giving me the side-eye, like he knows something is up but neither Dad nor Leo have said anything to him. I don't want to just blurt my issues out for all and sundry to hear, but his perspective might help me decide whether I'm going to text Leo or just turn up on Toby's doorstep, seeing as that's where he's apparently living at the moment.

When Dad told me as much, I'll admit I felt a pang of irrational jealousy. I mean, why is it okay for him to live under Toby's roof but not mine? We're all friends, aren't we?

But then I remembered that he wanted space, and he wouldn't have gotten that if he had stayed living in the apartment with me.

So then I circle back to the dilemma at hand. Dad's advice isn't exactly bad, but it feels kind of impersonal. I really want Leo to understand that my feelings weren't fleeting, nor did they exist only because he was there and 'convenient', or whatever.

I've spent the past two and a half weeks missing him like crazy. Not a day has passed without me thinking about him. The boys miss him, too. They miss the way he let them help him make breakfast, even though they usually made a huge mess. They miss the way he would Google things for them whenever they asked random questions about the universe.

Mom is great with them, don't get me wrong, but she doesn't seem to have the same enthusiasm for teaching them that Leo did. She's more interested in watching them play with toys or taking them on 'adventures' to the local shopping malls, where she proceeds to spend way too much money on clothes that they're only going to outgrow within six months. At least I can pass the clothes down to Vicky, seeing as Dad and Connor

Chapter Nineteen — Jack

don't care if she's dressed in shorts and tees or pretty dresses, as long as she's clothed and content.

Anyway, the point I was trying to make was that Leo was more to the boys than just their nanny. He was their friend and partner in crime. And to me? He was a friend, a confidant, and a support system.

I need to get him back.

"Earth to Jack," Evan ruffles my hair, and I glare up at him from where I'm still seated with one boot on and the other dangling in my hand. He grins. "You with us, mate?"

"Shut up," I huff, hurrying to get my other boot on and the laces tied, "I was lost in thought."

"Yeah, we noticed," he juts his bearded chin towards the group of guys gathering on the pitch. "Game starts in three. You up for it?"

"Of course I am."

He's quiet for a moment. "You wanna talk about it?"

Raising my eyebrows at him, I counter, "You wanna talk about whatever's been keeping you from the past few games?"

Evan blushes and shakes his head. "It's complicated."

"Yeah, well, welcome to my life." I haul myself up and plant my feet wide, running through a few lunging stretches. Then I jog on the spot to warm up a little more.

He observes me for a few more moments, then quietly confesses, "I think I'd be better off talking to Connor about my issues. No offence or anything."

I stop mid jog and slowly lower my raised knee until I'm standing straight and awkwardly. "Why Con?"

Evan fidgets and clarity hits me. He has no idea that I'm bi, but he knows Con's gay. Remembering how frustrated I was at being outed before I was ready, no matter how well-meaning my sister's intentions were, I back off.

With a shrug, I say, "You know what? It's not my place to ask. You've got his number, right?" I introduced Connor to the team when he and Dad started seeing each other, but outside of our games or going to see the A-League teams play, I don't think Connor socialises with the guys as often as I do. Evan nods, seemingly relieved that I've let the subject drop. I smile. "Cool. He's a good guy and a great listener. I...actually need his advice, too."

Evan blinks at me in surprise, but then seems to come to the wrong conclusion. "Oh, because of the kids? I figured you'd ask your dad any parenting type questions, not your stepdad."

I groan. "Stop calling him that. Even if you're technically right, it's weird."

"Oi!" Brett calls from the pitch. "Are you ladies planning on joining us?"

"You wish we were ladies," I jog over to my place as centre back, "have you seen how freaking aggressive the women's league is? We'd kick major ass if we played like them."

"I'll kick your arse if you're not careful," he banters back. "Try not to let the ball near the goal this game."

"Uh, hello, you're the striker," I gesture towards the other goal, "it's your job to put the rolling black and white thing into that goal, okay?"

He flips me off just as the ref blows his whistle to start the game, and I laugh.

The game is enough to distract me from my dilemma. Despite this being a friendly, casual league, the other team is competitive and seem to be taking themselves a little too seriously. One of their midfielders earns himself a yellow card fifteen minutes in with a dodgy tackle, and from there

Chapter Nineteen — Jack

the plays only seem to become more intense.

We battle it out for the first half, with neither team scoring. Our team is too exhausted during the halftime break to do more than guzzle water and rethink our strategy for the second half.

The game picks up again and is somehow even more aggressive and competitive than it was earlier. I lose track of the number of fouls within the first twenty minutes and swear under my breath when one of our strikers, Mitch, is called on an accidental handball. At least it didn't happen inside the penalty box, but it still hands possession back to the other team.

With five minutes left, Brett finally gets lucky and scores a goal, causing our team to erupt into cheers as though we've just won the World Cup. The other team's goalie is screaming at the ref that Brett was offside, but the ref counts the goal and the final five minutes of play are brutal. I'm half convinced that it's going to end in bloodshed.

When the final whistle blows, we exchange fist bumps and obligatory acknowledgements of 'good game' with the other team, but they're still grumbling as they head towards the side of the pitch where they dumped their stuff before the game.

"Jesus," Connor complains as he snatches up his water bottle to guzzle whatever he left after half-time, "that was rough."

"Mmhmm," I agree, but even I can hear how noncommittal my response is. I tug off my boots and shove them into my duffel bag, pulling out my sneakers. I'm sweaty and gross, but I'll grab a shower at home.

"Okay, stop." Con interrupts my movements, frowning at me. "You okay?"

It's funny how before the game I really wanted to talk my

thoughts out with him, but now I'm just agitated. I stop myself before I snap at him, though. It's not his fault I've gotten all up in my head.

"I think I fucked up with Leo," I allow the admission to tumble out of me before I can think twice about it.

Connor gapes at me as Brett and Evan pause in the middle of picking up their stuff.

"Leo, your manny? That Leo? Roar games Leo?" Evan asks, not even bothering to pretend he wasn't listening in.

"Fucked what up?" Brett also sidles in a bit closer, his head cocked to the side. "Being his boss?"

"Yeah, well, a bit of that, too," I lift my chin towards Brett in acknowledgment. "I'm a total cliché at this point."

Connor narrows his gaze at me, but it's Evan who snorts and asks, "What? Did you sleep with the barely legal nanny?"

Even though I want to argue that twenty-one is hardly 'barely legal', I can feel my cheeks heating up and it has nothing to do with the exertion from the game we just played. "Um…"

"Holy shit," Connor collapses back onto the bench, staring at me like he's never seen me before. "You didn't!"

Scrunching my nose, I confess in a much higher pitch than my usual voice, "I kinda did."

"Good for you, man," Brett claps me on the shoulder with a meaty palm. His long, dark hair is plastered to his forehead, and there are wisps escaping from his man bun. "Except… what's this about fucking it up?"

The whole story comes pouring out of me in a hastily summarised rush, brushing over the sexy stuff for obvious reasons. Those intimate details are only for me and Leo to know. I do tell the guys that we broke our self-imposed rules twice after the first time we fooled around, though,

Chapter Nineteen — Jack

acknowledging that for me, that's kind of a huge deal. Then I get to the part where my mom basically announced that Leo was no longer needed in my home and all three men wince and make matching sounds of empathy.

"...I tried to talk it out, practically begged him to stay with me, but he asked for space," I finish in defeat. "That was over two weeks ago and now Dad seems to think I've given him too much space and...*argh* how is dating a man even more complicated than dating a woman? Aren't we all supposed to be less high-maintenance and less...emotional?"

Evan holds his hands up in surrender. "I am not touching that one," he declares, then he points at Brett. "I swear to God, if you say 'that's what she said', I'll—"

"Children," Connor arches his eyebrows at them until they quieten down and have the grace to look sheepish, muttering apologies. Satisfied by that, my Dad's husband turns back to me. "Jack, I love you, but you're an idiot."

"Hey!" I protest, but it's half-hearted at best. I already know that the joke was in poor taste and was kind of sexist. I was just trying to lighten the mood, I guess, not that it's any excuse. And now I've set Con off on a rant.

He starts counting the reasons for his declaration on his fingers. "One, you've never really *dated* anyone. Ever. Right?" Pursing my lips, I nod. "Two," he continues, "if the temper tantrums we just witnessed from that other team tonight prove anything, it's that men are just as emotional as women. Probably more so, because a lot of them don't know how to deal with their feelings like big boys. Please correct me if I'm wrong on that front."

I watched a grown-ass man stomp his feet and scream like my four-year-olds over the ref's decision not fifteen minutes ago, so, no, I can't say he's wrong there, either.

"And three," he keeps going, "I've dated some men who were more high-maintenance than any pop diva has been rumoured to be, and *I'm* the twink."

I recall the things Dad told me about Connor's ex, who he had been living with when Dad first met him, and cringe internally. "Sorry," I apologise, feeling like a chastised little kid. I wish I could get away with toeing the ground and offering him puppy eyes like Huddy and Prez do. Somehow, I don't think he'd find me anywhere near as adorable. "I was just venting."

He softens and his cheeks flush. "I know. And I know you're not actually a sexist dick—"

"Even though he was totally a manwhore until the kids came along?" Brett chimes in helpfully, and I give him the finger while Connor snorts.

"Even then," he teases lightly. "But…stuff like that? It's a trigger for me, so I get a little…intense."

It takes me a moment to understand that he has probably been accused of being girly over the years, and with that comes the very stereotypes I just threw out there about dating women.

Yeah, I'm still a dick sometimes, apparently. Great. What is it Leo sees in me, if he even still does?

And we're back to Leo again.

"It was a dumb thing to say," I acknowledge, prepared to grovel. "But you hit the nail on the head just now. I've never dated anyone before: women or men. I'm clueless and I feel like I've already messed it all up by giving him too much space or whatever."

"Hmm," Connor picks his gym bag up and throws the strap

Chapter Nineteen — Jack

over his left shoulder, and by unspoken agreement the guys and I fall into step with him as he starts leading the way out of the indoor sports complex. "So, I think Will's right in a way. I think you need to talk to Leo. But…I wouldn't text."

"No?" Evan asks before I can, and I shoot him a curious glance over my shoulder.

"No," Con agrees. "It's been, what, almost three weeks now, right? A text is going to be too little, too late."

I frown. "But—"

"He asked for space. Yeah, I know." He pauses and exhales slowly. "He's also a guy whose life experiences to date have shown him that it's easier to be the one to cut ties and control his own heartache." He arches an eyebrow at me as we cross the threshold of the sports complex's door and step into the cooling early evening air outside. It feels good on my heated skin. "I know you didn't experience the sort of rejection that he has, but you didn't date beyond casual hookups for a reason, Jack."

I stop short midway across the parking lot, gravel crunching pleasantly under my sneakers. "How'd you…"

"Really? Because I don't think commitment-phobes are afraid of the companionship or the sex on tap. I reckon they're afraid of not having control of their feelings. They're afraid of having their hearts hurt."

"To be fair," Brett adds, still following us even though I can see his car parked on the opposite side of the lot, "some people avoid commitment because they have FOMO and they feel like 'settling,'" he emphasises the word with finger quotes, "means they're missing out on God only knows what opportunities, or that they're choosing the wrong person or whatever." There's derision in his tone and I'm not used to my jovial friend sounding so bitter. "Relationships are *mundane* to them. Or they're against the idea of any kind of responsibility and losing their independence."

Connor's keys jangle as he fishes them out of the side pocket of his gym bag, and he's clearly not as curious about Brett's sudden emphatic anger as I am. He's too busy proving his point. He leans against the side of his SUV and asks, "Yeah, well, do you think Jack's like that?"

Brett and Evan both shake their heads and Connor smirks. "Neither do I. So, that leaves my hypothesis…which was right, by the way." He looks over at me. "Wasn't it?"

I shrug. "Pretty much, yeah." I'll never admit it out loud, but Brett was kind of right about the responsibility thing, too. That passed the second I realised I was a dad, though. There's no greater responsibility than raising kids, as far as I'm concerned. After that, what's so scary about maintaining a relationship?

Connor bobs his head. "So, I'd say Leo's feeling similar. You also said he was a bit wary about your age gap. Maybe remind him to look at my relationship with Will, yeah? Because our age gap is bigger."

Evan snorts. "Are we playing 'mine is bigger than yours' now?"

Connor waggles his eyebrows at him. "Don't start a competition you'll lose, man."

"Okay," I forcibly drag the conversation back on track while I try not to laugh at Evan's playfully affronted expression, "so you're saying that I should go talk to him?" My heart thuds rapidly in my chest as the thought turns from a suggestion to a likely reality.

"Jack." Connor's tone is firm and, even though he's shorter

Chapter Nineteen — Jack

and smaller than me, and only a couple of years older, he's definitely got that whole 'stepdad' authority going on right now. I straighten up and meet his gaze. "Do you miss him?" I nod. "Do you care about him?"

What kind of a dumb-ass question is that? Would I be beating myself up over having let him walk out of my home if I didn't? Would my heart be hammering inside my ribcage over the thought of talking to him again if I didn't? Would I be pining for him to come home and complete my family with the boys if I didn't?

"I love him," I snap back as the irritation at having been asked such a stupid question gets the better of me. "Of *course* I care about him."

Silence descends on our little group, broken only by the low buzz of insects and the white noise of traffic from the nearby road.

I'm about to apologise for my harsh tone when it hits me that the silence isn't because I got shitty with them. It's because of *what* I said.

"I love him," I repeat in awe, realisation sweeping over me in a rush. Even though I'd felt myself falling that last night we'd made love, I was convinced that I'd stopped myself from going any further. I'd been falling, but I hadn't fallen. I'd been safe. *Womp-womp.* Apparently, I'm still the master of denial, because putting those three words out there lifts a weight from my chest that I hadn't even known was there.

I love Leo.

"Then you've gotta talk to him," Connor repeats with empathy.

I can't argue with that.

Chapter Twenty – Leo

"Can you teach me how to contour?" Vi asks from where she has leapt up onto the countertop, swinging her legs as she waits none too patiently for my answer.

From where he's pushing veggies around a wok with a plastic spatula, Toby snorts. "Vi, honey, I didn't think you were interested in makeup. Last I checked, you said it was all some kind of conspiracy to make girls feel like they're not good enough as they are." He turns and looks over his shoulder at his daughter. "Which I'm pretty sure you read online."

She shrugs. "Well, I'm changing my mind. Leo wears makeup sometimes and it's cool."

I've only been living here a few days and I'm just as surprised by her change in attitude as Toby seems to be. As far as I knew, Vi was more into traditionally masculine pursuits than feminine ones. She's the kind of kid my mum would have haughtily called a tomboy. But she's right: she's totally allowed to change her mind or interests if she wants to.

Chapter Twenty — Leo

I share a quick glance with Toby and his expression is full of amusement. With Vi's back turned, he bats his eyelashes at me, reminding me of his theory that she's got a crush on me. I want to make a face at him, but she's still watching me and waiting for my reply, so I can't flip him off or anything.

"I can teach you if your dad says it's okay," I finally reply, and she spins on the countertop to beg and plead until Toby relents.

With her back to me, I give him the finger.

"No makeup at school," he finally says, and the rest of his rules are lost to her gleeful cheers as she hugs him and leaps around in excitement.

Preteens are something else.

Vi's just turning around with a wide, expectant smile when the doorbell rings. It echoes off the tiled floors in its *very* dated chimed tune, and Toby and I both jolt at the sound.

"Expecting anyone?" I ask him, and he shakes his head.

"No. You?"

The flat expression I give him in response should be answer enough.

He chuckles and flicks the burner on the stove off, moving the wok aside while I start making my way through the kitchen and towards the entry hallway. Ever playful, Toby hurries to catch up with me, nudging me out of the way. We push and shove each other, laughing like five-year-olds as we fight over who gets to open the door.

He wins and turns the handle, swinging it open and blocking the open doorway with his taller, broader frame.

"So, here's the thing," I hear a familiar voice say, his deep timbre and sexy accent firing up my nerves even though I can't see him, "I'm just putting it out there before I lose my nerve."

"Jack," Toby tries to interrupt him, and I peer underneath the tanned arm which is holding the door open to see Jack on the other side of the threshold, staring at his feet and biting his lip.

He takes a steadying breath and continues talking to his shoes. "I miss you, Leo. So badly. And I know you asked for space, but I couldn't leave it another day..."

"Jack..." Toby tries to cut in again, and I can hear the building amusement in his voice. Behind him, I can't see the smirk on his face, but I know it's there.

Unfortunately, Jack is clearly in his own head right now. His words have made my stomach flip over and my heart race, though.

He misses me.

I miss him, too. So, so much.

"...and I realised that, even though we never really dated or anything, you've been the most important romantic relationship I've ever had and," he swallows roughly and finally starts to lift his head, "I lov—*ah! Shit!*"

Toby loses it, leaning against the open doorframe as he cackles in delight. "Hi to you, too," he teases, while the visible skin of Jack's face turns red with embarrassment. Then, finally, Toby steps back and pushes me forward. "I think this one's for you," he adds playfully, then pats my shoulder. "Have fun. I think Vi and I might go out for dinner tonight. The stir-fry looked a bit lacklustre now I come to think of it." He shoots me a wink and then wanders away before I can protest. Or thank him. Or both.

"So, um," Jack clears his throat and my attention swivels back to him. He shuffles awkwardly on the doorstep, all six

Chapter Twenty — Leo

feet something of him, looking delicious in a tight, black t-shirt and painted-on jeans. But the expression on his face makes him seem so much younger and more vulnerable than the confident, sexy Adonis I know him to be. "How much of that did you get to hear, anyway?"

Instead of answering with words like any sane person might do, I launch myself at him. He stumbles back but manages to catch himself, and me, as we collide. My legs wrap around his waist and while his hands instinctively shift beneath my butt to support my weight, I kiss him like my life depends on it.

It's like I'm coming up for air for the first time in months. I've been submerged beneath the mire of my inappropriate feelings for him. I've been drowning under all the negative thoughts —*I'm too young for him. It'll upset the boys. He's just experimenting. He doesn't do long-term relationships. What will his family and friends say?*— but after hearing his short yet impassioned speech, those thoughts have been silenced. Plus, Jack's lips on mine are life-giving.

As our tongues tangle and our breathing mingles, my head turns all floaty and light. My heart beats rapidly, and I am giddy with joy. Excitement thrills through my veins. I feel alive in a way I haven't since the last time we kissed.

"I love you," I tell him when we part for air. I have to blink back unexpected tears, however happy, as the weight of my confession hits me. But Jack's hands tighten their hold on me, and his smile and the answering sheen in his eyes reassures me that I haven't made a mistake. "We're doing this all arse-backwards, I know, but…"

"I love you, too, princess," he says with a delighted, if slightly unhinged, chuckle. "Even if you totally stole my thunder just now. *I* was making the big declaration."

"Yeah," I snort, "to *Toby*."

I yelp as he playfully smacks my butt, and I cling tighter to him lest he get any wise ideas about dropping me.

"I was nervous," Jack sulks. "The door opened, and I had to say everything I was thinking before I chickened out. I don't know why I didn't think about what I'd do if Toby answered the door."

It's the sweetest, cutest admission ever. I can't resist pecking his lips in a quick, chaste kiss before resting my forehead against his. "I mean," I snicker lightly, "it's Toby's house…"

"Shut up," there's no venom in his complaint, just a bit of embarrassment, "I was in the moment."

"It was sweet," I acknowledge, taking pity on him. Then I sober up a bit. "I've missed you, too." The lingering pain of being ignored for almost three weeks sets in and I unwrap my legs from his waist and he helps me back onto my feet. "We should talk."

Before Jack can leap to any conclusions that I'm going to mess him around or tell him that kissing him and declaring my feelings was a mistake, I take his hand and lead him inside. He closes the front door behind him and we cross paths with Toby and Vi who are now heading towards the garage.

Vi narrows her eyes up at Jack before she smiles sweetly at me. "Dad's taking me out for sushi, but he said you can teach me how to contour when we get back."

"Later," Toby stresses. "I said 'later'. Maybe another day, kiddo."

She shrugs, completely ignoring him. "So, will you?"

I laugh. "I need to replenish my supplies and get you your own set of makeup brushes, so let's set some time on the weekend, hmm?"

Chapter Twenty — Leo

Vi tosses her hair over her shoulder and sighs dramatically. "Fine. I guess I can wait." She gives Jack the stink eye again. "I get him on the weekend."

Jack sputters for a second while Toby gently admonishes his daughter for her attitude. She's still complaining that she made plans with me first as he guides her through the internal door to the garage, and it's not until we hear the car's engine rumble to life and the sound of the automatic garage door squeaking and rolling up that Jack starts to laugh.

"Guess I've gotta get in line, huh?" he asks with a sexy grin.

I almost forget that we have issues to resolve. Now that we're alone in the house, it's much more tempting to drag him into my room and push him to his knees on the soft carpet.

Clearing my throat, I shrug lightly. "What can I say? I'm in demand."

"That's because you're awesome," he responds, wrapping his arms around my waist as he tugs me towards him. I go willingly while he continues. "You're clever, and funny, and sweet. You're hot as fuck and when you get all bossy? God..." He chuckles and shakes his head, then brushes his lips over my forehead. His beard tickles, but I love the sensation. "How could anyone not want you?"

"About that," with my hands planted on his chest, I push myself away with reluctance. "We really do have to talk."

"I'm sorry," he blurts before I can even tug him towards the living room. "You asked for space and I should have at least sent you a text or whatever, but I didn't know if that would be coming on too strong or breaking my promise to give you space and I left it too long, didn't I?"

"Yeah, you did," I answer honestly. "But that's on me. I should have given you some sort of time limit or sent you a text when I was ready to talk." And this is the thing, isn't it? Jack and I have been so good with communicating and anticipating each other's needs that we both took it for granted.

"Yeah, well, you've got a history of being rejected and hurt. I don't. I should have known better."

"I think we both dropped the ball." It's a relief to put that out there, so much so that I smile at him. "I should have understood that whatever was going on with us was new for you, and not just because I'm a guy. And I should have been clearer about what giving me space meant. But you could have asked, too. Or at least sent me an update about the boys." I can't help the way my throat tightens when I say that last bit. My eyes fill up and the pang of loss hits me harder than I expected.

They're not my kids. I have no rights where they're concerned.

And yet...

"They miss you so damn much, baby," Jack interrupts my thoughts, fishing his phone from his pocket and bringing up his photos app. He holds the device out to me and I start flipping through the photos with avid interest, soaking in every little detail.

"How were they on the flight?" I ask him when I get to photos of their promised weekend in Melbourne.

It sucks that I missed it.

Once they'd learned it was happening, Preston couldn't stop talking about going on a plane, and Hudson had decided that he wanted to be a pilot. We'd spent a lot of time Googling about planes and flying after that.

Jack's expression becomes pained, if only fleetingly. "Prez threw a tantrum because you weren't there," he admits. "We

Chapter Twenty – Leo

compromised and he got to take as many pictures on his camera as he wanted, with the promise that he can show you when you come over to see them. So, um, prepare for a few hundred blurry pictures of the inside of an A320."

I snort, but it comes out as a sob.

"Fuck, I'm sorry," Jack apologises again, then he pulls me into his arms for a strong hug. "I should have just—"

"No," I try to pull myself together. I clear my throat and take deep, measured breaths, enjoying the calming scent of his cologne. It's just as I remembered it: spicy, but with mellow notes. "No more 'should haves'. It's done."

"Please tell me you'll come home," Jack pleads into my hair and my heart squeezes.

It would be so easy to agree. To allow him to help me repack my few possessions and take me back to his apartment. But I can't do that.

I shake my head.

"Why not?" The way he whines the question makes me think of his sons and I chuckle wetly.

"We need to do this whole thing properly," I insist, hating myself for being the voice of reason. At least it's easier to put this all out there without having to see the disappointment on his handsome face. "You said it yourself: I've got a history of being hurt, and the last time came from moving way too fast with my ex." He tenses, so I quickly continue, "And you've never really done the dating thing before. I think it would be better for both of us to experience a more traditional kind of relationship."

Jack's quiet for a long moment, but I give him the time to process what I'm saying. As much as I want to move back in with him and the boys, I know it would be healthier for both of us to take things slowly.

Well.

Not *too* slowly.

"To be clear, I don't mean that I don't want to sleep with you," the embarrassing words are tumbling from my lips before my brain can catch up with my mouth.

His laughter rumbles up from his chest. "Oh?" he sounds amused and I bury my face into his shirt. His arms tighten around me.

"I just…I just think we should date. Get to know each other socially, while I'm working a job taking care of kids that aren't yours and while you get to have some space away from me when you're at home. But, y'know, the horse has already bolted on the whole 'falling in love' thing, so…"

"So sex is still on the table?" I can still hear him smirking, the bastard.

"I was thinking in a bed, but we can probably do it on the table, too." I yelp as he lifts me off the ground again, encouraging me to wrap my legs around him like I did earlier.

"Thank God," he says, backing me against the hallway wall and kissing me hungrily. "Because I'd totally wait for you to be ready, but…" he grinds his bulge into me and it's my time to smirk.

"Did someone else miss me?" I tease.

"Uh-huh. Turns out my hand isn't good enough anymore."

Just the thought of him jerking himself off has me going from half mast to completely hard within seconds. "Fuck, Jack."

"Well, that's what I'm hoping you'll do, yeah."

"*Jack*," his name comes out on a groan, and I'm unable to resist the images he's put in my head. "Bedroom. Now."

Chapter Twenty — Leo

Instead of putting me down so I can lead the way, he turns on his heel and demands, "Directions?"

Laughing, I guide him towards my room and he carries me as though I weigh nothing, proving that his big, broad body isn't just for show. One day, I'll encourage him to pin me down underneath his bulk and fuck me senseless, but today is not that day.

I bounce on the mattress when he drops me onto it while he simultaneously toes out of his shoes, but we're barely separated for a few seconds before he's clambering over me, his hands tugging up my t-shirt while his mouth fuses itself to mine again. His fervour is endearing, but I don't want to rush this.

Covering his hands, I still his frantic movements. "We've got time," I murmur against his lips. "I'm not going anywhere. And," I rub my nose against his affectionately, "I'm not setting any limits this time. No more 'one night only', I promise."

"Thank fuck for that," he whispers back, before kissing me again.

This time, the kiss is softer and sweeter. His tongue begs entrance into my mouth and I part my lips willingly for him. I sigh happily as our tongues reconnect, slowly caressing each other, and he grinds his clothed erection against mine in the same rhythm.

It's not long before I curse myself for telling him to slow down, my body ramping up its desire to rut against him —*in him*— and come hard. My own words echo inside my head: *we've got time*. Making out with Jack is addictive, even more so now that it doesn't feel forbidden or like we're crossing a line. He's my boyfriend now. We've exchanged the big, scary I-love-yous.

Yeah, we've done this all backwards. We started with the fucking, declared our love, and *then* agreed to start dating, but somehow it feels right for us.

"Baby," Jack pants as he pulls away from our ongoing kiss, "I need you inside me."

It still boggles my mind that this big, burly fireman wants twinky little me to top him, but I love that this dynamic works for us. I love that Jack's never been ashamed to tell me that it's what he wants, that despite looking the part of an alphahole, he's anything but. Some part of me wonders if I have Will's influence to thank for that, but thinking about my friend while I'm about to fuck his son is probably not a great idea, so I shelve the thought for the time being.

"Roll over," I instruct, and Jack complies without hesitation, flopping onto his back beside me.

"Too many clothes," he complains, reaching for my shirt as I climb onto my knees, preparing to straddle his thighs.

I laugh and reach behind my head, tugging the offending item up and off my body, throwing it to the floor.

Jack's hands move to the waistband of my jeans and deftly pop the button. He nibbles at his lower lip and looks up at me from beneath hooded eyelids, his eyelashes sinfully long and dark and almost too pretty — a stark contrast to his otherwise rugged appearance.

"Are you wearing them?" he asks me in a voice turned gravelly with need.

I frown for a moment. "Wearing what?"

His calloused fingertips dip beneath the denim band, teasing the soft skin of my lower belly. "The lace, princess."

My cheeks heat, but I nod. Unless I'm at work, I always wear my panties these days. They make me feel sexy, empowered,

Chapter Twenty — Leo

and like I have a secret from the rest of the world. They also remind me of Jack's reaction to them, and I've found wearing them has made being separated from him a little easier to bear (even though you'd think it would have been the opposite).

The way Jack moans and bucks his hips makes me glad for the choice, though.

"Fuck, Leo," he all but whines, "I need to see them. To see you in them. Now. Please, baby. *Please*."

There's that feeling of empowerment again. It rushes through me, pulling my lips up into a grin I can't contain. Just the thought of seeing me in my skimpy, lacy underwear has reduced this big, hyper-masculine man to begging and writhing on my bed.

Taking pity on him, I shuffle back off the mattress and stand at the foot of the bed. Boldly, I tease him with the slowest lowering of my zipper *ever*, delighting in the way he props himself up on his elbows to watch me intently. His blue eyes are dark with lust and it looks like he's attempting to use x-ray vision on the crotch of my jeans with how laser-focused his gaze is.

"Princess," he pleads, "don't leave me hanging."

If I wasn't out of my mind with how horny I feel right now, I'd probably make some kind of pun about that.

"Patience, honey," I practically purr at him, finally hooking my fingers into my waistband and pushing the figure-hugging denim down over my hips, thighs, and to the floor. I watch what I'm doing as I step out of them and, when I look back up, it's my turn to smother a groan of approval.

Jack is watching me with that same burning intensity in his blue gaze, but he's undone his own jeans and has let his cock distend the soft cotton of his boxer briefs through the gaping fly. He rubs himself unashamedly as he takes in the sight of me wearing my black, lacy boy shorts.

"Turn around, princess," he demands, his voice low and sensual.

Doing as he says, I turn to face the wall and, because I'm a tease, I arch my back, giving him the best possible view of my butt, popping it out in what I hope is an enticing way. I can feel the lace stretching with the movement, tightening against the curves of my cheeks, hopefully emphasising their shape. With the amount of yoga I do, it should look damn good framed by the lace's scalloped edges.

Unable to help myself, I peek over my shoulder to sneak a glance at Jack. A gasp escapes me as he groans and fists his freed cock, then his eyes meet mine.

"You're so fucking hot, Leo," he practically growls, stroking his length slowly. I can't help focusing on the movement of his hand, or on the glistening tip of his erection, his precum dribbling out with every pass of his fist. "Now turn back around so I can see that sexy-as-fuck dick of yours."

Any concerns I might have had about him enjoying me in lace because of its feminine qualities vanish at those delicious words. He knows I'm a man and he wants every part of me. I already knew that, of course, but the reminder after so many months of uncertainty is nice.

No, it's better than nice.

It's just what I needed to hear.

I hadn't known it until this moment, but my niggling fears about his desire being temporary or in spite of my sex clearly needed to be put to rest, and he's managed that without even realising it. While telling me he wanted me inside him again went a long way towards achieving it, it took hearing him

Chapter Twenty — Leo

admit that he finds my dick sexy to fully trust my instincts.

"You want my cock?" I ask him, feeling bold and empowered all over again. The appendage in question strains at its lacy confines, leaking and desperate for his attention. I trail my hand down my chest and over my abdomen slowly, watching as his eyes track its motion. Much as he did a few moments ago, I rub my bulge over the material, squeezing it for a little relief as I do. "Want this?"

"Yes. Yes, please. Inside me. Toys don't feel anywhere near as good."

His babbling spurs me on, igniting a fire deep inside me. "What kind of toys, honey?"

A blush travels over his chest and up his neck. It kisses his ears and rests on his cheeks. "I bought a dildo," he confesses, making my heart race. "W-with a suction-cup base."

My eyes flutter shut as I imagine him riding the silicone toy. "I'm going to want to see it in action," I tell him, forcing my eyes back open so I can pin him with what feels like a heated stare. "And maybe you can use it on me, too."

"Fuck, Leo…" His fingers flex and tighten over his shaft. "You're gonna make me come before you're even on the damn bed with me."

"Mmm, one day I want to watch that."

But not today.

I go to remove my panties but Jack shakes his head. "Leave them. I want to pull them off."

I have no reason to deny him, so I don't. I climb back onto the mattress as he launches into action, scrambling to shuck his jeans and underwear. They hit the carpet with a dull, crumpled-sounding thud, and I can't help but enjoy the sight of him spread out on my bed, naked and wanting.

He's every bit as big and broad as I remember, with his dark tattoos standing out on his tanned skin. He's let the hair on his chest grow a little wild, almost hiding the ink over his pecs, and his beard is decadently full. He's kind of a bear of a man and he's willingly submitting to me.

Me.

Twinky, much younger, makeup-and-lace-wearing *me.*

This man could literally throw me over his shoulder like a sack of potatoes, but instead he wants me to set the pace. He wants me to rock into his bigger, stronger, arguably more traditionally masculine body and fuck him to orgasm. He wants *me* to control *his* pleasure.

God, I love him.

Jack's fingers hook into the thin waistband of my panties and he rubs the material between his thumb and index finger. Lust-darkened blue eyes look up at me and he says, "I just want to rip them from your sexy body…but they look so good on you that it would be a waste."

Precum leaks from my slit and wets the lace, turning the spot where the fabric is straining all shiny and slick. "I can buy more," I reply, sounding throaty to my own ears. "My previous employer paid me very well."

His answering chuckle is deep and rich with affection. "He sounds like a good man."

"Mmm," I pretend to consider it, "he's okay. A bit slow on the follow-through, though."

"Oh, is that so?"

There's no time to respond before he's propped himself on his side and has grabbed handfuls of lace on either side of my hips. A ridiculously sexy growl emanates from his throat and the tendons in his tattooed forearms draw tight as he tugs.

Chapter Twenty – Leo

The delicate fabric tears under his assault and he pulls the ruined panties from my body and tosses them over his shoulder. "How's that for follow-through?"

Instead of answering, I tackle him to the mattress, kissing him as I move to position my body over his. The moist head of his dick rubs my belly and I'm briefly distracted by it until I remember that I am on a mission.

When I pull back from the kiss, I lean over to open the drawer of my bedside table and pluck out my half-empty bottle of lube and a condom.

"Do we need that?" Jack asks me, his gaze drifting to the little foil square. "I've never…" he clears his throat. "Despite the twins' existence suggesting otherwise, I've only ever used condoms and I…I get tested every six months for work. Anyway," his Adam's apple bobs and his expression turns earnest, "I'm negative, and if I was gonna have unprotected sex with anyone, it would be with the person I love, right? I mean, if you were comfortable with it."

Oh, my heart.

"I'm negative, too," I assure him as my heart thunders in my chest, "and I haven't gone bare before, either. So…yeah, I'd, um, I'd love that. With you." I add the last two words in case my feelings weren't clear. Then, toying with the lube, I add, "But that means I'd be coming inside you." A thought that's way hotter than it has any right being, but there's every chance he won't feel the same way. "You're sure—"

"Leo," he cuts me off, his smile gentle and warm. "Why do you think I asked? I don't want any barriers between us and I want to feel you when you come. Mark me up inside, baby. I'm all yours."

The condom is sent flying to parts unknown as I launch

myself at Jack all over again. I practically maul his mouth with my own, all restraint having fled my senses. It's nothing but primal need and desperation now.

The kiss is far from perfect as we roll about on top of the sheets, lost in the sudden, overwhelming urgency to connect in every way possible. It's sloppy, and our teeth clack, and I'm pretty sure I'm getting beard burn from the intensity of our faces rubbing together.

While we writhe, our cocks also seek attention and I'm more than aware that we're both hard as steel and leaking all over each other. Occasionally, our erections brush against one another and each time sends jolts of pure desire racing through my veins.

Somewhere along the line, I have the presence of mind to grab the lube from where it has rolled to a stop beside my knee. I wrench my mouth away from Jack's and start to kiss a path down the strong planes of his chest, hair and all, and over his firm abdomen.

His cock, thick and practically pulsing, seems to reach for me as I finish peppering kisses over the top of his Adonis belt, and I take a moment to reacquaint myself with it. The uncut flesh has slid back to reveal the darkly purpled head, sticky and glistening and begging for my mouth.

As with the rest of Jack, I just can't say no to it.

He practically arches off the bed as I hold the base and then wrap my lips around the tip of his cock, licking and sucking on it like a lollipop. The salty, tangy taste of him makes me hum happily. Jack's fingers thread into my hair.

"Oh, baby, I've missed your mouth," he declares, rocking his hips gently. "Fuck, it's like you were made for sucking my cock."

Chapter Twenty — Leo

I want to tell him that I think I was, but that would involve removing the appendage from my mouth, and I'm not willing to do that right now. Instead, I uncap the lube with my free hand, delighting in the familiar *click*. Proving that perhaps I'm too experienced with one-handed manoeuvring of the bottle in question, I manage to upend it until a sufficient amount of viscous liquid has gathered in my palm, then turn it upright again and snap the cap shut, all without pulling away from Jack's dick.

I manage to spread the lube from my palm to my fingers and Jack spreads his legs without me even needing to ask. His hips buck upwards in a silent invitation to hurry this along and I smirk around the shaft in my mouth.

"Please," he begs me when two of my slick fingers circle his rim, "Leo, I need—*yes*." The 's' turns long and sibilant, drawn out as he bears down on my fingers, his greedy hole practically sucking the digits inside.

"More," he begs, raising himself on his elbows to look down the length of his body at me. "Give me more. I don't want to come until you're inside me, but if you keep sucking my cock like that…" He trails off with a groan, his eyes fluttering shut while I dip my tongue into his slit.

Using his distraction, I add a third finger. He hisses a little, and I pause and give him time to acclimate before he rocks his hips again, alternating between bearing down on my fingers and thrusting up into my mouth.

"I'm getting fucking close," he growls out. "Leo. Fuck me. *Now*. I'm ready."

I can't help laughing lightly as I release his spit-slicked dick and sit back, resting my butt on my heels. "You're a toppy bottom, aren't you?"

He flops back onto the mattress with a huff. "I swear to God, Leo, if you don't put your dick inside me, I'm flipping you over and riding you hard."

"Don't threaten me with a good time," I sass him, slicking my cock up with a little more lube. He raises back up onto his elbows when I bring my leaking tip to his entrance, and I'm torn between watching his expression or watching his body take me in.

In the end, I settle on watching the rapture play out over his features, realising with a start that this is the first time we're doing this face to face, not counting the frotting on his couch which kickstarted our crazy not-relationship.

Back then, I never would have imagined that we would be exchanging declarations of love. I certainly never would have guessed that I would ever see him spread out underneath me, writhing on my cock and begging for more.

But that's what's happening right now.

Thick, hairy thighs lock around my hips as Jack arches his back, encouraging me to sink all the way inside his welcoming heat. It's almost overwhelming feeling his channel without the latex to dull the sensations. He's tight and warm and gripping my shaft so perfectly that I'm convinced this will be over within a couple of embarrassingly short minutes.

"I love your dick," he grunts as I start to thrust back and forth. His hands, previously gripping the sheets at his sides, traverse the lightly haired skin of my arms and then toy with the fair hair across my pecs. "And your chest hair." He gasps when I change the angle of my movements and graze his prostate, "Baby, I love your chest hair."

I'd snort in amusement, but there's a soft, vulnerable twist to his expression that tells me he hadn't meant to blurt the

Chapter Twenty — Leo

confession out.

"So," I pant, grateful for the distraction from the overwhelming pleasure of his arse practically milking my cock, "no waxing for me, then?"

"Don't you fucking dare!" The hand which had been exploring my chest snakes behind my neck and yanks me down towards him, where his lips claim mine in a bruising kiss. "The hair is hot as fuck. It's like a secret treas—*oh!*" His thighs tighten around me as his back curves off the mattress once more. "Fuck, Leo, do that again."

All thoughts about manscaping are forgotten while I do as requested, nudging his prostate again and again with every increased snap of my hips. Words disappear, replaced by gasps and groans and wet kisses. At some point, Jack's hand sneaks between our bodies and he strokes his weeping cock in time with my thrusts.

"Fuck," he mutters, rolling his hips, curving his spine again. His skin glistens with sweat, and his eyes squeeze shut. "I'm coming. Shit, fuck, Leo, I…" Whatever he was about to say is replaced by an unintelligible shout of pleasure. His abdomen tightens at the same time as his cum sprays between us, streaks of it landing on both our bellies and even a little in his beard.

I'd be tempted to lick that up, but the clenching around my cock is too hard to ignore, and my orgasm tears through me with a similar intensity to his.

"Oh my God," Jack bucks against me as my cock pulses, "that feels so good, you filling me up like that."

Breathing hard, I hold my position just a little longer, relishing in the new feelings surrounding my slowly softening dick. I eventually pull out slowly, but I can't resist spreading his legs further apart to stare at the mess I've made.

There's something primal inside me that's stupidly proud of seeing my cum slowly leaking from inside him.

"One day," Jack says in that low, seductive tone of his, "you'll have to get a plug to keep it all inside me."

Jesus fucking Christ, who is this man? And how did I get lucky enough to find him?

I swallow roughly at the ideas he's putting in my head and tear my gaze away from his hole to meet his eyes. His smirk is self-satisfied and knowing. "Like that idea?" he asks me.

"You know I do."

"Good," he flops back onto the bed and I crawl back up alongside him, nestling myself in the crook of his outstretched arm, uncaring of the sticky mess I'm spreading over his side. "Because one day? I'm gonna do the same to you."

A slow smile tugs my lips upwards, and I crane my neck, angling for a kiss. "I can't wait."

But that's kind of a lie, because for Jack? I'd wait forever.

Luckily, though, I don't have to.

Epilogue – Jack

"Daddy..."

"Shh."

"But, Daddy..."

"Huddy, we've been over this."

"But..."

"What, bud?" I sigh and turn my attention towards my son. He's squirming in his tan-coloured cargo pants and white linen shirt.

"I gotta pee."

Mom snorts from where she's not-so-surreptitiously waiting around the corner to whisk the boys away once they've done their job. I fight the urge to pinch the bridge of my nose.

Never work with animals or children, they say. And this is why.

"Go...pee in the bush over there," I tell him, pointing to the shrubbery lining the driveway.

He scrunches his nose at me, shifting from side to side in his shiny dress shoes. "But Toby has a toilet inside. I know, 'cos one time, Grampa broughted us here and Prez had an accident and Grampa said why didn't we use the toilet here and we didn't know there was one so—"

Mom is giggling from her hiding spot while I hold up my hand and shake my head. "Okay, okay, I get it. But we're here to surprise Leo, remember?"

It was a great plan in theory. Leo and I have spent the last six months dating. He was a bit awkward with Mom when I introduced him as my boyfriend, but after she fell over herself apologising for accidentally chasing him away, he came back out of his shell and, as with Dad, has become good friends with her. So, when I told her that I miss having him at home with me and the boys, she suggested 'The Grand Gesture Moment'…which brings us to why me and the boys are standing uninvited on Toby and Leo's doorstep with signs that read 'Please Move Back In With Us'.

"I'm gonna give him a bad surprise if he doesn't hurry," Hudson insists, much to his brother's (and grandmother's) amusement.

"Nobody's surprising anyone with the racket you're all making," Toby's voice cuts in and my attention shifts to the open doorway while my heart lurches. I scramble to right my sign, but Toby shakes his head and holds his hand up in the universal 'stop' signal. "Hold your horses, it's just me."

"Toby! Can I go pee in your toilet?" Hudson yells the question, because of course he does.

Toby snickers and steps aside. "Be my guest."

"I gotta go, too!" Preston declares and takes off after his brother as they both race inside the house.

Their signs, complete with drawings they made of our apartment with Leo joining us for our usual domestic activities, lay

Epilogue – Jack

discarded on the front lawn. I sigh and pick them up.

From inside the house I hear Preston's chipmunk-like voice squeal, "Leo! You gotta go outside! Daddy is gonna ask you to live with us as a surprise!"

Mom loses it, collapsing against the side of the house in a fit of hysterics as my shoulders slump and I look down at my feet. "Include the boys, you said. It'll be sweet, you said." I look back up to give her a withering glare. "This is the last time I listen to your suggestions."

"Awww, but it's so cute," Leo says from the doorway where Toby had been leaning only moments ago. He gestures over his shoulder. "He's gone to help the boys." Then, cocking his head, he looks at the pieces of cardboard dangling uselessly at my side. "Well? Aren't I getting my *Love Actually* moment? Only, y'know, without the creepy 'trying to steal my best friend's partner' vibes."

"I…" My cheeks flush. "The boys were supposed to do the sales pitch." We'd practised for days.

"Getting your cute four-year-olds to do all the work for you? Tsk-tsk, Mr Bradford."

Mom snorts again.

"Hey, Jen," Leo leans his sexy body around the corner of the entryway to wave at her.

This whole thing has gone really pear-shaped.

"Just…please move in with me?" I ask him, feeling ridiculous and a little deflated.

The corners of his lips twitch. "Now try that with the signs."

"I swear to God, Leo…"

Hudson comes running back outside before I can finish my threat and he grabs one of the signs, holding it up to face Leo. His reads 'With Us?' and he's standing on my right side now,

257

where he should be on my left.

"See?!" he demands of the man who is arguably his favourite person in the whole world. "We made the surprise pretty like you! Will you come live with us again?"

"Hey!" Preston cries before Leo can answer, and he tears out of the house to grab his sign. There are water stains on his shirt and pants, and his hair is all messed up. He holds his 'Please Move' sign upside down, and the stick figure drawings of the family eating dinner together are now recreating that scene from *Mary Poppins* which the boys love so much. It's kind of fitting, really. "I get to ask him!"

"That's not what we practised!" Hudson argues back hotly. "*Daddy* gets to ask!"

"But you already asked!" Preston whines.

Hanging my head, I gesture for Prez to get on with it. "You can ask, too."

"Good." He huffs, then looks at Leo with a sweet smile, like he wasn't just on the verge of a meltdown. "Will you come live with us again? But you gotta share Daddy's room, 'cause he said me and Huddy will get our own rooms…which is dumb, 'cause we play together, but he said—"

"That's enough explaining," I cut him off and hang my head. "I could have done this romantically over dinner, but noooo…"

"Daddy," Hudson nudges me. "Hold up your sign."

Ignoring my mother's ongoing giggles, I hold up my 'Back In' sign and force myself to look back over at Leo. His amusement has faded and his smile is wobbly, his eyes suspiciously wet. Suddenly, this does feel romantic again, imperfections and all. Maybe it's even more perfect for all the chaos, because that's how our lives will probably be for a while.

"The boys and I miss you living with us," I tell him softly,

Epilogue – Jack

smiling as he brings his hand to his chest. "You're part of our family, Leo Martin, and we want you to come home officially and forever. Not as a nanny, but as my partner and equal. So…what do you say?"

"I want nothing more than that," he answers, sniffling through happy tears. "I love you all so much!"

The boys cheer and throw their cardboard to the ground, racing forward and tackling his legs. "And maybe," Preston says, "you and Daddy can get married like Grampa and Grampa Connor, and—"

"—and then we can call you Papa, and have a Daddy and a Papa like Vicky does," Hudson adds with excitement while my heart seizes.

It's not a fear of commitment or even of marriage, but a fear that maybe that's going to push Leo too far, too fast.

Everything about our relationship has been unconventional, though, so it really shouldn't surprise me when he grins up at me and says, "I'll have to talk to your daddy about that, but I'd love it very much."

"Can we call you Papa now?" Preston asks with wide eyes, and I'm not surprised that my mom's giggles have now turned to quiet sobs. Even my eyes are feeling a little moist.

"If your daddy's okay with that," Leo tells him.

Hudson cheers and hugs him tightly around his hips. "Yay! Now we have a Mummy, a Daddy, *and* a Papa!" he grins up at us both, oblivious to the tears and soft expressions Leo and I are sharing. "Does that mean we can have a baby sister, too?"

I can feel the colour draining from my face at the prospect, but Leo swoops in with the save, like always. "Well, maybe not." My relief is short-lived, though, because he cheekily adds, "What about a puppy instead?"

"I take it all back," I protest playfully as the boys start screaming with excitement. "You're nothing but trouble."

"Always have been, always will be," he agrees, stepping in to wrap his arms around my waist while the boys run wild around the front yard. He brings his lips to my ear and whispers, "But if you want to try some old-school baby-making, I'm down with that."

My laughter drowns out the squeals of the kids before I cup his cheeks in my hands and bring our lips together in a deep, lingering kiss.

Eighteen months ago, I never would have believed you if you'd told me I'd be happily settling down in a relationship, and I would have asked if you were on crack if you'd told me it would be with another man. But now? I can't imagine my life any other way.

I guess I never really knew myself after all. But I do now, and I'm super happy with the man I am and the future I can see ahead of me.

I can only wish this kind of happiness for all of my loved ones, friends and family alike. Of course, my story is the only one I can tell, and I'm grateful to say that it's ending with a Happily Ever After.

Well, as long as I can talk the kids down from that puppy.

I wonder how they feel about cats instead…

(Just kidding, we're totally getting a puppy.)

THE END

Epilogue – Jack

Thank you so much for reading *You Don't Know Jack*. I had far too much fun writing this one, so I really hope you enjoyed it.

I'd love it if you could leave a review on your retailer of purchase or on Goodreads.

Reviews not only tell the algorithms that our books deserve attention, but honest feedback also encourages and inspires me to keep writing. Even a star rating helps, and I greatly appreciate you making time to do so.

Speaking of my writing, if you want a glimpse into Book Three of the Dads & Adages world, titled *A Match Made In Evan*, keep turning the pages because the prologue is waiting for you.

And if you'd like to read Will & Connor's wedding and honeymoon night (which functions as an extended epilogue for Book 1, *Where There's A Will*), you can subscribe to my newsletter and snag a copy at:

https://annasparrows.com/newsletter-subscription/

If you're already signed up and still want a copy, you can visit:
https://books.bookfunnel.com/annasparrowsbonus
to claim copies of the bonus content you don't yet have.

Please also consider following me on my socials at:

Website:
https://annasparrows.com/

Facebook:
https://www.facebook.com/AnnaSparrowsAuthor/

Instagram:

https://www.instagram.com/annasparrows

…And now, without further ado, the sneak peek of *A Match Made In Evan* awaits!

Sneak Peek: A Match Made In Evan

Prologue – Evan

"Ev!"

I swivel on my barstool and grin at the guy I've been waiting for. "Jay!"

My best friend snorts and runs his hand through his lush, blond hair, sweeping the floppy fringe up and back. I swear he does that just to stir me up seeing as I am follically challenged. "Why do you insist on shortening my name? It's already one syllable."

"Because all four letters of my name don't need to be shortened either?"

It's an ongoing joke between us. James insists on calling me Ev, and I, in turn, call him Jay. I'm pretty sure that if we ever revert to using one another's actual names, it'll be a cry for help.

"Careful," he jokes while sliding onto the stool to my right and flagging the bartender, "or I'll shorten your name to 'Anne' again."

"That threat hasn't worked since we were twelve."

The bartender, a gorgeous buxom redhead, cocks her head at James. "What can I get you, hun?"

"A Bundy and coke, please," he answers, then slaps me on the shoulder. "He's paying, so make it a double."

"You're such a dick," there's no malice in my tone, just laughter. "You're lucky I love you, man."

We've known each other since grade four and have been thick as thieves since then. We practically grew up in each other's houses, and we've always thought of each other's families as extensions of our own. There were even a few years there where we combined our families for Christmases, but things changed once we graduated high school.

We went to separate universities —with him staying on the Gold Coast while I moved to Brisbane— and then he knocked up his girlfriend. Life changed significantly for him after that, while I continued the plan I'd set for myself: finish uni, become a Certified Practising Accountant, land a job at one of the Big 4 accounting firms and live comfortably ever after. I'd never really planned on settling down, but I hadn't avoided it either. Of course, most of the women I'd dated over the years had pushed for more and I had always found reasons not to marry or have kids. James covered the 'kids' thing for the both of us, as far as I'm concerned, considering how close we've stayed over the years.

"How's Mia?" I ask once he's settled with his drink. I adore my Goddaughter, but she recently turned fifteen and suddenly her dad and his friends aren't cool enough to hang out with anymore.

Sneak Peek: A Match Made In Evan

James groans. "She's *dating*."

I wince. *Uh-oh.* There's no reasoning with James about his little princess. She's been the centre of his world since she was born and her birth mother gave him full custody. I could try to argue that she's her own person, with autonomy and rights, but James still sees her as his little girl and not a young woman almost at adulthood. I can't exactly blame him: he put his entire life on hold to raise her, never once resenting her or begrudging his life choices. Of course she's his little princess. She's his entire world.

"Please tell me you haven't threatened or maimed any teenaged boys lately," I beg lightly. "I can't afford to bail you out of jail again."

"You never actually had to bail me out," he sulks. "It was just a misunderstanding."

Poor, sleep-deprived, nineteen-year-old James had let himself into his neighbour's flat by mistake after a night spent driving his colicky newborn around the suburbs to get her to sleep. His eighty-year-old neighbour —who really should have locked her front door— had called the cops when she'd discovered him passed out on her couch with the baby fast asleep in her capsule seat on the coffee table. He'd called me from the station in a panic, not wanting his parents to find out about his embarrassing mistake, mostly because he didn't want to worry them. Even though I lived over an hour and a half's drive away, I'd ditched my morning classes and come to his aid…and I've never let him live it down.

"Either way," I reply, "please tell me I don't need to call in any favours with my lawyer mates."

"I don't think finance law would help me, unless you've made other lawyerly friends?"

I roll my eyes. "Are you saying that just because I'm an accountant I only know other people in finance?"

"That's exactly what I'm saying."

Turning to face him properly, I rest my elbow on the shiny wooden bartop and arch my eyebrow. "You know, when you asked me to meet you because you had a favour to ask of me that you *absolutely* couldn't put into text or ask over the phone, I thought it would involve a lot more buttering me up and a lot less spending my money and insulting me." I study him intently as he sips at his drink, still facing forward and not looking at me. "What's going on, Jay?"

I'm concerned by the tremble in his hand, which makes the liquid inside his glass quiver and the ice cubes clack against the sides. It's been a long time since I've seen my best friend so unnerved and I don't like it.

"You know," I figure injecting a bit of humour might loosen him up a little, "short of murdering someone, I'll do pretty much anything for you. And, hey, even then, it's not a hard limit. I'll even help you hide the body if you ask nicely enough." I wait another beat and frown. "Unless you really did kill some teenage punk for dating your daughter. If that's the case, you're on your own."

James finally snorts and turns his head to look me in the eye. His smile doesn't quite reach his grey-green eyes. Instead, within them I see apprehension and uncharacteristic nerves. He licks his lips and sets his glass down on the coaster in front of him, the condensation marring the bar's logo of a deer or elk or whatever the hell it's supposed to be. Either way, the circular mark from the water obscures the antlers from view.

After hanging his head for a moment, my best friend finally turns sideways in his seat to face me directly. He takes a deep, steadying breath, then says, "I need you to date me."

I blink at him, aware that I'm gaping. "Say what now?"

James lifts his glass and gulps down his drink as though fortifying himself further with the alcohol. "Ev," he pleads, "I need you to be my boyfriend. Well…my fiancé, actually, if I'm putting all my cards on the table."

And, even though we're both straight (or, at least, I think we are), I find I still can't deny my best friend anything.

Without tearing my gaze from James', I signal for the redhead to return, and I hold up my half-empty glass. "We're going to need another round." Not waiting for her response, I lift what's left of my current beverage and raise it in a faux toast. "To our impending nuptials."

Then I skol the whole thing in an eye-watering gulp.

What the actual fuck am I getting myself into now?

About the Author

I've been writing* for as long as I can remember. I started with silly short stories as a kid, moved on to fanfiction in my teens (and still write it now), and am also a published MF romance author under a second pen name.

I have been an avid reader of MM romance my whole life. (Ask me about my beginnings with *Buffy* fanfic, haha.) I wrote a sweet and kinky MM romance novel in 2022 and the reader response changed my life. From there, I knew I had found my niche.

And thus Anna Sparrows was born.

*All of my writing is 100% my own. No part of it is generated by Artificial Intelligence (AI) software of any kind. Yes, that means that it's sometimes flawed, but I'm okay with that.

You can connect with me on:
- https://annasparrows.com
- https://www.facebook.com/AnnaSparrowsAuthor
- https://www.instagram.com/annasparrows

Subscribe to my newsletter:
- https://annasparrows.com/newsletter-subscription

Also by Anna Sparrows

I write ridiculously sweet & steamy MM romance with guaranteed HEAs…and sometimes with a side of kink.

Littles & Lace series
The Littles & Lace series is an MM Age Play series, following a group of like-minded friends in the BDSM community. You'll find mild ABDL, light Pet Play, Femme Play and more here.

Book 1: Asher's Answer

Book 2: Matteo's Mettle

Book 3: Ted's Temerity

Book 4: Spencer's Satisfaction

Book 5: Chance's Choice

Book 6: Josh's Jackpot

Dads & Adages series
Visit Australia's sunny Gold Coast where an assortment of single dads find love and even learn a few life lessons along the way.

Book 1: Where There's A Will

Book 2: You Don't Know Jack

Book 3: A Match Made In Evan (release TBA)

Shifters Sanctuary Series
In a world where alphas are thought to be extinct, a number of 'human' men are about to have their worlds rocked.

Book 1: His Alpha Unlocked

Book 2: His Prodigal Alpha (release TBA)

Milton Keynes UK
Ingram Content Group UK Ltd.
UKHW051134240324
439834UK00001B/15

9 780645 876260